Drifting Shadows

Drifting Shadows

Christina Green

ROBERT HALE · LONDON

ISBN 978-0-7090-9357-2

Robert Hale Limited
Clerkenwell House
Clerkenwell Green
London EC1R 0HT

www.halebooks.com

2 4 6 8 10 9 7 5 3 1

ACKNOWLEDGEMENTS

I am grateful to the authors of many books about Dartmoor
for information which has helped me write this book, and also
to friends and family who have driven me around the 'special
places' on the Moor which set me thinking about Becky and
Joseph. I must also thank many writing friends who have
given me their interest, comments and encouragement.

Typeset in 11/15pt Classical Garamond
Printed in Great Britain by the MPG Books Group,
Bodmin and King's Lynn

CHAPTER 1

The darkness of the great grey rock pile loomed over them as they made their way home. Thirza held two baskets of small dark fruit against her hips, her sunbonnet slipping down over her wrinkled neck, and her breath coming in hard worked puffs. But Becky was in another world. Her baskets, too, were heavily filled with whortleberries, her hands purple stained from picking the small ripe fruit, and her whole body sweating with the heat and the labour, but her mind was free and light. Even the shadow of Bowerman's Nose, sliding down over the moor as the sun began to sink, didn't bother her. She thought of other things – exciting, hopeful things.

Until Thirza's slow voice brought her back to the burden of the day. 'We'm late, Becky. – Will'll be waiting fer his tea. Get on, maid.' And then the heaviness of the baskets, the knowledge that brother William would shout at her and that she must try yet again to ignore his quick temper, all returned, twice as heavy as before, igniting the familiar rebellious thoughts. *Nothing but work and shouting. Want something better. Different. Don't know what or how but – yes, one day I'll find it.*

Now they were out of the shadow, passing the rough grassy mound lying in the middle of the lane where the track down to High Cross Farm met the road. Becky saw Thirza pause, put down her baskets, bow her head and touch the small headstone, then continue on her way. It was a familiar ritual, all the villagers touching the grave as they passed. *'Pore soul,'* they muttered. *'Should never have happened.'* Becky, too, stopped now, put down

5

her baskets and then leaned sideways to pick a stem of mauve sheep's bit scabious from the wayside. She laid it on the top of the grave, thought for a long, hard moment about the girl who had hanged herself, so said the old story, a good eighty years ago now, and then, retrieving the baskets, followed her mother down the narrow, rocky track.

High Cross Farm was half a mile away and they were both even hotter when they reached it. Thirza sighed with relief as she traipsed into the cool, shadowy kitchen and told Becky to put the baskets in the dairy. 'We'll do 'em tomorrer,' she said. 'Wash your hands, maid, an' get the 'taties. Will'll be in any minute.'

As if summoned by her words, he came through the doorway, stocky but thin, ragged carroty hair uncombed, dun coloured trousers and shirt stained and creased. Becky looked at him and saw not the arrogant young tenant farmer who thought he knew everything and treated her and Thirza like mere labourers, but her brother, trying hard to prove his worth and turning himself upside down in doing so. She hid her smile, knowing resignedly that there would probably be shouting and arguments before the night was out, but hoping that one day Will's maturity would shine through and life would improve.

He scowled at her as he sank into the cane chair by the range and kicked off his boots. 'You look a mess, Becks. An' we got Nat Briggs comin' after tea. So do something to clean yourself up.' Boots flung into the drying warmth of the ashy hearth, he got up, went over to the stone sink below the window and dangled earthy fingers in the bowl of water waiting for the 'taties.

Behind his back, Thirza made a face at Becky. 'Go on, maid. Do as he ses. You're all stained and hot.'

Reluctantly, but knowing better than to argue and so start an evening of cross words, Becky stood in the middle of the stone floored room, staring first at Will and then at her mother. But, despite the good intentions, her mind was instantly full of refusal. Why not say she had nothing to wear, and what was wrong with a bit of hurts stain, a good natural colour? And why all this fuss because that Briggs man was coming? But Thirza was coughing, turning away and pulling out pans and bowls in preparation for the meal, and Becky knew she must banish the wayward thoughts.

'All right,' she said and nodded at Thirza, deliberately ignoring the sharp blue eyes watching from the fireplace. 'I'll only be a minute. Leave the dumplings to me, Ma, I'll do them.'

As she went towards the door, Thirza asked, 'So why's Mr Briggs comin'? Same old thing, is it? I hope—' But Becky was on her way, so didn't see her brother shake his head, nor hear him answer, 'He's been talking 'bout it, Ma, but we'll have to wait an' see.'

The cross passage outside the kitchen was cool and Becky sucked in a huge breath as she went through towards the narrow stone staircase. No good losing her temper. Will did enough of that. And don't argue, either, because he always won an argument. She didn't know how long she could continue giving way to him, but with Ma so pale and now that old cough bothering her, it was important to keep a quiet life. Sometimes she thought he didn't seem like a brother. More like somebody else – someone more in control of things – and then again came the old thought: *one day, one day.*

Up in the hot little bedroom under the thatch, she rinsed hands and face, threw down the stained work dress and slipped into the other one, the printed cotton that was kept for church and market, and then went back into the kitchen. The silence in the room was oppressive and she avoided looking Will's way although she heard him muttering as he picked up last week's newspaper. And then she was making dumplings, mixing lard with herbs and flour and dropping them into the stew that had been slowly cooking all the long day while they were out there picking hurts. Tea then in silence, Will slurping his hungrily, Thirza picking at her plate and only Becky herself eating properly.

While the meal went on, her thoughts were redeeming ones. Thankfulness to Thirza for sending her to the dame school in the village, in spite of Will's arguments about wasted pennies. Gratitude for being taught to read and write and to have better manners than the other wild children. Hope for the future which she knew waited for her. And a plea for patience until she found it.

When the knock came on the outer door, she went to answer it, not seeing the look that passed between Thirza and Will. 'Mr Briggs. Good evening. Come in.' She didn't like anything about him, not his slight, nimble body encased in clothes as dark and dirty as his raggle-taggle hair. Not the leery smile which he produced directly he saw her. Nathaniel Briggs was the maister's bailiff who ran the estate for him. He usually brought trouble when he called. So what was he doing here now?

He followed her into the kitchen, accepted the cane chair which Will, smiling amiably now, had vacated, took a tankard of ale from Thirza and produced from one of his vast pockets a clay pipe which he lit. Smoke furled around their heads as they all sat and waited for the pronouncement that surely Mr Briggs had brought.

'Harvest comin' up,' he said after a stretching silence, small, closely set eyes moving from Will to Becky and then back again. 'And then supper. The maister wants to make a do of it this year. Got a new lady, so it's said....' His smile was lustful and Becky felt prickles run down her back.

'So got to make a show, see?' The pipe stabbed into the smoky air. 'Big meal, us all dressed in our best, everyone perlite and thankful. Must impress the lady.'

Will said impatiently, 'But we got to get the harvest in, first ... not ready yet. An' where do I get the help from? You gonna help, Mr Briggs?' He grinned briefly, like the mischievous boy he'd been only a couple of years ago, before the running of the farm turned him into a grim man concerned only with weather, crops and stock.

Nat Briggs regarded him with hooded eyes. 'You got George Meldon. Mebbe I'll give a hand, too.' Quickly he looked at Becky. 'An' you got a good healthy maid here – she can toss a few stooks onto the wagon, can't she?' He eyed her up and down, mouth lifting, showing gappy teeth.

Becky felt anger rage through her. How dare he look at her like that? Like a heifer at market – was that all she was? Something to be assessed, valued and then used. Her cheeks flamed and she jumped up from her stool at the table. 'I'll help if I want to, but there's enough to do without pretending to be a man,' she snapped and saw the gleam in his eye grow brighter.

'Who's pretendin'? No one'll make any mistake 'bout you, Becky Yeo. Woman all through, I'd say.' He laughed and Will nodded and she knew she was being made fun of. Angrily, she marched to the door. 'Time to shut up the hens.' The door banged as she slammed it and again she heard laughter following her.

The cross passage was dark and comforting. She wouldn't stay in the kitchen any longer with that man making personal, rude remarks about her. She didn't care what he thought of her, or whether Thirza would tell her off for not being polite to the all important bailiff. He couldn't do any harm anyway; they worked hard, paid their rent, and the farm belonged to Mr Fielding at the Manor, not to slimy, sly Nat Briggs.

With the hens shut into the roost and the door firmly latched, she returned to the yard, leaning against the warm house wall after patting Prince's head as the old collie lay in his kennel. The sun was at its lowest, vibrant and beautiful, painting the wide evening sky with flaming drifts of cloud. Stretching fields darkened into heavy hills beyond the farm boundary and where the rolling clouds piled up in the west, colours slid into grey, bluey green, violet and orange. Suddenly there was a flash of kingfisher brightness, quickly concealed behind the oncoming grey mass, and, watching, Becky felt all the rage and problems ease out of her. This was what she loved and needed, the vast, uncaring Dartmoor landscape with its beauty – yes, even with its cruel indifference and sometime brutality.

These moments of dimpsey brought ease and comfort, height-ening her senses. Nat Briggs's cob fidgeted on the cobbles. A sweet smell of hay drifted from the barn and a hunting cat slunk across her path, stopping, eyeing her with emerald pinpoints and then disappearing. And it came to her, as she stared, listened and wondered, that, despite Will and his temper and the hard work of the farm, she would never leave Dartmoor. Could never go anywhere else, not even if fate suggested otherwise. All the dreams of a new life that had been flying around her mind lately were suddenly unimportant. This is where she belonged and where she must always be.

She could have stayed out there in the enclosing dusk for ever, dreaming and wondering, until she heard a distant footfall – someone going down the road to Manaton, she guessed. And then a voice filling the quietness, deep, rich, singing words she recognized. One of the songs George Meldon sang when he was grooming the horse, or hedging and ditching, or even just when he sat and drank his cider at crib time. Something about John Barleycorn....

'O! Barleycorn is th' choicest grain, that e'er was sown on land, And it will cause a man to drink....' She smiled as the voice and the words penetrated her mind before passing on into the distance, and found her world was content.

But then louder footsteps down the passage roused her, and she quickly hid behind the ash house to watch Nat Briggs unleash his cob, mount and then, coughing and spitting as he trotted across the courtyard, disappear into the lane. Only when the silence was complete again did she leave her hiding place and return to the kitchen.

'Well,' she said, pulling a stool up to the hearth, 'so when's the maister's celebration going to happen, then? And what do we have to do about it?'

Without looking up, Will grunted over the crumpled page of newspaper, and Thirza moved uneasily in her chair opposite him. Becky stared at them both. What was wrong? She needed an answer. Raising her voice she said, 'Well, come on – we must make plans, surely? We need help for the harvest, and then Ma and me will have to think about new dresses for the supper. Will, don't just sit there – tell me.'

Again, that uncomfortable lack of reply. Until Thirza lowered her head to look at the darning in her lap, and said, very quietly, and with a hint of trouble in the slow words, 'We aren't going, Becky. It's just – well, best that we don't.'

'Why ever not?' Ridiculous, everyone always went to the harvest supper, and this was going to be a special one. It would be such fun – good food and drink, gossip and chatter, jokes, dancing, someone telling tales, perhaps someone singing. And then there would be Mr Fielding's new lady who would probably wear a wonderful gown.

Becky's quick temper flew to the surface. 'I never heard of anything so stupid. Not going? But if you don't want to go, Ma, well I do. And I shall. Will, you'll have to give me something towards a new dress. Goodness knows, I work hard enough for a bit of a handout.'

The paper fell to the floor and his eyes blazed. 'You'll do as Ma ses, Becks. She don't want to go, nor you to go neither so that's it. So stop going on about it. And another thing – no need for you to cheek Mr Briggs like you did. Come the day you'll be sorry 'bout that. No—' as she opened her mouth, words flying to question such a statement. 'No, I'll not talk 'bout it any more.' He and Thirza looked at each. Will nodded and Thirza bowed her head. The blue eyes stared at Becky's astounded face. 'An' now you can make us all a cup o' tea before bedtime. Go on, maid, an' stop your natterin'.'

Becky got up very slowly, her mind awhirl. Not to go to the harvest supper. Why not? Not to cheek Mr Briggs, even when he was so rude and personal. Again, why not? And why was Will reluctant to say any more? *Why, why, why?*

She made the tea, handed out mugs and then went to bed. But not to sleep. Instead she lay awake, listening to noises in the thatch overhead and the rising wind blowing down from the moorland heights and then, sleepily, remembered the voice she had heard down the road. *John Barleycorn* – yes, one of the songs the old men sang.

But this singer had sounded young and full of life, full of cider, too, she guessed, if he had just come out of the Hound Tor Inn. Singing was part of Dartmoor life and she, too, often sang as she worked. The *Sprig of Thyme* was her favourite. Sleepily, she whispered the words. *In my garden grew plenty of thyme, it would flourish by night and by day....*' She smiled.

And that took her onto thoughts of the coming harvest supper. Before sleep claimed her she told herself that, never mind what Ma and Will said, she would definitely have a new dress and go to the Manor celebrations; go into market next Friday and see what Mrs Hannaford had at her old clothes stall.

She slept, dreamlessly, until dawn lit the sky, slowly shafting into her small room, when the cow's lowing and the cockerel's boastings broke into her rest, and then there was routine awaiting her, as usual. Another day. And more work.

CHAPTER 2

The August sun blazed down as Will and George set off for the corn field, old Prince and George's terrier, Tricksy, frisking and barking at their heels, and already nosing into the corn, on the scent for rabbits and hares.

In the farmhouse Thirza and Becky set about the usual chores, milking, feeding the animals and cleaning the night's litter, doing the dairy work and then preparing food and drink for the harvesters who would all too soon be thirsty and sweating. A basket was filled with bread and cheese and bacon for crib and a cider jar filled from the cask in the granary. Thirza poured cold tea into as many bottles as she could find, and then she and Becky set off for the field, preparing themselves for hard, hot work, tying on their sunbonnets as they went.

The four men were steadily cutting, sickles rising then sweeping low, bodies moving in rhythm, one behind the other. The sun flashed on each lifted blade, and every so often a hand paused from its acceptance of the cut sheath, coming up to wipe a sweating brow beneath a low pulled hat. Becky put down her basket in the shade of the big hedge oak where work bags and jackets had already been thrown, and squinted into the sun, looking at the harvesters. Will, George Meldon and Nat Briggs. She remembered that he'd said he might help, but somebody else made up the team, a tall, heavy figure she didn't recognize.

Very soon they were ready to stop and drink, George sprawling on the ground and Will talking to Nat as they poured the cider and cold tea. Becky offered a bottle to the newcomer. 'Have this. It's hot work.' She looked at his weathered face, with its generous mouth and laughter lines reaching up to the handsome nose, and watched as one large hand swept off his hat, revealing thick, untidy corn-gold hair that fell over keen grey-green eyes.

'Thank you.' He had a low, resonant voice, this stranger, and she liked the sound of it. He drank deeply, then wiped his mouth with his forearm and smiled at her. 'That was good.' They looked at each other curiously, and Becky said, 'I'm Becky Yeo, Will's sister. Who are you?'

The observant eyes gleamed. 'Joseph Freeman. Mr Briggs said he had work here, so I came with him. I travel around, just come down from Tavistock way. Harvest's a good time to scrape a living.'

So he was a harvest man, a traveller. She knew such men went from farm to farm at hay and corn harvests, and then had to find other work during the winter months. She wondered what else Joseph Freeman did besides cut corn and smile at every girl he met in this confident way. He seemed sure of himself. Something made her say sharply, 'And where are you off to when this job's done?'

His tanned face lifted into an expression of amusement. 'Want to know my address, do you, then, Miss Yeo? Gonna send me a postcard?'

'Course not,' she snapped. 'I was only being friendly. You can go where you like for all I care.'

'And I probably will. I always do. Freeman, that's me, by name and by nature. My life's my own. I don't have to kowtow to any maister.' The smile had gone and he looked at her with determination written all over his handsome face.

Becky nodded. She was irritated by this unusual, far too self sure man. She took the empty bottle from him and moved away, but something made her turn, look over her shoulder. He was watching her, smiling again, pulling his hat down over that mop of thick fair hair and making her feel – how did she feel? Shock filled her. She discovered she was pleased, glad to be noticed, willing to be made fun of if that was what he wanted. As she tried desperately to sort out these strange emotions, suddenly the deep, quiet voice, broke into her thoughts. 'But wherever I go, I'll remember you, Miss Becky Yeo, Miss Freckles. Because not every maid has all those lovely sunkisses. No, don't blush.'

But yes, she was blushing. How terrible. She felt the colour sweep up her throat and into her cheeks, and had to look away in embarrassment. She dropped the bottle into the basket and kept looking down at the grass and for once was thankful when Nat Briggs said, just behind her, 'Ready to start work, then, Becky? You and Thirza do the tying and then stook the bundles.'

He pulled her round to face him, grinned, looked back at Joseph Freeman, still standing there, and then said, as if he understood how she felt, 'Don't trouble with this chap, Becky, reckon he's got maids on every farm where he goes.' And then, his voice sharp and edgy, 'So what you waitin' for, Freeman? Get on wi' it.'

No reply, just a nod and then the tall man turned away, sharpening his sickle and taking his place behind Will and George, already at work.

Such heat. The sun blazing down from a cloudless sky, insects flying and buzzing, tormenting the horse standing in the shade of the hedge, the dogs yapping, occasional rabbits bolting from the oncoming blades and a linnet singing in the far hedge. Becky felt her cotton dress, tied up around her knees, grow damp and uncomfortable as she and Thirza began gathering the bundles of cut corn, tying them and then putting into stooks of seven or eight, to stand in rows through the field.

She was thankful when Dinah Meldon appeared, carrying her father's dinner in a basket. Becky stopped, looked at the plump, plain girl who nodded back at her.

'Morning, Dinah,' she called. 'Give me a drink, will you? I'm so hot and thirsty. Oh, that's good.' She straightened up as she swallowed down the cold tea, smiled at Dinah and then looked up at the sky. 'Must be nearly dinner time. Sun's overhead. Let's sit down for a while.' In the shade of the oak tree she called over to Thirza, still tying and propping up the stooks. 'Come on, Ma, have a rest. Men'll be stopping in a minute.'

The three women sank gratefully onto the rough grass beside
the hedge and Becky said, as they took food out of the baskets and
shared it, 'Heard about the harvest supper have you, then, Dinah?'

Dinah nodded. 'Father has,' she said and Becky knew that was
all she'd get in reply. If one word could be used instead of two or
three, then Dinah used it. But now, even as she sank small teeth
into a lump of bread, she smiled at Becky and added, 'Lookin'
forward to it.'

Becky gave Thirza, beside her, a quick glance as she said, 'So'm
I. Gonna have a new dress, too. What'll you wear, Dinah?'

A long thought while the bread was slowly chewed and swallowed. Then – 'Me ole blue.'

Becky hid her grin. 'Nothing new? I'm going to see what Mrs
Hannaford's got in the market on Friday. The maister's got a new
woman, so we need to look smart for the supper. Want to come
with me?'

'You're not goin'.' Thirza's voice was slow and purposeful.

Becky stared at her mother. 'Yes, I am. And you.' She watched
the tired face become suddenly more alive than usual. 'Why not,
Ma? Give me a good reason.'

'I've nothin' to say.' Thirza met her eyes and frowned as she
shook her head. And then, reluctantly, contradicted herself. 'Maid,
long ago there's things been done as shouldn't have – so it's better
we don't meet Mr Fielding.'

Becky watched the colour on her mother's face flame. It was all
wrong to upset Ma like this – but she tried a last time. 'Something
he did? But he's old so it's probably years ago. All forgotten. Come
on, Ma, of course we'll go....'

Now the men were around them, sitting down, taking off sweat-
stained waistcoats and neck scarves, reaching for drinks and filling
the quietness with loud voices. Becky looked up, saw Joseph
Freeman talking to Will as he put a bucket of water down for Ruby,
the work horse standing patiently in the wagon shafts, and then
watched Nat Briggs making his way towards her, cider jar in hand
and a grin on his sweating face. Quickly she got up, finding an

excuse to move away, to take bread and cheese across to Will, and offer some to Joseph. She avoided meeting his watchful eyes and instead went back to sit beside Dinah, stolidly munching her way through a hunk of rabbit pie.

Dinah looked sideways at her and said, between mouthfuls, 'Course we're goin' to the harvest supper. An' you?'

'Yes,' Becky replied forcefully. 'I'll be there.'

Harvest continued for three days, by which time conversation of any kind had seized up as the exhausted men and women worked side by side, completing the cutting and carrying of the field. Becky only knew that Joseph slept in the barn at night, for Thirza had taken him a blanket and he had eaten a huge meal with them every evening before disappearing into the humid darkness. She thought she heard his low voice singing sometimes, but perhaps she imagined it. If she had any thoughts of him, they were confined to the few times when the work was thankfully finished and before the next day began. Her mind, instead, was full of the coming harvest supper and her determination to be there with Will, even if Thirza refused to go.

Nat Briggs ate dinner with them and did all he could to corner her in the cross passage afterwards, or as she went into the pantry, even following her into the yard when she went to shut up the hens. But Becky was sharp with him and stepped away when he accosted her.

'Mr Briggs, I'm busy – let me pass please ...' and then stepped around him, hurrying back to the kitchen as soon as she could. She knew from his expression that she was causing his quick anger to grow, but it was necessary to keep her distance. But, on the last evening, he was too quick for her.

'Becky, you an' me gotta talk.' He snatched at her as she tried to pass and suddenly his arms were around her. She kicked at his legs and he swore. 'You little bitch – I'll give you somethin' for that.' She was pulled close, the breath almost knocked out of her body. She smelt his dirt, tobacco and cider fumes, saw the light in his small eyes and felt wiry arms tighten around her. 'I'll scream if you don't let me go, Nat.' Her voice was shrill, but her courage quickened and she fought to free herself.

'Let her go, Briggs. You hear me?' On his way to the barn, Joseph Freeman saw them and his voice fell on Becky's ears like comforting honey. She cried, 'Help me, help me, please!'

Nat's arms dropped and she pulled away from him, turning to see Joseph's great fist striking out, hearing it connect with bone and flesh, followed by Nat's shout of pain and rage. He almost fell over but recovered his balance, glared at them and then instantly plunged towards the stable where his cob was stalled. Obscenities and threats filled the air, but she was only aware of Joseph at her side, nursing his fist and looking at her with concern in his light eyes.

'You don't want to have no more to do with that clodhead, Becky Yeo.' His deep voice was quiet and she heard a note of something that made her shiver.

She looked up at him and nodded, trying to control her breathing. 'I know. But he followed me.'

'He won't do that no more. Not while I'm here. Didn't hurt you, did he?'

'No,' she said, wondering. 'No, it was just that he held me so tightly ... and I was afraid.'

'You're with me now. No need to be afraid no more. I'll take you into the house.'

His big hand enveloped hers as he led her back, through the shadowy cross passage, into the lamp lit kitchen where Thirza was making the last pot of tea and Will was already snoring by the fire.

Joseph said nothing, but nodded at her as he let go of her hand, then gave her a hint of a smile. 'Don't dream no bad dreams, Miss Becky.' The words were quiet and just for her, she knew. And then, louder, 'So I'll say goodnight, all.' And he was gone.

Thirza looked at her. 'Something wrong, maid?

Becky swallowed and bit her tongue. 'No, Ma. Just a bit of a row with Mr Briggs, but it's all right now.' She went to the dresser and got down the mugs, avoiding her mother's anxious eyes. Thirza said nothing, but once the tea was drunk and Will was stomping upstairs to his bed, she put a hand on Becky's shoulder, and said, very carefully, 'Try and keep in with Mr Briggs, maid. He's got an eye for you, and he's a good man under all that temper, you know.'

By now Becky had recovered her self control. She smiled tightly at her mother, and said, as they left the kitchen together, the oil lamp doused and candlesticks in their hands, 'He's not a good man, Ma, and I don't plan to keep in with him. I'm sorry, but I've decided.' She halted at the door of her bedroom, before adding, 'And I don't reckon he'll be keeping his nasty eye on me much more now.'

'Why, what happened out there?' Thirza's face was taut.

Becky kissed the cheek that had paled beneath the day's sunburn. 'Nothing to worry about, Ma, now get a good sleep. We've still got to work in the morning.'

The last sheaf cut, dried stooks loaded on the wagon, Ruby heaved it out of the field and towards the rick yard. Will, poised on the top of the wagon, waved the last handful of corn and shouted, 'We got 'un, we got 'un!' his words taken up by the harvesters following behind. A joyful, satisfied time with smiles overtaking the weariness etched on sunburned faces, and a glow of pride replacing sore backs and aching arms. The harvest was gathered in and another year's living safely stored.

Becky, Thirza and Dinah followed the men to the rick yard, but then went into the house, longing to sit down and thankful for its shade and coolness. As the humming kettle was pushed closer over the flames and they waited for the tea to be made, they smiled at each other, relishing the quietness and the serenity of the old house. Yes, the rick would be built by the men outside, but here, in the stillness of home, they could return to age old women's work and push thoughts of the long hard hot days they had just endured behind them. It was a good feeling.

And so, with the burden of the harvest taken off their minds, the thoughts of Mr Fielding's feast at High Cross Manor began to be talked about, bodies stopped aching and thoughts grew freer. In the evening George Meldon and Dinah traipsed home, Nat Briggs rode off with a last leery grin at Becky and Joseph Freeman vanished.

But Will took out what was left of his usual ill temper on Becky even more than usual. 'Don't think you're going to the supper. I told you no and it's still no. You'll stay 'ere and keep Ma company.'

Becky glared as she watched him shaving over the sink, his red face seeming to cast a shadow over the whole kitchen. 'I've worked hard, I'm going. I don't care what you say.'

He turned, glowering back at her. 'You 'eard me!' he shouted. 'Ma don't want you to go and that's it. I'll lock your door, see if I don't. Now get outta here an' go to yer bed.'

No point in arguing, but her mind made itself up. Of course she would go. New dress or the old faded just-for-church-and-market brown check, she was going to the harvest supper. Lock the door, indeed! She laughed aloud. She knew a thing or two about escaping from locked doors. Just let him see.

Thirza fussed around Will as he put on his best coat. She brushed hay seeds from his dark beaver hat and smiled at him. 'You looks really smart, Will boy. Enjoy yourself. Becky an' me'll be all right here.'

He nodded, and pecked her cheek. 'That's it, Ma. You wants a rest after all that harvesting – don't want a crowd of rough men around you, do you?' He grinned as he opened the door. 'Reckon your days of dancing are over – I'll tell the maister as how you're too tired to come.'

'And me? What will you tell Mr Fielding about me, Will? Perhaps I'm too tired and too old, too – but give him my apologies, please, and say as I wanted to come but there was something about a locked door.' She laughed at the rough face he pulled, then joined Thirza in the open doorway, watching him mount the pony and clatter off out of the yard.

'So what'll we do, Ma? Get out our darning? Make some harvest dollies to sell at market? Give ourselves a nice meal without having to keep some for Will?'

Thirza looked at her with a puzzled expression. 'I'm meant to lock you in your room, Becky, but o' course I can't – no lock, is there? So just promise me you'll not open that door once it's shut, maid.'

Becky closed her eyes, hiding the secret excitement welling up inside her. 'I won't open the door, Ma. I promise.'

They parted on the small landing at the top of the stairs, Thirza kissing Becky and smiling at her. 'You've worked well, maid. Now have a good rest.'

Becky nodded. 'And you, Ma. See you in the morning, and let's hope the old cockerel don't crow too early.'

Thirza's door shut and Becky sat on the edge of her bed, eyes agleam, mind working out the best escape route. She looked towards the window and remembered childish pranks of climbing down the honeysuckle that grew all over the cob wall. Were her feet too big nowadays to find those old thick stems that provided safe footfalls? Getting up, she washed herself, brushed and knotted her hair and put on the faded brown checkdress that had seen better days, but would now enjoy itself at Mr Fielding's harvest supper. The hope of getting to market had been just a dream, a ruse to irritate Will enough into agreeing to her going to the supper. Now it no longer mattered. She was going, and the brown dress would have to do.

Looking down from the window the ground below seemed a long way off, but she was determined. One foot over the sill and yes, the old safe branch was there, waiting for her, she thought, and grinned happily as she climbed down and then jumped the last three feet.

She was on her way to High Cross Manor and no one was going to stop her.

CHAPTER 3

Instinct told Thirza something was wrong. Not that Becky would break her promise, but....

Hurrying across the landing, she found the small window opened to its fullest extent, not latched and clearly offering extra space for someone to put a foot on the sill and then step out onto the sturdy honeysuckle limb. Standing staring out into the silent landscape, memories of the small, mischievous Becky escaping this way flashed through Thirza's disturbed mind.

She must go, find her, bring her home before anyone at the harvest supper gossiped. It must be kept clamped down in the past. No one must tell Becky. Mr Fielding mustn't see her, mustn't have a reason to trail his thoughts back into the long ago years. Dear Becky mustn't be hurt – she mustn't know.

A shawl snatched up and thrown around her shoulders, the faded work frock dusted down and shoes hastily cleaned with a wet rag, Thirza pulled her shabby straw hat on to her head and set off down the lane towards High Cross Manor. She went as fast as her aching legs let her, thoughts in chaos, and with each step becoming more and more aware of the shadows of oncoming dusk rolling up around her.

Shadows, she thought wildly; there had always been shadows, and now they seemed to be overtaking her.

The big barn was filling as all the tenants and workers from Mr Rupert Fielding's many estate farms crowded in, voices ringing through the lofty timbers. Old friends caught up with gossip and the latest harvest news, while their women, all in best dresses and flower bedecked hats, chattered and laughed. It was a time of reunion, and a celebration of the satisfaction of hard important work which wove its way through the merry cacophony of noise as they awaited the coming of the maister and his new lady.

Becky paused at the door before entering. Yes, she knew some of the farmers and their wives there, and Dinah was not far away so she could go and talk to her, but something kept her waiting. She hoped Will wouldn't see and order her home; and that Nat Briggs wouldn't make a nuisance of himself. Secretly, she wondered if Joseph Freeman was here. Then someone behind her pushed and she was in the barn, swept along by a new crowd of shouting harvesters from the farm up the valley, and she lost her sense of shyness.

She made her way to the bench where George Meldon, his wife May and Dinah were sitting and smiled at them, nodding as they squeezed up and made room for her. 'Thank you,' she said, voice rising above the noise all around them. 'What a crowd. Time the maister came, isn't it?'

Suddenly, the voices hushed and quietness fell. Heavy boots crunched aside, women took deep breaths of excitement and then there they were, a tall well dressed man with grizzled hair and hooded dark eyes, his arm supporting one hand of the woman beside him. No one said anything but caps and hats were doffed and instinctively, the body of people moved away, leaving a space at the top of the barn. Becky saw Nat Briggs following on behind Mr Fielding, and grudgingly realized that Nat was an important figure in the running of the estate. Hate him as she did, she knew he had a good position, and, for all his personal faults, fulfilled it well. As long as he kept away from her.

Rupert Fielding was looking around his workers, recognizing them, nodding, and then speaking, his gentrified voice friendly. 'I welcome you here this evening, and thank you, too. Harvest's been brought in without any trouble and we're stocked for the coming year so I feel you deserve a celebration. But before—' Here there was a movement of men and women turning and grinning at each other, quickly stopping as he went on. 'But before the feast begins, I want to introduce my fiancée – my bride to be – to you all. Mrs Felicity Richards lives in Moretonhampstead, but before long she will come to High Cross Manor as my wife. Now, will you please welcome her?'

The smallest pause and then the voices rang out. Cheers, saucy, even bawdy side remarks about him finding a likely widow at his age, all hidden beneath gales of laughter, and finally quietness growing as expectations rose. Becky stared at the woman standing by Mr Fielding's side and at once envied everything about her. She was a little younger than him – and personable in a way that Becky knew she would never be.

Such clothes. Smart, close fitting, with a high collar and small waist. Large sleeves in a pale almond green dress that, thought Becky critically, drained the colour from the rather long, thin face. But such posture and poise. A contained smile as brown eyes looked from face to face, nodding and smiling almost regally. And then the voice, high and lazy. 'Thank you all very much for your welcome. I so look forward to being here at High Cross Manor and meeting you all.' A pause, a moment when again everyone grinned and nodded, and then Mr Fielding stepped in.

'So now we can start eating!' he said heartily, 'and afterwards Mrs Richards and I look forward to some entertainment.'

That went down well. Old Charlie Hobbler fished his mouth organ out of his shirt pocket and waved it in the air, while a couple of lithe, heavily booted youngsters kicked out a couple of raps on the ground beneath their feet. Becky joined the Meldon family in fighting for a place at the laden table in the middle of the barn, and knew that once all the food had gone the evening would become loud, louder and uncontrollably wild. She just hoped that Will wouldn't drink too much cider and ale. The thought made her look around for him, and there he was, at the far side of the long table, sitting down and talking to his neighbour.

And then she stopped smiling because Ma had appeared, her

careworn face over his shoulder creating a hush of sudden silence in the people sitting nearby as she bent over and whispered to him. Becky held her breath and automatically got ready to run. As she watched, she saw Will arguing, and Ma shaking her head but then Will's next door neighbour, a burly old chap from a farm lower down in the valley, took her by the arm, pushed up along his bench, and pulled her down beside him. 'C'mon, maid,' he roared, 'always fancied you, so now you're here we'll make the most of it, eh?'

There was loud laughter from onlookers, and Becky saw Thirza's face crumple, as if she didn't know whether to smile or shout. But then all attention was turned to the arrival of the goose on the table, decorated with apples, followed by pies and hams, chickens and pastries, jellies and fruit, and even Thirza began to smile. Becky watched her mother slowly settle down, her plate piled with slices of everything passed down the table. How good it was, she thought, as she ate and chatted to Dinah, that Ma had come after all, and, by the look of things, was enjoying herself.

When the gargantuan meal came to its close, plates emptied, ale mugs refilled and an atmosphere of easy jollity filling the barn, the entertainment began. The mouth organ piping out some of the well known tunes, *The Old Grey Mare, Off to Widecombe Fair, John Barleycorn,* and several others of doubtful content with the audience joining in with enthusiasm; the two Ridge brothers doing their heavy, noisy dance on a large slab of timber; Bert Hannaford telling his old tales, well known but always welcome at such celebrations, and then a deep voice rising above the others, singing *The Sprig of Thyme.*

In my garden grew plenty of thyme ... o'er the wall came a lad, he took all that I had ... and the audience grew quiet, as if caught in the spell of the old words and the richness of the voice.

Becky knew that voice. She looked around her and saw Joseph Freeman at the back of the barn, leaning against a piece of rusted machinery, catching all eyes as he sang the song that she had known and loved from birth. Her song. So why was he singing it?

Did she imagine it or was he looking at her, grey eyes seeking hers above all the other faces? Instinctively she bowed her head, wondering why she did so. Dinah, beside her, caught the movement, turned to her. 'He's lovely – he's lookin' at you,' she whispered, plain face caught in a transforming smile.

Becky shook her head. Something made her want to run. She took the chance as Joseph's song ended and applause burst out. Dinah caught at her arm, but too late. Becky pushed her way out of the barn. In the cooling dusky air she breathed deeply, wondering why she was behaving in this way, and then pushed away the memory of Joseph's voice and his eyes looking for her, forcing herself to return to an old, childish longing: to see inside High Cross Manor, to know how the maister lived, what the rooms were like, and were the comforts greater than the neglected old cottage that was home? And then, like a whisper from an unknown world, what made it possible for one man to live a better life than another?

It only took a few minutes of concentration to find her way through the farmyard to the entrance of the old house, standing grey stoned and a bit mysterious in the deepening shadows. A dog barked, horses whinnied in the stables, but Becky crept in through the unlocked door and found herself in the huge kitchen. That enormous sink and wooden draining boards. The huge dresser, piled with handsome blue and white china, copper pans and bowls catching the last sunlight drifting through the big bare window. She imagined herself working here; what would it be like? Better than scraping about in the small kitchen at home. But what lay beyond? Too late now to realize that she was trespassing, that she might be caught and a huge fuss made. Will would be furious. Ma would weep and say she should have known better. But to be here – to see how other people lived…. Becky, wandering through the big marble floored hallway and looking up at the sweeping stairs, at the mercy of her desire and forgetful of any caution, had the strangest feeling that she felt at home in this ancient house.

She walked into what she supposed was the parlour. Perhaps the drawing room that she had heard a girl who had once worked here talk about. 'The Manor's got pictures in the drawing room, all the maister's family. Talk about lovely furniture … and oh, that carpet….'

Now she stood in the middle of the spacious room, and felt a sort of joy sweep through her. And a decision. She wanted to work here, to be part of the Manor with its wonderful decorations and heavy, shining furniture.

Yes, she would seek out Mr Fielding and ask politely, but firmly, for a position in his household. Perhaps in the kitchen to start with, but then, because she had been educated, why not as a house-maid, or even a parlour maid? Working here, in these beautiful surroundings, this was what she wanted. Well, she could only ask. She smiled and all the niggling doubts were dismissed. Never mind what Will and Ma might say, what the villagers would think, this was where she wanted to be. Turning away, Becky swiftly made her way towards the kitchen and then heard footsteps approaching.

Instinctively, she stopped, heart racing. What should she say, found in here without permission? Was it a servant returning? Someone who might agree to say nothing about her appearance here? Even as she thought so furiously, a figure appeared, and she looked straight into the dark, hooded eyes of Rupert Fielding. She let out her breath in a gasp and his frown deepened.

'Who are you? What are you doing here?' His voice was raspy and quick and immediately her excuses fell away. She could only stare at him and feel telltale colour rush into her cheeks.

'Well? Answer me. Are you deaf, girl?'

And suddenly her head was clamouring with words. 'No, I'm not deaf. I'm Rebecca Yeo, Will Yeo's sister. And I was just – just….'

The long, lined face lifted into an expression of distaste. 'Looking around? For something easy and useful to filch? Is that it?'

'No.' Courage grew. He was clearly very angry, but she might not see him alone again, so perhaps this was the moment to ask….

She drew herself up very straight and smiled nervously. 'I'm sorry, Mr Fielding, I know I shouldn't be here. But I haven't taken anything, of course not. I just wanted so badly to see the Manor. And it's – beautiful….' Her voice faded.

There was a pause and she watched curiosity replace the unpleasant expression on his face. He seemed not to know how to reply. She waited, holding her breath and then, when at last a hint of a taut smile lifted his thin lips, said very quietly, 'I would like to work here, Mr Fielding. In any sort of position. Please forgive me for coming in like this – but do you need a kitchen maid? Or perhaps –' she tensed even further – 'a housemaid? I can read and write, and I work well. You see, I have to, helping my mother and my brother at High Cross Farm.'

Rupert Fielding twisted his mouth and stared at her. 'You're an unusual girl, Rebecca Yeo. But I can't excuse you for breaking in like this. '

Without thought, she said, 'I didn't break in. The door was unlatched.'

Again, that controlled smile and a new expression in the dark eyes. 'Yes, well – I'll think about your request. Now go back and join the party – your brother will wonder where you've got to, and I don't want any search parties coming along. Very well, I'll say no more about your appearance here. And I may just have a word with Mr Briggs in the morning, as to your character and so on.' He turned away and then looked back at her. 'If I do employ you – mind you, only if – how will your brother manage without you?'

'He could get an apprentice from the workhouse. A strong lad would work even harder than me.'

A brief flash of amusement. 'Got it all worked out, haven't you?'

Becky swallowed and bowed her head. 'Just that I want to come so bad,' she muttered and then, looking up, saw him nod, give her another very straight stare before going up the staircase and out of her sight. She let out all her pent up breath, looked around her for a last time and then fled.

*

Outside she heard revelry continuing in the barn, where the oil lamps were lit and voices were raised as all the old songs were sung. Becky stopped in the yard, suddenly wondering what to do – go back and join Thirza and Will? Or go home and keep out of their way when they finally rolled home, full of food and ale? She knew there would be something to pay for her wickedness in not obeying Will – but he could only shout at her, which she was used to. But Ma, who had been so firm that she mustn't go to the Manor, what would Ma say – or do?

The sky was heavy now with dark night rack rolling up from the east. Becky slowly walked out of the farmyard and across the rough grass path leading to the yard where the shadows of the newly built rick loomed black and tall. She felt she wanted to be alone, to think, to imagine, perhaps to come to some sort of decision.

But, even as she stopped, instinct told her that someone was near, and arms came out of the night and wrapped themselves around her. 'Becky. Miss Freckles.' The deep, velvety voice, softened now by ale fumes and tobacco.

She gasped, twisted around and stared into Joseph's eyes, their lightness dimmed but still powerful enough to keep her staring. They looked at each other for a long moment and he shifted his arms to pull her closer. 'You shouldn't be out here alone,' he murmured as he pulled off her hat and lifted her face towards his. 'Bad men about after all that drinking and rowdiness....'

'Are you bad?' she whispered, feeling the heat of his body reaching into hers, enjoying it but knowing that this was the way young girls should never allow themselves to go.

He chuckled and whispered into her hair, 'Of course. All men's bad. But some's badder.... I won't hurt you, Becky, just want to love you a bit....'

She had never known such feelings that swept through her. Such swamping emotions longing to say, *Yes, she felt the same* ... but Thirza's slow, anxious voice was there, telling her, *Never let a man take advantage of you, maid,* and so, slowly, grudgingly, she pulled out of his arms, stepped away, put a hand on the sturdy rick beside her as if seeking help, and said, 'You're wicked, Joseph Freeman. And you've drunk too much. Go on your way and let me be.' But the last words died in her throat, unwilling to emerge.

Through the half darkness she watched his face slowly change to an expression of regret and then, surprisingly, to lighthearted humour. 'But you don't really want me to go, do you? Sending me away without knowing any more about me? Want to know if all Mr Briggs said is true? A girl in every farm, have I? Well, why not find out for yourself, Becky? Just a kiss? Just one? It's there in your voice, in your eyes – that want – so what's the harm, eh?'

How could she stop herself? She closed her eyes, longing again for the arms that had been so warm around her; the big body over-powering her with its strength, and yet, at the same time, such gentleness. Slowly now she moved nearer while he waited, until she dared slip an arm around his neck and breathed out all her doubts and knowledge of her wickedness as he lowered his head, found her lips and kissed them.

A moment of wonder, of joyous sensation, and then Dinah's voice, calling, 'Becky? Where you to? Father ses you must come home with us.'

Becky drew away from Joseph, looked around and saw Dinah entering the yard. When she turned back again, he had gone.

CHAPTER 4

Thirza slipped out of the hot barn before the last songs were sung, the final tales repeated and embroidered still further and before people began drifting homewards in various degrees of drunkenness. The noise had left her a bit moithered, but one thought pounded through her aching head. Becky had disappeared from the barn and was still missing and Will had been too far gone to even listen when she told him. But thank goodness, Mr Briggs had seen how confused she was and had put a hand on her shoulder as he said 'Don't worry, Mrs Yeo, I'll find the maid and see she gets home. Now, you go on. You wants your bed, I'm sure – it's bin a long day an' a half, all right.'

So Thirza slowly walked down the dark lane, praying that what-ever Becky had been up to, she would soon be home and safe again. Yet her thoughts still roamed. Had anyone gossiped to Becky? Tongues could well be loosened on a night like this – she caught her breath: Was it the time to tell the maid the truth? Or continue to keep quiet, as she had done for the last nineteen years?

She felt old and tired. The harvest had left her depleted and anxious. One thing crowded into another – what should she do? But, even as she reached the farm and left the night behind her, she knew that she was going to carry on in the same way – keep quiet and hope no one would ever talk about what had happened.

Nat Briggs found Becky as she joined the little crowd of returning harvesters walking up the lane back towards the village. She was with the Meldon family, so she was safe, and he knew it wouldn't do to drag her off and ask what she'd been up to. But he shouted goodnight as he passed them and then turned to see Becky, taller than Dinah, upright, and with a curving bosom pushing up her old faded dress. He felt his lust stir and knew that tomorrow he would find out where she'd been this evening, all on her own. By God, she needed a man to take her in hand. He nodded and told himself it was time to ask the question – why wait any longer? So he halted until she reached his side and then bent down, his face close to hers. 'I'll be along tomorrer, Becky. Some'at I got to ask you.' She made no response, except stepping away and not bothering to look at him. Nat kicked the cob into a fast trot up the lane, throwing stones and dust as he went. Little bitch. She'd be sorry soon.

In the morning farm noises aroused late sleepers, Will frowned and pushed aside his breakfast, saying he'd never go to a harvest supper again, didn't do any good, all that food and drink and chatter. 'Give me some'at for me head, Ma,' he growled as he paused at the open door, where Thirza had a herbal drink all ready. She knew about harvest suppers.

'This'll do it, boy. Betony'll help. An' take things easy.' She watched him snatch the cup and drink down its contents, his face reacting to the vile taste, before shouting back at her, 'An' tell that lazy maid to come an' help. Why's she not down yet?' He strode out into the yard and the waiting work and Thirza, retrieving the empty cup, sighed. The day was going to be a difficult one.

But Becky was in a new world. Something wild and almost wanton had leaped into life within her, and she felt she would never be the same. She was a woman now, no longer a girl, a woman who had found something wonderful and would always be searching, longing to find it again. She went about the usual duties and while she was feeding the pigs, pausing finally to scratch Flower's broad back, her ever present thoughts of Joseph strayed to the chance meeting with Mr Fielding last night and what he'd said about talking to Nat Briggs. Character, he'd said. Well, hers was good. Apart from a few childish scrapes and rebellions she had done nothing to be ashamed of. She gave a final pat to Flower, then picked up the empty bucket and returned to the farmhouse. Even the dairy work didn't stop her dreaming, although the butter was slow to come and Thirza's anxious questions about last night pushed aside those memories of Joseph.

'Stop going on, Ma. I didn't do anything wrong. It was just so hot and rowdy that I had to get out. And anyway, Dinah came looking for me and we all walked home together. No, I don't care if Will did see me—' She stopped, grinned to herself and decided not to tell Ma about meeting Mr Fielding and what she had asked him. Let things lie and see what might happen. At last the butter came, the eggs in the dairy were all washed ready for market, the whortleberries taken out of their baskets and made into pies, and then it was dinner time. Becky counted the hours. No sign of Nat Briggs.

He came just as Becky and Thirza were piling empty plates into the sink. Will was by the door, looking back over his shoulder. 'Taking the cart down to the field,' he told them. 'Shovelin' all that dung and then forkin' it in – hot work. Bring George an' me some tea later, Becks,'

Becky nodded. No need to answer, she knew she'd have to be there or else. And then Will's voice changed as he went into the yard, polite, eager to please. 'A'ternoon, Mr Briggs. Good feast, eh?'

And Nat's voice, surly as usual. 'Something to say, Will. Leave your carting for a bit.'

Hands about to plunge into hot water and soda, Becky stopped, her body stiffening. Iron-tipped boot steps on the cobbles of the cross passage and then the two men came into the kitchen, eyes at once finding her. Her pulse raced, but she simply nodded at them and carried on with the washing of the dishes. Thirza, beside her with a linen cloth, raised an eyebrow and then picked up the first wet plate.

'Better if you come an' listen, Mrs Yeo. An' you, Becky.'

The women exchanged glances, stopped what they were doing and crossed the room to stand, looking at Nat Briggs as he took the chair Will gestured him towards. Becky saw Will frowning, guessed that he expected a rebuke for not keeping an eye on her last night. Quickly she glanced at Nat, sitting with his feet outstretched and apart, hat on the back of his head, clearly preparing to say something important. Her breathing quickened. *Come on, tell me, tell me….*

'Word from Mr Fielding, Becky. He's offerin' you a situation in the house while it's being done up. Talked about a month. What d'you say, then?'

A second's pause and she felt the room instantly fill with thoughts, fears, memories – but then, in a flash of brightness, her own hopes overwhelmed everything. Thirza gasped and all but collapsed onto a stool beside the table. Will frowned and slowly said, 'What? Becks goin' to work at High Cross Manor? But I can't do without 'er.'

Nat Briggs twisted his mouth and said roughly, 'Maister said as how you can get an apprentice.'

Will let out an explosion of breath. 'But that'd be just a lad – and I needs a worker, not a skinny little hedge boy from the work-house.'

Silence and Nat Briggs shrugged his shoulders. Excitement pulsed through Becky, dismissing any difficulties. Nothing must stand in her way. 'Yes, Mr Briggs,' she said quickly, her smile radiant, 'I'll take the situation. For as long as it lasts. Please thank Mr Fielding.' She smiled into the narrow set eyes watching her so keenly, for once at peace with what she saw. 'I'll start tomorrow.'

Thirza grabbed her arm, looking up at her. 'No! You can't go – not up there. No, Becky, no. You must stay 'ere.'

Becky pulled her arm free. She saw Thirza's wild anxiety, but could only think of her own excitement. 'Of course I'll go, Ma. It's what I want – to work somewhere better'n an old farm like this. An' I'll be paid – a few more shillings, not so much pinching and scraping, Ma.'

'But—' Thirza wailed as she slid from the stool, falling to the floor, arms scrabbling and sounds of her despair filling the room.

Beside her, Becky's guilt overflowed. What had she done? Why was Ma in such a state? What was it about High Cross Manor that so upset her? But at once the men were pulling Thirza from the floor, looking at each other for a few seconds, and then clumsily carrying her up the narrow stairs.

On her bed, Thirza blinked up at them, shook her head and wiped her eyes. 'I got some'at to tell her. Where's Becky?'

Nat stepped back. 'Here she be, Mrs Yeo. You lie quiet like – got any brandy, Will?'

Becky heard Will clump downstairs and then return with the bottle always hidden in the cupboard in case of accidents and illnesses. He gave his mother a cupful and they all watched as she sipped, saw the colour return to her face. She stared up at Becky. 'Want to tell you....'

Becky shook her head dismissively at the two men, heard them go downstairs and then turned to her mother. 'What is it, Ma? Tell me.'

'Just that you mustn't go to High Cross Manor. Not while he's there.' Thirza struggled to sit up, clutching her skirt with twitching fingers. She looked at Becky with wide, wild eyes. 'He's bad all through. I don't want you goin' there, maid, in case he – in case....' Words died and she sat there, staring at Becky with tears running down her cheeks. 'Don't go—'

Becky had never in her life had to make a decision like this one. Now she knelt down beside Thirza and took her hands in her own, warming them, smiling into the wan face that stared at her so desperately. She felt torn in half. Of course she wanted to go to the Manor to work. It was the chance of her life. But how could she disobey Ma who so clearly was in fear of what might happen there? And what *could* happen? She thought back to last night, when Mr Fielding had stood beside her, talking to her, and immediately cast aside Ma's fear that he might, well, what did '*in case he*' really mean? She guessed it was another way of saying *keep away from that bad man, Rupert Fielding, in case he tries to take advantage of you.*

Becky hadn't lived in a small village for nineteen years without hearing all the gossip, all the fears and hopes and scandals that naturally erupted. She knew that Rupert Fielding was disliked as the squire of his estate and was said to care only for drinking, hunting and the associated social events. There had been whispers about women, too – well, what was so dangerous about that? All men were that way inclined. Just for a second she remembered what Joseph had said – *some men are bad* – and at once her determination grew. If Mr Fielding tried to take advantage of her then she would resist. She had physical strength resulting from the hard labour of farming. He would have no chance with her. Ma must realize that and let her go.

'You don't want to worry about me and Mr Fielding, Ma,' she said firmly, but with a smile. 'I'll be a match for him if he tries anything. No, stop worrying – there's no need. And think, I'll be paid a wage, even if it is only for a month. Come on, Ma, cheer up and think of what we can spend a few extra pennies on.'

She and Thirza looked at each other, Becky nodding her head and smiling, until finally Thirza sighed deeply, patted the hand that still held hers, and said weakly, 'If you're sure, maid. Then I'll have to let you go, I reckon. On'y,' she paused, looked into Becky's eyes, and then added, 'tell him you wants to sleep at home. Then you can come back before it's dark.'

'I don't know about that, Ma – we'll see what he says. Now, up you get an' I'll make you a nice pot of tea when you come down.' Becky left the room and went down to the kitchen, where Nat Briggs and Will were sitting looking at each other across the table, their conversation stopping the moment they heard her footsteps. Becky looked from one to the other. 'What's up? More trouble?' No answer, both men looking down, and so she said, 'Will, go and talk to Ma and tell her it's safe for me to go to the Manor. Tell her that Mr Fielding isn't the big monster she imagines him to be.' She thought for a moment as, grudgingly he got up and walked towards the door. 'An' tell her that soon she'll have a skinny little orphan from the workhouse to fuss over. That'll make her forget

I'm somewhere else.' And then, with a straight look at Nat, 'Well, Mr Briggs, stopping for a cup of tea, are you?'

He stared, frowned, opened his mouth, then clamped it shut and she knew that whatever he had been saying to Will when she was up with Ma was not to be shared. 'No,' he said shortly, getting up. 'Got work to do. I'll tell the maister you agreed.' He walked to the door, looked back at her and added, 'So make sure you're there at eight o'clock, Becky, an' no nonsense.'

As he left, she wondered what it might have been they were talking about, but then pushed away any ideas that came into her mind. At the moment all she must think about was persuading Ma that everything was all right, and then, tomorrow, going to the Manor and starting work there. Making the tea, she smiled at the smoky range and let herself imagine what the kitchen would be like at High Cross Manor.

The morning was hazy with a threat of storm clouds beating up from the southwest. Becky was thankful that the harvest was safely in as she left the farmhouse, bundle of belongings in her hand, kissing Thirza and saying she would be back for a visit when she could manage it. Thirza seemed less worried, but still had a word of warning. 'Don't forget what I said, maid.' Becky smiled, said 'Stop worrying, Ma, I'm a big girl, you know,' and went down the lane feeling as if she were walking on air.

Everything seemed brighter and more interesting this morning. She looked at the ferns on the roadside walls and loved their sharp greenness and sword-like shapes. Small flowers of sheeps' bit and chickweed caught her eye and, hearing the music of a gentle wind sweeping down from the tors, and the lark singing in the field beyond the hedge, she thought of her favourite song, *The Sprig of Thyme*. Her voice rose as she sang a few lines, clear in the quiet air, and then she remembered Joseph singing it, too. '*O'er the lane came a lad, he took all that I had....*'

She added the final line, *and stole my thyme away*, thought about it, and then walked on silently, wondering just what it was that Joseph had stolen. Because she knew now that he had taken a bit of her – some secret part that she had never shown to anyone before. Something warm and yearning that she still preferred to put aside. Then she told herself determinedly that her position at High Cross Manor was more important than a brief kiss with a man who never stayed still long enough to have an address.

It was with a mind full of hope and restrained excitement that she presented herself at the kitchen door of the Manor and was met by an old woman whom she had never seen before, although the whole village knew that Nellie Mudge was the only servant left from the many who had kept the Manor going when Rupert Fielding's parents were still alive.

'You're Rebecca Yeo? Maister said you were comin'.'

Becky thought the hooded eyes, almost invisible among folds of wrinkles, were not welcoming. She stepped inside the doorway and looked around as the old woman turned and limped across the room.

She knew that this had once been a kitchen full of maids and steaming pots and pans. Gossip said that dinners at High Cross had been popular among the gentry of twenty years ago. Ma had once chatted about working there herself when she was a girl. How Mr Fielding had been a handsome young man who charmed everyone but then, after his parents died, had seemingly let himself go, allowing the house to become neglected, dismissing most of the servants, living in a few rooms and not seeing friends any more. He'd let himself go, said the village, forever watching and tattling.

Becky put all this out of her mind and stood beside the huge scrubbed table in the middle of the big kitchen, watching Nellie turn slowly and stare at her. 'You looks strong,' was all the old woman said before turning again and leading the way through the house. She stopped at the foot of the grand staircase which circled the vast hall, leading to a gallery above, looked back at Becky and said, in her cracked old voice, 'Your room's in the attic. More stairs above these. Put your things there and then come down. I got a list of things for you to do. Maister gave it me just now. Said as 'ow you can start right in on them.'

Becky nodded, still looking about her. 'Get on, then,' said Nellie Mudge roughly. 'No time to lose if this ole house is goin' to be made tidy again. I don't want no fly-by-nights 'ere, so move sharp, maid.'

Up the stairs she went, noticing the carved oak banisters, looking at the huge portraits hanging on the wall, wondering who these aristocratic people were. Across the landing with its many closed bedroom doors and on to another flight of stairs, uncarpeted, narrow and creaking, with knots in the old wood, and finally there was her room at the top. Becky saw an iron bedstead with a grey blanket and an uncovered shabby bolster. There was a chair, a small table and a washstand with a cracked bowl and matching ewer. Something made her shiver. It was a cold, lonely room with a bad feel to it. She didn't want to sleep here. She wondered if Nat Briggs had given Mr Fielding her message, if the maister would find her, tell her she must do as he wanted and dismiss her own wants. Indeed, for the few minutes it took her to look around the attic, put her few clothes in the rickety drawers, soap and hairbrush on the washstand, then go down the stairs again, longing to explore some of the rooms with their closed doors but knowing she shouldn't, Becky wondered about being here at all. Had she been right in accepting the position? The house seemed unwelcoming and she feared she and Nellie would never get on.

But then her natural brightness banished the bad thoughts and she returned to the kitchen more sure of herself and willing to do whatever work was needed. Maister's list, Nellie Mudge had said – so what would the first task be?

'I needs wood for the fire,' said the old woman, frowning and nodding her head towards the door. 'Out in the carpenter's shop there'll be a heap o' bits. Take this basket and bring in as much as you can. An' get a move on,'

Becky took a deep breath and went into the yard. So she was to be treated just as harshly as at home? What on earth had made her come here? Tonight she'd leave. This was no place for a decent girl to work. Maybe Ma had been right.

Outside she looked around. There was a clutter of buildings spread down the yard, sheds and outhouses, stables and a granary – so which could be the carpenter's shop? And then, slowly, all her fears and annoyance died, for someone was humming in the furthermost shed. A deep, low, contented sound which made her smile and run towards it.

The shed was unlit but a weak sun filtered through a bleary window on its far side. It smelt of wood and tar and paint, and with each step she took her feet were covered in shavings. But nothing mattered because she saw that the big figure leaning over a bench with a chisel in his large hand was someone she knew, just as she knew that lovely, velvety voice.

Joseph Freeman, of course, singing as he worked.

CHAPTER 5

He stopped working, looked over his shoulder, turning to meet her gaze. 'Miss Freckles! So – come to find me, have you? I knew as you wanted my address.'

Excited as she was to see him, Becky's mouth pursed. His words were cheeky, but his eyes, a silvery light in the dim building, held an irrepressible gleam she couldn't ignore. Sharply it dawned on her that there was much about this attractive man that she had to discover. Casual kisses were all very well, but what went on in his head? In his life?

She stood quite still in the doorway, stiffening with irritation. 'What a thing to say! I work here, didn't know as I'd find you here as well. What're you doing?'

Joseph leaned against the bench which held tools and a big carved piece of wood. He grinned, stood up straight, rubbed his back and stretched his arms, still looking at her. 'Might say the same to you, Miss Becky. I'm taken on to do some joinery. Didn't expect to see you. Last time 'twas at the harvest supper and then … afterwards.' His deep voice died away, the final words lingering with a resonance that sent colour flushing up her throat and into her cheeks, remembering.

'Yes, well.' She cleared her throat, put a hand to her face to hide the blush and decided to bring this cheeky clodhead to heel. 'I'm employed by Mr Fielding to help as he renovates his house. Like you, I expect.' Already she had forgotten her earlier decision to leave once the day was over. For now she knew, like it or not, that if Joseph was to be here, then life would be much more exciting, intriguing even. She couldn't go home, not now.

He moved towards her, a big shadowy presence, and she stood still, captivated by what was happening. 'So we shall be seeing a bit of each other, shall we, Becky? That's good.' Gently he put a hand, large and strong, on her shoulder and she felt again that extraordinary sense of meeting someone who understood her, who would help her on her way, who would be good to her. And even good *for* her. But Joseph was an unknown labourer with perhaps, as Nat suggested, a girl in every farm. Becky's natural defiance brought a speedy warning. If he thought he could treat her in the same way as all the others, then he was wrong.

With a sudden burst of knowledge, she realized that, one day, when she met and loved a man, there would be no other. So she must be careful with Joseph, with this stranger. Not allow herself to appear easy and flirtatious. She took one step away from him, felt his hand leave her shoulder and instantly regretted it.

He was watching her, not moving, and she could find nothing more to say to him. It was as if she had become stricken down, like a rabbit when the ferret searches it out. This man was powerful and too attractive to be any good. Perhaps, after all, she should change her mind yet again, and leave High Cross Manor and return home. She took in a deep, noisy breath and frowned. But then she might not see him again and that was unthinkable.

Joseph turned to the bench, body bending as his left hand picked up the chisel, right hand reaching for the mallet, and began working again on the oak panel. But as he did so, he said quietly, 'No need to be scared, Becky. I'll do you no harm. But we must be together again, like the other night. So wait for me, eh?' And quickly he glanced over his shoulder, the message in his eyes forcing her into speech.

'All right. I'll be working here, at the Manor. I'll be busy, but – when I have time off, I'll wait....'

A last gleam in the green-grey eyes and the soft, seductive voice, saying, 'That's good. I'll find you – when I can.'

And then, abruptly Nellie's cracked voice ringing through the yard. 'Rebecca, where're you to, for goodness? Bring in that kindling, quick as you can.'

Becky felt the spell shatter. Hurriedly she went towards the corner of the shed where a huge pile of offcuts of timber and broken branches stood and grabbed handfuls, filling her basket. She didn't look at Joseph, but sensed that he watched. She went back to the kitchen and Nellie's grumpy rebukes with a light heart and a sense of adventure. He would find her, she was sure of it. And then – her heart raced – what would happen?

Rupert Fielding returned from escorting Felicity Richards back to her home in Moretonhampstead. It was early evening and he felt the need of his usual drink, but once the carriage had been drawn into the mews, and the horses taken to the stables, he found time to speak to Tom Butler, the groom who was working with the stable lad, Eddy.

'How's that new young gelding coming on, Tom? I'd like to try him out next week when we go cubbing. Promising, is he? Steady? Getting used to moorland work?'

Tom Butler nodded, pausing in his work. 'Yes, sir. Justice seems a likely young'un, I'd say. Next week, is it? Friday, as usual?'

'That's it. I'll see how we get on. Goodnight, now.'

Rupert stopped momentarily at the stall where Justice was standing, pulling hay from the tallat above and whickering as he heard voices. A hand on the smooth, firm rump, and Rupert smiled to himself. Hunting season again. Good. The summer had been boring without the customary adventures over the moor and the ongoing conviviality of his country friends. Returning to the house and his shabby, comfortable study, he wondered briefly if Felicity, when they were married, would resent his many disappearances during the hunting season. She was certainly a very social woman, always out somewhere with her many friends. He sank down into the old leather chair by the fireplace and reached for the bottle Nellie had, as usual, put on the table beside him. He lit a cigar, took a long, relishing sip of the whisky and felt himself ease into the familiar, drowsy, shadowy evening state when he could forget the world and its problems and sink back into the simplicity of taste, smell and comfort.

If, during the evening, Felicity entered that world then she was quickly cast out again. He had told her bluntly that this proposed marriage was simply a convenience; he needed an heir and she had said she was keen to have a child, which should be possible, as she was a good fifteen years younger than him.

Felicity. Still pretty and nubile enough to excite him, even though he found her determination and bossiness hard to deal with. He shut his eyes. It would be pleasant to take a woman to bed again. Something he had been used to doing frequently in his youth, but nowadays – well – perhaps he was getting too old for it. He opened his eyes, smiling at the foolish thought, and memories began coursing through his mind.

There had been so many pretty little maids, some in the house, others daughters of his parents' farming tenants. It had all been so easy – and no problems. No comebacks, no arguments. A handout and a stiff warning about the future of the tenancy usually dealt with any possible complaints. Although…. Suddenly his smile died and he eased himself up a little straighter in the creaking chair. There had been one, of course, who had come back and said defiantly that he'd made her pregnant and what was he going to do about it? Rupert poured another measure of whisky and tried to push the unpleasant memory out of his mind. All gone. All done, in the past, and today just the faintest memory, so easy to forget.

But something still nagged at him. He frowned, forcing himself to confront it. That girl, the one who had had the audacity to come into the house uninvited and then asked him for a situation. Freckles, a clear speech, and that thick chestnut hair.

Something about her.

Yawning, he drooped back into the welcoming chair. Cigar ash fell unheeded on his chest as the evening light faded, the sun slipped away and the comforting shadow land returned. He slept.

*

Becky worked hard all morning, stopping only for a meal in the kitchen at crib time when she was thankful to sit down. Now she was able to go anywhere that she chose in the house, it had become increasingly clear that Mr Fielding had let things go for too many years. Dust, cobwebs, even dry rot in some of the panels and beams of the main rooms – she wondered why she had ever thought their homely farmhouse old and dirty. Thirza would be shocked if she saw this neglect.

As she sat at the long table, with Tom Butler and the lad, Eddy, opposite her, she listened to Nellie wheezing on about the past. 'Once this was all clean and shining. When Mr Rupert were a boy. His parents were fussy, oh yes, they was. But after they'd gone, well, the maister seemed not to care about the house any more. Always out, hunting, parties....' Nellie frowned as she paused, a hunk of bread spread with dripping in her hand. She stared at Tom. 'What you grinning at, then?'

'Nothing,' he assured her. But the grin grew. 'Just remembering all the stories 'bout the women. . . likes a bit of warm flesh, does the maister.'

Becky saw the lad drop his bread and bend down to hide his laughter. She looked at Tom, who met her gaze, then said apologetically, 'Sorry, maid, but that's how it was. Nellie knows.'

But Nellie looked at her plate and said nothing, leaving Becky to understand that Mr Fielding's reputation was in no way different from the tales she'd heard in the village. Perhaps it was worse than that. She recalled Thirza's anxiety, and told herself that she must be careful. Not that he would ever think of her as a possible victim. Needing reassurance, she looked at Nellie and said, 'He's old now. He can't do things like that any more.'

But her thoughts raced on, wondering what made a man behave in such an uncontrolled way. Surely he must have been unhappy in those days? Uncertain what life held for him? She even felt slight pity for such a man and the thought surprisingly made her want to see him again. To find out what he was really like.

Nellie drank her ale, pushed the empty plate away and scraped back her chair. 'Time to get on.'

In the afternoon Becky worked in the main guest bedroom, sleeves rolled up and a hessian apron tied around her waist. The four-poster headboard was carved with angels and flowers and leaves and the dust had become engrained. One pillar of the board was missing and at once she knew what Joseph had been working on. With difficulty she took down the faded, musty bed curtains and carried them down to the scullery, ready for the next wash. Up again to clean the big mullioned windows, at the same time looking down into the neglected garden and stretching paddock and meadows beyond.

She was ready to stop work, ready for a cup of tea and a breath of outside clean air after all the dirty, musty atmosphere up there, when Nellie called up the stairs, 'Rebecca, come down 'ere.'

Nat Briggs stood in the hallway, watching her. 'Workin' hard, then, Becky? I reckons you owes me something fer getting the maister to take you on.'

His smile sent a shiver through her and she stiffened. 'I don't owe you nothing, Mr Briggs. I spoke to Mr Fielding myself and asked and he said—'

Nat cut in quickly. 'Asked me 'bout your character, he did, Becky, and I gave him a good account of you. Course you owes me.' He came closer to her as she reached the bottom of the stair-case and looked into her eyes, his leery smile repulsing her. 'But not now. There'll be other times. Soon, I reckon. And me being around, 'cos Maister needs me to help out with his papers, he says. So I'll be here. Like you. Plenty o' chances to be together. Proper, eh?'

'No!' He made her feel dirty, the way he looked at her. She pushed past him and almost ran into the kitchen, his voice following as she went. 'You wanted to be here, Becky, so you can't blame me for charging my payment, can you?'

Nellie looked up as she entered. 'What you doing with that Briggs? Keep clear of him, maid. Always after the girls, he be. Now – done that bedroom, then?' And, looking at her more closely, 'Sit down an' rest now. Kettle's on the boil. We'll have some tea, get ready for the next job.'

Becky was grateful for the understanding and the chance to stop working. She wondered again just what secrets Nellie knew about the house and its occupants. Perhaps she could get the old woman talking one day…. Mr Fielding's image flashed into her mind, and she felt again the urge to find out more about him. Smiling at Nellie as she poured water into the big enamel teapot, she knew she must make the old woman her friend.

She could hardly believe it when the day ended. Working on the farm had always been in accordance with the routine duties, the weather and the seasons, but here, contained in four stone walls, time passed without her noticing it. Straightening up after removing dirt and fluff from under the bed in what Nellie called the second guest room, Becky's thoughts were suddenly full of home. And Thirza. And how she must, somehow, get a message to Ma that she wouldn't be coming back this evening, or any evening, until she was given time off.

Back in the kitchen, glad to sit down and watch Nellie preparing dinner for the maister, she asked quietly, 'Can I have an hour off, Mrs Mudge? I need to tell my mother that I'm sleeping here. She didn't want me to, you see.'

Nellie looked up from basting the chicken in the big black pan set on top of the range.

'What, Thirza nervous for you, was she?' She chuckled and Becky thought, *Why?* Carefully, she asked, 'You remember Ma working here, I expect?'

Nellie turned and looked at her. 'I remember lots o' things,' she said sharply. 'Yes, she was here.'

Becky thought she was going to say more, but abruptly she moved away to the dresser to get down dishes and plates and put them to warm.

'So – can I go, for an hour or so, Mrs Mudge?'

'Work's done fer the day – yes, you can go – but door's locked after ten o'clock.'

Rising, Becky said, 'Thank you,' and went up to the attic to change her stained dress for the old print hanging in the curtained cupboard, wash her hands and face, brush her hair and then escape.

Outside it was nearly dimpsey, with rooks shouting in the elms nearby and a scent of gorse sweeping down from the moor. Becky left the yard without wondering whether Joseph was still at work, for her mind was full of other things. She walked down the lane towards home, filled with anxiety. How had Will got on without her help? Had he forced Ma into taking her place? Was anything being done about getting an apprentice from the Union? Had Mr Briggs helped in any way?

And then, like a sinister cloud darkening her mind, she remembered that Nat Briggs was going to spend time at the Manor, so he said. How could she avoid meeting him? And would he really demand payment for his small service? As she walked, Becky increased her speed, as if to escape from the image of him, thankfully reaching the farmhouse before any more anxieties mounted up. The yard was empty, but Prince barked and then gave her a mad welcome, while the cob whickered in the stable shed. Becky smelt cow dung and hay and wood smoke and breathed it all in with a sense of relief. She went in through the open kitchen door and smiled, knowing she was home and safe. The thought puzzled her for a second: *Safe from what?* But she pushed it aside, as Thirza came to greet her.

'So you're back! Oh, maid, I'm that glad to see you.'

It took a while to let Thirza understand that this was just a visit, and Becky patiently softened the blow by telling her mother about the work she had been doing all day. 'So you see, Ma, there's so much to do, and I've been given this little room, which isn't bad.' A small lie, but necessary. 'And Mrs Mudge is good to me.'

'Nellie Mudge? Her still there? My soul, she must be gettin' on now. Her was there when—' Thirza bit off the words and Becky said quickly, 'When you were there? Yes, she remembers you.'

There was silence for a moment while Thirza sat down, apparently lost in thought. Until Will came stomping in, stopping in the doorway when he saw Becky.

'You back, then? Didn't last long, that job.' With his familiar lack of manners, he pushed past her, heaving himself into the chair by the fire and beginning to unlace his boots. 'Got the sack, did you?'

'No,' said Becky sharply. 'I'm just here to tell Ma that I shan't be coming home nights. I'm to sleep there.' She frowned at her brother. 'It's a good position and I like it so don't you go saying bad things.' She stopped, remembered what her loss must mean, and then added, 'Done anything about getting an apprentice, have you?'

Will turned and looked at her, boots slowly being kicked off. She thought he seemed reluctant to answer, but slowly, he said, 'No. Gettin' a 'prentice is too much of a to do with indentures and suchlike, so Dinah's comin' to help.' He paused, blinked. 'I know she's slow, but she'll learn. An' she said it's right for you to get a better sort of work – you can read an' write. So I thought 'bout it and well, all right then, Becks. I hopes as you're happy at the Manor.'

Becky was taken aback. She had never thought Will would come round to saying such brotherly things. And then she wondered at Dinah, making him change his mind; it was all very surprising. She felt a new warmth as she looked at him, and said slowly, with a wry smile, 'That's the nicest thing you've ever said.'

Will sat back in his chair, eyes on the beams overhead. And then he looked at her and nodded. 'You're a good worker, Becks, I'll give you that, an' like Dinah ses, all your education gone for nothing if you stay here. Well, no need for you to worry 'bout leavin' us any more.' Surprisingly, he smiled. 'Come fer supper, have you? Ma's got a plump rabbit – shot it this morning. Let's sit down, then.'

It was a good hour later when Becky knew she must leave and go back to her cold, musty attic. But now she was full of hope and all the worries about Ma and Will had slipped into the background. They would manage without her and she could give her wages to them, which would be something in place of her work. She walked down the dark lane, pulling her shawl about her shoulders, for August was rapidly slipping into autumn and the evenings growing cold.

The hedges threw dark shadows and the rough road was a thread of moonlit stones taking her back to High Cross Manor. Shadows, thought Becky, walking quickly and surely along the old familiar way. Life seemed full of them. But she was recognizing, slowly, that very often shadows lightened and became different. Just think of Dinah talking to Will. It was almost as if they could even become sunlit paths, easy to follow and enjoy. Her mind lightened, and she hummed a bit of *The Sprig of Thyme* as she walked.

She found the key in the door waiting at the Manor, the kitchen empty, but a kettle was on the fire, and a mug stood on the table holding milk and she knew that Nellie had left it out for her. Going up first the elegant staircase and then, with her candle wavering in the draught, up the narrow creaking stairs above, Becky accepted that being here at High Cross Manor could well become one of those newly sunlit paths – if that was what she truly wanted.

CHAPTER 6

The days slipped past increasingly rapidly. Becky found the work hard but satisfying, seeing the dusty and neglected house becoming once again the elegant home Nellie Mudge told her it had originally been. Even her attic was more welcoming after a good clean, with some wild flowers on the creaky washstand, an extra blanket. and the one window cleared of raindrops and bird spatterings. And Nellie was more inclined to be friendly, and talk. Or so Becky thought.

'How's Thirza these days, then? Don't never see her now.' Nellie's sharp eyes fixed on Becky. 'Must be gettin' on a bit. Not all that young when she were here.'

'I don't know.' Becky found the idea of Ma *getting on* surprising. To her Thirza, with her grey hair and slight cough had always been the same figure. 'We don't count birthdays much at home, too busy. Except that I was nineteen in January.'

Nellie's wizened arms worked at the dough on the table in front of her. She said nothing but Becky watched the expression on her face and wondered where these questions came from.

She waited, uncertain whether to ask, but Nellie was silent, immersed in bread making, her face intent, her lips tight, and so Becky slowly learned to be quiet and not ask anything.

But vaguely, she realized that Nellie knew secrets and was unlikely to share them. The knowledge gave a sense of frustrated excitement to her hard work, a source of wonderment when arms and legs and back ached and the day seemed never ending.

Gradually, too, she accepted that Rupert Fielding was a complex man who spent periods sitting alone in his study, drinking, smoking cigars, eyes closed, but seemingly aware of what went on in the house, in the yard, around the estate. When Nat Briggs came, which was every few days, Mr Fielding became more active and Becky heard their voices in the study as she passed the closed door. At those times she made sure she was upstairs when Nat arrived and when he left. She had a fear of meeting him again, of seeing something in his small, close set eyes which scared her. And she remembered the looks passing between Will and Ma not long ago when Nat was around. It was as if they had arranged something – about her? Becky put all her energy into her work and banished Nat Briggs from her mind.

Joseph was still working in the carpenter's shop. She heard him whenever she went into the yard for something, but he never appeared, looking for her. And, although she wanted to do so, she didn't allow herself to go and find him, because if she did, and he showed no more interest in her, how would she feel?

He's a wild man. No good. He'll be off somewhere before I know it – all that about coming to find me was just rubbish. But, oh, the memories of his kiss, of his voice and of the wicked smile on his handsome face refused to disappear. Becky swept, dusted and polished all the harder, resolving never to think about such a useless fly-by-night again.

When Rupert Fielding came into the kitchen one morning after breakfast, she and Nellie stood up, at once seeing something different about him. Dressed in tweed jacket, breeches and riding boots, bowler hat in hand, he was clearly the man of means, the owner of the estate.

Even his voice was different, clearer, crisper. 'I'm bringing some friends back for dinner, Nellie. We'll be ravenous after hunting – do one of your tasty dishes, please, and plenty of it.' He stopped in the doorway, glanced back at Becky, and gave her a stiff smile. 'I understand you work well. Mrs Mudge is pleased with you.' A pause, and then the stiffness resolved slightly. 'Like it here, do you? Want to stay?'

Becky almost gasped. He hadn't spoken to her since that awful confrontation in the kitchen after the harvest supper. And now there was a hint of a more open smile on his long, lined face.

'Yes,' she said quickly and bobbed neatly, 'Yes, sir. Yes, please, I do.'

'I'm glad you're happy here.' Rupert Fielding nodded, turned away and disappeared into the yard where she heard him shouting for Tom Butler.

She went to the door, watching as Justice, the gelding, was held and Mr Fielding mounted. She saw him clip clop out of the yard with Tom Butler on the cob behind him, before she turned back to Nellie. 'Hunting? Cubbing, is it? End of August, killing the young foxes? Meeting his friends and then hacking out somewhere?'

'Yes,' said Nellie, pushing her dough into a pan, covering it with a cloth then putting it close to the fire. 'They generally meet up by Swallerton Gate. Dunno where they goes then.' She sighed. 'Company for dinner, so I'd better get that cockerel you plucked yesterday and get it ready to cook. You can do the 'taties.'

Rupert Fielding rode away from the Manor, wondering at his remarks to the new kitchen maid. She was an attractive and lively young woman with a clear voice and good manners, but she knew her place. Then the disturbing thought returned; something about her. An air of vitality and charm. He frowned; she had a presence that seemed to lighten the old house.

But then Tom was at his side and they discussed the venue of the morning's meet. And soon then they were passing Bowerman's Nose, standing huge and grey beyond the Gate where already a group of horsemen had gathered. Forget the girl; this was the time of his favourite pastime and nothing must intrude.

'Morning, Squire.' Doffed hats from the estate farmers.

'Morning, Fielding,' from the gentry and a patronizing nod from the master, holding court, hounds restless beside him, and then they were off and everything in Rupert's mind fled, save the moment. The rhythm of the horse and his body responding to it;

sweat on his forehead as the sun beat down and the scent of heather in the air as hoofs left the road and plunged across open moorland.

Hounds found and one young fox ran so they let it go, to grow into good healthy maturity. But then hounds were in the covert, noisy and ready to kill. Enthusiastically the inexperienced and excited gelding headed down the rough, pitted slope towards the copse. Abruptly off balance, Justice fell, Rupert clinging on for the first seconds, but then falling heavily while the gelding stumbled to its feet and stopped, confused.

Rapidly Tom Butler dismounted, took hold of Justice's reins, shouted for help and for someone to find a hurdle, on which Rupert was carried home, eyes closed and his back causing him what was clearly agonizing pain.

Becky and Nellie waited in the kitchen while the doctor, brought from Moretonhampstead, arrived to examine Rupert. Tom and Eddy were in the stables, Nat Briggs hovered on the stairs, and Becky saw that Joseph, hearing the commotion, had left the carpenter's shop and was outside the kitchen door. No one spoke, for the hurdle and its occupant had been enough information on its own. The maister was badly hurt and no one could do anything until the doctor spoke.

When Dr Gale came downstairs he stood in the hall and called for Nellie. Wiping her hands on her apron, she quickly went out of the kitchen. Becky followed, loitering in the shadowy passage between kitchen and hallway. She listened, anxious about the maister's progress, and surprised at herself for feeling such an emotion.

'Mr Fielding needs rest,' said Dr Gale gruffly. 'His back will recover – slowly – but he took a fall on his head and I fear might suffer concussion for a while. I've given him drugs to help him sleep, but someone should be in attendance. Have you a girl who can sit with him?'

Nellie said slowly, 'There's only Rebecca here with me. I s'pose she could do it.'

'Is she sensible? Capable of making decisions if necessary?'

Becky was about to step through the doorway, when she heard Nellie say grudgingly,

'She'll do that all right, Doctor.' A pause and then, her voice softening anxiously, 'Will the maister – will he be all right?'

'I hope so. A fall at his age needn't be fatal, but his heart isn't all that strong. We can only hope for the best, Mrs Mudge. And now I'm off. Send the boy for me if I'm needed.' He went out into the courtyard where Tom waited with the pony and trap.

Nellie turned, saw Becky behind her and said slowly, 'You heard then?' She sighed heavily. 'Go on up and see that he don't want for anything – just sit there and watch. And so I reckon I gotta do the best I can on me own. Just when I was getting used to having you help out. Well, at least there'll be no big dinner tonight.'

Alone in the passage, Becky stood still for a moment, thinking. And then she took off her apron, smoothed her work dress, pushed some wayward hairs under her cap and went up the sweeping staircase. If Mr Fielding needed her care, then she'd give it to him, and willingly.

She met Nat Briggs at the head of the stairs, standing there watching her. He said, very sharply, 'You an' me gotta do the best we can. Maister can't do nothing for himself for a while. So you to sit with him and me to see to the estate. Understand?'

'Yes.' Becky saw the start of a new expression on his tanned, leathery face, and knew it was a growing realization of power. Her mind seethed with words of distaste, of warning, of her hatred of him, but then realized this wasn't the moment to confront him. She had a duty to do, and caring for Mr Fielding was more impor-tant than bringing Nat Briggs down a peg or two. She walked around him, knocked lightly on the bedroom door and entered, closing it behind her.

Rupert Fielding lay there, stretched straight out on the length of the four-poster bed. A green quilted coverlet rested over his chest and arms and his head was slightly turned to one side, his closed eyes and pallor making him almost unfamiliar.

Becky was shocked. She had only known him for a short while, but his long frame and once handsome face had already become familiar, and now he had suddenly changed into an old man whose unsteady breathing filled the silence of the big room and made her own heart start to race. What could she do to help? Surely there must be something, other than merely sitting beside his bed and waiting for him to open his eyes?

Her mind flew in circles, suddenly remembering Thirza's husky voice from childhood, crooning to her when she was poorly, and then words came unbidden, and she began, very softly, to sing.

'In my garden grew plenty of thyme, it would flourish by
*   night and by day.*
O'er the wall came a lad, he took all that I had, and stole
*   my thyme away.'*

Sitting there in the large, sunlit room, her thoughts slipped back to the warmth of her childhood. To memories when Will was more friendly and of both of them playing around the farm. And then, growing, working together, helping out by holding the horses, rounding up the sheep, feeding poultry and washing eggs for market – all the common tasks of a small farm struggling to keep the family alive, striving for as much comfort as they could afford.

As she reached the last word she sighed. The thyme in the song had gone, and so had her childhood. Yesterday, gone for ever, and here was today and poor Mr Fielding lying beside her, eyes still closed, breathing shallow and slow. What could she do for him other than sit here and wait patiently until he regained consciousness? And why should she feel this unexpected sympathy for him? She got to her feet, walked to the window and looked out across the garden to the stretching moorland beyond. Something moved along the rough path leading from the adjacent yard to the road and she looked more intently.

A man, tall and heavy, with a bag over his shoulder and a hat clamped down over his wind-blown corn gold hair. He carried a staff and she thought he looked eager to get away into the freedom of the moor. Joseph, of course. Going, and without a word to her.

Becky sucked in a huge breath, trying to stop the anger and the depth of longing that suddenly raged through her. She had known the sort of man he was, a traveller, a fly-by-night, so why feel like this? Why waste her thoughts and feelings? She was here at High Cross Manor with a special duty to perform. Her situation was confirmed. No need to worry about her future. She turned back to the bed and sat down, looking again at Mr Fielding whose breathing had become noisier.

As she looked she saw his eyelids fluttering. And then suddenly he was awake, dark eyes looking directly at her, a hint of a smile lightening his grey, lined face.

'Grace,' he said. Just the one word.

Anxiously, Becky leaned over him. 'Mr Fielding? Can I get you something?'

No reply. Eyes closed, and the suggestion of a smile vanished. He slept.

Becky remained where she was until, later in the afternoon, Nellie came with a dish of beef tea and a drink. 'I'll sit for a while. You can go down – get some fresh air.'

Becky nodded. 'Thank you. I'll come back soon.' She felt the need to get up and move away from the sick bed. From the uneasy thoughts that were swirling around inside her. Who had the maister thought she was? Who was Grace?

She went downstairs quickly, eager to get out of the house with its strange echoes of what she sensed were haunting secrets. Passing the study she heard movement and knew it was Nat Briggs, reading papers and books that he had no right to read. But someone must run the estate while Mr Fielding was ill, so it had to be Nat, just as he had said. And she was the one to look after the maister. So she supposed there was a sort of unwanted bond between them.

Out in the breezy air of the yard, Becky took in great lungfuls and felt herself respond to more cheerful thoughts. She went into the carpenter's shop and saw the wooden slab of timber Joseph had been working on propped on the bench. It was finished, a cleverly restored part of the panel forming the head of the bed in the guest room. His tools had disappeared, so had his jacket hung on the door and the big bag beneath it, but his presence remained. She could sense him there, turning, looking at her, smiling, saying wicked words that he had never meant. And although she knew she must forget him, she also knew that she had to find him again. Somewhere. Somehow.

It was a happy thought, and enabled her to return cheerfully to the patient's bedside an hour later where she found Mr Fielding awake and looking around him, with Nellie and a half-emptied bowl of beef tea at his side. 'He's come to,' whispered Nellie, standing back from the bed. 'Ses he must get up, see to things. I told him as doctor ses he has to stay there, but he wants to get up. Asked where you was – where's the girl, he said, clear as anything. Well, see what you can do, maid.'

She left the room and Becky stood by the bed, saying quietly, 'Can I get you anything, Mr Fielding?'

He drew his arms from beneath the coverlet and asked harshly, 'What happened?'

'You took a fall. Dr Gale came from Moreton. He said you must rest.'

'Good God! I can't rest.' He pulled himself into a sitting position, wincing as pain struck. 'My back, is it? Well, it's not the first time. It'll mend.'

Becky thought she should reassure him after the shock of the accident, so she said, 'Mr Briggs is here, looking after things, Mr Fielding. No need for you to worry about anything....' And then the words died away as he stared at her, dark eyes wide and intent.

'I know you, don't I? Seen you before somewhere.' His voice was rough and hoarse.

She smiled, trying to calm him. 'I'm Rebecca Yeo, your new kitchen maid.'

Silence, and she saw thoughts tightening his pale face. 'Rebecca? Not Grace?'

Again, *Grace*. She took a deep breath. 'No, sir, I'm Becky.' And then sympathy for what he was obviously suffering made her add, 'You had a blow to the head, sir. Can I get you something to help the pain?'

He dropped back onto the pillows, grimacing as he allowed his body to slide downwards. 'Nothing. I don't want anything. You can go.'

'But the doctor said—'

'Damn the doctor. I'll be up tomorrow. Just want a good night's sleep. And then, so much to do. Must tell Felicity. Get Briggs to go to Moreton, I'll write a letter and tell her....' The words weakened and died.

Becky nodded her head. She had tried to help but all he wanted was to get his life back. She walked to the door and then stopped as he called after her, voice suddenly weak and only just audible. 'Stay here. Till I sleep.'

'Yes, of course.' She went to the window, drew the curtains against the afternoon sun, and then returned to the bedside.

She felt him watching her every movement. When she sat he nodded and turned his head to look at her, dark eyes taking in every feature, freckles, her strong chin and thick chestnut sparked hair. What did he see in her, she wondered uneasily and wished she was somewhere else. Safely at home, perhaps. Somewhere with Joseph. Anywhere away from this haunted room and the unsaid thoughts flickering in Rupert Fielding's dark eyes. 'Grace,' he murmured, and then turned away.

She sat there, wondering, imagining, until at last the curious eyes closed, he slept and then she crept from the room, thankful to escape.

Going downstairs, two words echoed through her uneasy mind. *Grace. Escape.*

But – escape from what?

CHAPTER 7

'Mrs Mudge, who is Grace?'

Becky asked the question quietly, looking at the grey haired woman bending over the hot range in the kitchen. The stirring hand stopped abruptly and Nellie turned, looking over her shoulder, narrowed eyes and wrinkled face tight with a grim expression that surprised Becky.

'Why d'you want to know?' Her voice was quick and harsh.

'Because Mr Fielding said her name. He'd just woken up, then he looked at me and said, "Grace".'

Nellie turned back to her stock pot and the steady stirring. 'Just a girl who worked here once.' It seemed a casual remark, but Becky heard her voice crack. 'Oh, long ago. Now, we must think about something for the maister's dinner – I wonder if he might like a bite or two of that old fowl if I makes it really tender. Fetch it out of the larder, maid.'

Knowing she was being put off, Becky went to the larder with determination hot inside her. Nellie wouldn't tell her. Very well, she would ask Ma, who had also worked here, if she remembered Grace and what was so special about her. Well, special enough to make Mr Fielding remember her. And it would be easier to make Ma tell than keep questioning awkward old Nellie.

Returning with the fowl and putting it on the table, she smiled and asked politely, 'If the maister doesn't need me for an hour while he's asleep, I'd like to run home, Mrs Mudge. I expect Ma and Will have heard the news and they'll want to know how he is. Can I go?'

Nellie stared across the table, hands already busy about the bird. 'Well – wait till he sleeps proper after his meal and then p'raps you can. Wonder if we can get Mr Briggs to sit with him – or p'raps Tom, though he do smell of the stable.'

Becky started cleaning potatoes in the scullery, her thoughts busy. Perhaps tomorrow the maister would like her to carry on sitting with him – at least until he could manage on his own. She breathed deeply, saw him in her mind's eye, pale and tense with pain, and knew she would gladly give time to looking after him. Uncertain why, she felt at ease with him. And she sensed that he liked her enough to allow her to be beside him. She shook her head. Everything was very strange today.

Returning to the kitchen she put the potatoes on to cook, aware of Nellie watching her, and suddenly she turned to meet the thoughtful gaze, hoping for something about Grace, but then Nellie turned away and the moment was gone. By the time the meal was cooked, she had laid a tray to take to the invalid and was about to carry it up the stairs when Nat Briggs came down, forcing her to step back and wait. He looked at her very keenly, deep set eyes seeming to pierce her mind. 'So he's awake, is he? Tell him as I needs to see him. Things he must decide.'

Becky said firmly, 'He's not ready yet. He needs to rest more.' And then she remembered what Mr Fielding had said. 'But I know he wants you to take a letter to Mrs Richards in Moreton tomorrow.'

Nat frowned, stretched out his hands and took the tray from her. 'Give it here. I'll take it to him. Then he can tell me what I gotta do.'

'But—' She hated the idea of Nat forcing the maister to try and think straight when clearly he wasn't ready for it.

'Never mind but,' he growled. 'Go on back and tell Nellie I'll be down for me dinner soon as I can. Tell her to keep it hot.' His frown grew more ferocious; watching her, he waited and she could do nothing but obey. Seeing him go up the stairs and barge straight into the maister's room without bothering to put down the tray and knock, she knew she hated Nat Briggs with a force that frightened her.

Downstairs, Nellie looked at her. 'Some'at wrong? Not the maister?'

Becky told her about what Nat had said. Nellie snorted. 'That's him, all right. But the maister'll tell him off, I don't doubt. He's a strong man, maister is, and that little hayseed'll have to give in if he wants to keep his job. Now,' She smiled at Becky. 'Sit you down, maid. You deserve a good meal and then you can go home fer a bit. I'll watch the maister meself if Nat don't do so.'

It was in the middle of the shared meal around the kitchen table that they heard a knock at the door and a deep voice called out, 'Joseph Freeman. I gotta message for Mr Briggs.'

Nat, deep in his chicken and gravy, growled, 'What a time o'night to come.' He nodded at Becky and gestured towards the door. She rose quickly, avoiding his knowing eyes, and opened the door. 'Mr Briggs is here,' she said curtly into the shadowy dusk, and turned back into the room, not letting herself look at the man standing in the doorway. But, even as she returned to the table, something warm and urgent flashed through her. Joseph here; would there be a chance to talk together after he'd given Nat the message?

Nellie looked at the remains of the carcass on the big dish on the table, and then across the room. 'There's a few scraps left if you're hungry,' she said, and allowed herself a slight smile as she met Joseph's eyes. 'Just get the talkin' done first and then you can sit yourself down.' She turned to Becky. 'Leave 'em be. We'll do the dishes – an then you can go, maid.'

Go? thought Becky, full of confusion. But I don't want to go anywhere while Joseph's here. And then, suddenly, she caught the full force of Nat's eyes, staring at her, his mouth down slanted and his hand clumsily wiping gravy from his thin lips. He knew, she thought wildly. He knows that I want to see Joseph. And he'll stop me doing it.

Words came without thought. 'I'll go and fetch the maister's tray. He'll be finished by now.' She left the kitchen without looking at anyone and ran up the stairs, wondering at her wild feelings. She found Rupert Fielding slumped in his bed, asleep, his breathing calmer and some colour in his cheeks. His bedside table held a half emptied plate and a large, empty wine glass. Relieved to think that he was on the road to recovery, she folded the green coverlet closer over his chest and then took the tray downstairs.

In the kitchen voices rose and fell, but she hardly heard what they said, for her mind was filled with the longing to do the dishes and then find Joseph. Clattering at the sink in the scullery, she found Nellie at her side.

'So he ate his meal, then? It was almost an empty plate.'

'Yes. And now he's sleeping – maybe he'll sleep through the night.' Becky glanced sideways at Nellie. 'Can I go, when this is done?'

'Said as how you can.' Nellie's sharp eyes narrowed. 'But keep away from that Briggs. He's in an awful temper, all about the message Joseph brought. Run home quick and you'll be safe.'

Becky breathed in a great sigh of relief. Having Nellie on her side was a help, and yes, she knew the road home so well that even if Nat Briggs followed, she could easily disappear into the shadows before he saw her. And perhaps Joseph would follow....

And then she heard the voices in the kitchen grow louder. 'So when did you see the vicar? What you doin' in Manaton, anyway?'

'Heard as there was work in the church, carving of new pews, so I went and asked the vicar, Mr Broadland, showed him some o' my work an' he recalled I was with Mr Gosling and said good enough. I start tomorrow.'

A chair scraped back and Becky winced as she heard Nat's heavy footsteps on the flagstones. 'An' then he told you to tell me 'bout the service on Sunday? Important, he said? Have to find someone in maister's place? So how did he know you was goin' to see me?'

There was suspicion in every word and she waited tensely for Joseph's reply. She knew he was a man of action when driven to it, but his voice, deep and quiet, held no replying anger.

'Told the Reverend I'd be coming to High Cross Manor to ask about Mr Fielding. Said as I've done work for him – and hope as how he'll employ me again, so I must enquire about him.'

Nat's answering growl was to be expected, but suddenly Becky heard him stride across to the door, his last words for Nellie. 'Tell maister I'll be here tomorrer to get his orders.'

The door slammed to, the untethered cob clattered out of the yard and Becky, wiping her hands, returned to the kitchen and dared meet to Joseph's eyes. Putting dishes on the dresser on the side wall, Nellie glanced over her shoulder. 'Off you goes, then. And remember as I lock the door after ten.' She nodded, and Becky thought she saw a glint of amusement in the old, faded eyes.

'Yes. Thank you, Mrs Mudge.' She took up the shawl draped over her chair and, without looking at Joseph, let herself out into the yard. The evening was chilly and she walked very slowly down past the stables, the cow barn and the carpenter's shop, uncertain whether to run or to wait. Suddenly she was full of burning, terrible doubt. What if Joseph didn't want to find her? What if he really had come just to give Nat a message and convey his best wishes to the maister? What if he had already found a new girl in Manaton? What if—

No! She wouldn't allow herself to think such things. Instinctively, she turned back towards the kitchen door and stood there, half hidden in the shadow of the old lilac tree growing around the privy, bravely facing her fears and counting every slowly passing second.

She waited a good ten minutes before the door opened and his voice reached out. 'Thank you, Mrs Mudge – a good meal that was. I'll be on my way now – and my best wishes to the maister, if you please. I hope he'll be up and about again soon.'

He stood, big and strong, in the dark doorway, looking about him, not seeing her until she slipped out from the lilac and faced him. Her heart raced, and she smiled.

He said nothing, but smiled back, his eyes catching the pale moonlight as he put an arm around her, silently drawing her away out of the dusky patch of yard. They started walking towards the lane; he put a finger on her lips and Becky knew that she had been right to wait. She would wait for ever, if that was what he wanted.

In the lane the hedges threw heavy shadows onto the path ahead of them until the growing moon slipped out from its veil of drifting clouds, and Becky thought her life had never before been so full of joy and contentment as in these few happy moments, walking between the Manor and High Cross Farm. At first they didn't speak, until a fox suddenly slid through the hedge ahead of them, turned to stare, and then disappeared into the darkness.

And then Joseph laughed, put his arm around her waist and drew her close. 'We're not alone, then, but as good as. So tell me, Becky Yeo, what you're thinking.'

She said nothing, too busy enjoying the nearness of his body.

'Something about the maister? About your new position? About being away from home – on your own?' His voice lowered a tone, but she thought she heard concealed amusement. 'About being here, with me, a man you don't know much of except what that rogue Briggs told you?'

At once her voice was uncertain. 'A girl at every farm, he said. How do I know if he's right or wrong?' She wasn't going to let him see how she excited and joyous she felt. Not yet. Perhaps not ever. He must show her what sort of man he was first.

Joseph stopped walking, holding her more tightly as he did so. He turned to look down at her and Becky felt herself giving in, leaning against him. 'You know he's wrong, Becky Yeo. You know there's only one girl and she's here, now. You know that, don't you?' His voice was deep and quiet and she felt his breath on her face.

Of course she knew. Had known from the first time she heard him singing, walking down the road to Manaton when she was outside the farm, hiding from Nat Briggs. The voice, the song, the sense that there, walking away from her, was the man who would mean everything in her life. But she had been brought up by a mother who warned her all the time about men and their easy ways, their charms and promises, and then, never ending, their habit of going off and finding someone else.

So she drew away, tightened her lips and said coolly, 'I don't know anything, Joseph. I've only seen you a few times.' But then, because the urgent emotion inside her rushed out, the words refused to be stopped. 'I need to find out … what you're like. What sort of a man. And … what you want.'

For a moment he said nothing, then his steps slowed, stopped and he turned to face her.

'Becky, I want to tell you who I am. What I'm trying to do – and why. Let's find somewhere where we can talk. Shall we?'

The unexpected seriousness of his words touched her, made her nod, whisper, 'Yes. Yes, please, Joseph.'

He took her hands, smiled into her inquiring eyes and drew her along the lane until they reached a field gate. 'In here. I'll find you a comfy place to sit while we talk.'

She sat at the bottom of the hedge, cushioned by grass and weeds, sheltered by the dark windproof foliage, expectant and tense. What did he have to tell her? Did she really want to know this man's secrets? But his quiet presence, the comfort of his deep, low voice banished the doubts. He sat beside her, held her hand in his, warm and reassuring, and began his story.

'I come from the Union Workhouse,' he said quietly. 'My mother died having me and so I spent the first nine years of my life there. In Newton Abbot. I was called Jack Adams because Jack was one of the ten names used for boys, and the surnames had just come around to A again, and Adams was the first on the list.'

Something deep inside Becky stirred. She hadn't expected anything like this. 'But you said you were Joseph Freeman....

His hands tightened around hers. 'I am. I changed my name because once out of that prison I wanted freedom. And I chose Joseph because that was the name of the man who rescued me: the Reverend Joseph Gosling who found me living wild, took me in and found this little half starved creature had a mind that was curious enough to want to learn. He apprenticed me as a garden lad. And also he taught me.'

Becky was silent, her mind too full to see clearly. Then, 'And what did you learn?'

'How to live. How to read and write, to enjoy music. I sang in his church choir. He taught me how to garden, to carve wood, build pigsties, care for animals and labour on the land. Before he died he taught me all I needed to live a good life. And so – here I am.'

Wondering, she said slowly, 'So that's why you're always going somewhere new. Hay making, harvesting, mending Mr Fielding's bed panel....'

'And now I'm off to Manaton church to make new bench pews and decorate their ends.' His voice had lightened, holding a note of gaiety which seemed at odds with her own thoughts.

'But if you never stay in one place, you'll never have a home.' She frowned. 'Is that what you want? Always to be alone? Never to—' She didn't finish, for the picture she conjured up was up was too dark, too hurtful to describe. Her mind saw him for ever alone, on the move, always doing the next thing, having no roots, with no possibility of settled happiness. It was a wicked picture and she bowed her head, trying to push it away.

'I know what you're thinking. That I'm no good for anything. For – anyone.'

What could she say? Desperately, she searched for words. They came slowly, broken and hardly audible. 'I don't want to think that. I want you to – be someone. To do something.' She stifled a sob, ashamed to think he might understand how she felt and need to escape. The words faded. 'Love someone perhaps.'

She thought his silence was the end of it all. Now he would say something like, 'Well, I'm sorry but I've got to be free. That's my name, and my life must be the same.' But instead, after a long moment he said, very quietly, and with an arm slipping around her waist, 'I do love someone, Becky. I love you. Probably always will. But first, I have to find where I'm going. Find the thing that will settle me, help me know that what I'm doing is right. Can you understand that?'

Slowly and weakly she knew that she could. Strength grew. It dawned on her that working at High Cross Manor was, for her, the right thing. So of course he must find his own place in life. And even if it meant she wouldn't be with him, she understood quite clearly that this was what he had to do.

'Yes,' she whispered, pushing back her tears and drawing on all her strength. 'Yes, I know what you mean. And I hope you find it. I hope – so much....' She couldn't go on. Betraying tears fell and she turned away her head, but he pulled her close, his heart beating against her breast, his mouth whispering small love words into her hair, warming her, reassuring her, making a quiet but fervent promise she knew she would hold onto until he came back to her.

If he ever did.

CHAPTER 8

He left her at the farmhouse door, kissing her and whispering, 'Wait for me, Becky, won't you?' before turning and striding away down the yard.

She watched for a moment and then heard other footsteps. Will came out of the shadows, a gun couched on his arm. Face to face with Joseph, he stopped abruptly and said harshly, 'What you doin' here? We don't want you here, Freeman. You brings trouble. Leave Becks alone, get outa here and don't come back.'

Becky gasped, about to fly at him, but she froze as he raised the gun, leveling it at Joseph's chest. A bitter silence swept through the yard, broken only by hard breathing and then Joseph's deep, controlled voice saying, 'I'll go now, but I'll be back and you can't stop me, Will Yeo.' She saw him turn away, striding purposefully into the darkness, and felt a cold hollowness fill her body.

Will came up, stood looking at her and frowning. But his voice was warmer. 'He's no good. Don't think no more o' him – come indoors, maid.'

She went in slowly, not looking back, her mind a slough of thoughts, images and voices, so that Thirza's greeting – 'Ah, maid, I hoped as you'd come home' – didn't at once make sense. She looked blankly around the lamp-lit kitchen, smelling the familiar scents of fire, oil, food and worn clothes and then, gratefully, felt the old warmth of home banish the pain that was surging through her.

'We heard 'bout the maister,' Thirza said anxiously. 'Is he any better?'

Becky unwrapped her shawl, watched Will come in, set down his gun and claim his usual fireside chair. She decided not to burden Ma with this latest problem, so said quickly, 'Yes, Ma, he's sleeping now. That's why I'm here, 'cos he likes me to sit with him when he's awake.' She caught the look on Thirza's face and sat up straighter, meeting her mother's questioning, anxious eyes.

'He's poorly,' she said defensively. 'He needs looking after.'

Thirza bowed her head and turned to the fire where the kettle was humming. 'I'll make tea.' Her voice was low, and she looked, thought Becky, frowning, full of sorrow and anxiety.

'What's wrong, Ma?'

No reply for a moment and then, 'Will an' me, we wants to talk to you, maid. Somethin' serious.'

'Yes?' Becky tensed. She didn't want more problems – surely there were enough of them already, casting shadows over her life. But she had to release the anger inside her. Words burst out. 'I don't want to talk to Will, he's so hard and I don't—'

'It's for your own good, Becks.'

The blue eyes, looking across the room, had thawed. She stared, wondering what new game this was. Three years older than her, he had always tried to boss her around, and was still doing so, but there seemed some odd change in him tonight. Even his voice was more caring, the words slower than usual. 'Mr Briggs has offered for you, maid.'

Becky caught her breath. 'Offered? You mean—?'

She couldn't say it, but Thirza did. 'Wants to make you his wife. Wants you to marry 'im.' The thin voice grew stouter. 'It'd be a real good chance fer you, Becky, love – estate bailiff's wife, an' he promises to do up his cottage. Why, just think—'

'I'll never marry him! He's rough and dirty, hateful – how could you possibly think I might? And you want me to? Both of you do? No, you can't! I won't!'

She was on her feet, raging at them as she flung herself around the room, feeling all the anger inside her striking out; her eyes blazed, her fists belaboured the air and her strident voice echoed off the shabby walls.

Thirza was the first to answer, persuasive and loving. 'But, maid, you'll be set up for life. Safe. No more hard work like 'ere, chances of nice clothes, an', – an….' Meeting Becky's wild eyes, she faded, huddling on her stool, a sad, teary figure, shaking her head and dissolving into silence.

'She hasn't thought it through.' Will stood up, came to Becky's side and laid a hand on her heaving shoulder. 'Don't say no more. Let's have tea an' then I'll walk you back to High Cross Manor. C'mon, maid, sit down.'

Boiling water pouring onto twice used tea leaves. A slide of burning wood sending a glitter of ash onto the hearth. They sat down in silence, sipped the tea, each deep in thought, until Will said, more cheerily than Becky thought she had ever heard him speak, 'Wanna hear 'bout Dinah, d'you, Becks? How she's gettin' on?' and Becky knew that she owed it to her family to return to everyday matters and leave the awful suggestion of marrying Nat Briggs for another day.

But she had to accept that, like Will had said, she must think about it.

Later they walked together down the lane, heading for the Manor, as the fast moving clouds released the brilliance of stars overhead. The little owls that nested in the woodland were on the hunt, small voices carrying through the still quietness, and Becky slowly felt her anger drawn away into this peaceful night as she listened as Will, for once in his life, it seemed, talked easily to her.

'Dinah's doin' well, Becks. Hard worker an' she makes me laugh.'

Makes Will laugh? Becky found herself smiling at the idea, but also wondering what gift plump little Dinah possessed that was clearly making Will more affable, even more cheerful. Whatever it was, she felt a warmth of filial affection spread through her.

'So, in a way, it's good that I've gone and you've got Dinah instead.'

He didn't reply at once, but looked at her sideways, and then nodded, before saying slowly, 'So what 'bout that Freeman chap, eh? You don't want nothin' to do with him, Becks. I warned him off.'

'You and your gun,' she said with a quick blaze of returning anger. 'After a fox, were you, and then heard us come home?'

'Aye.' He said no more, but she knew from the slouch of his shoulders that this was a tricky subject and best to leave alone.

'Thank you for walking back with me, Will. I'll come again when I can. And in the meantime—' She stopped, turned to face him as the Manor farm yard opened up before her, and suddenly, on an impulse, kissed his hoary cheek. Her brother, with all his own problems and thoughts. He deserved her love. 'I'll think about what Nat wants, Will. But don't hope too much. And don't talk to him. Well, goodnight, now,' and she ran towards the kitchen door.

He waited, watching her go into the house, heard the latch bang to behind her, and then turned, striding rapidly back along the dark lane, going home. He wondered briefly if his warning to that useless Freeman chap was enough to keep him away, and then, half smiling, went back to thinking of Dinah and her funny ways.

Two days later, Rupert Fielding insisted on getting up. Nat Briggs brought the village midwife and general cottagers' helpmate to help dress and shave him and Becky brought up a breakfast tray to the study where the invalid somehow got himself to the table and chair and sat there, glowering into the brilliant sunshine that brought the dusty, shabby furniture into high relief.

'I shall write a letter to Mrs Richards and you can ride over and give it to her, Briggs.' His voice was crisp and testy. Becky, pausing at the door to make sure he had all he wanted on his tray, thought that this was a different Mr Fielding from the quiet, dour man she had first met. The accident had, in some way, woken him up. Now it was clear that he intended to move on, to make his life more important, to perhaps tend to the estate and look forward to his wedding to the elegant Mrs Richards. She felt glad for him and then, making her way back to the kitchen, wondered at the feeling.

Nat Briggs appeared in the middle of the morning, the letter sticking out of his coat pocket. 'I'm off to Moreton, back for dinner,' he said importantly. 'You, Becky, go up to the maister. Ses he needs you for something.'

She looked at Nellie, who sighed, nodded her head, and carried on making pastry.

About to leave the kitchen, she encountered Nat waiting in the doorway, looking at her with a grin which she immediately feared. Very low, he said, 'I'm gonna talk to you when I gets back. Make sure you're here, see?'

She made no reply, kept her eyes down and slipped past him into the escape of the hall. But going up the sweeping staircase her heart raced and she felt a return of the old anger and rebellion. She would have nothing to do with the man. Only one thing mattered: she would wait for Joseph to come back and save her.

Rupert Fielding looked up as she entered the study. She bobbed. 'Mr Briggs said—' but he cut her off at once.

'Yes, I want you. Pull that chair over and sit down. Here, by me.'

Becky could hardly contain her curiosity. Why should she be given this unexpected privilege? She bowed her head and murmured, 'Yes, sir,' as she obeyed.

'Now.' Rupert Fielding looked at her very keenly. 'You can write, and read?'

'Yes, sir.'

'Are you good with figures? Here, look at this.' He pushed an open book towards her.

Becky looked at it with trepidation. What if she couldn't please him? But as she slowly took in what the book contained, interest grew. It was a ledger, showing credits and invoices. Memories of her school arithmetic prowess rushed back – adding, subtracting, multiplying. Yes, she could make sense of all this. But what did he want of her? She looked up at him. 'I know what this is, sir.'

He smiled, an easing of the frosty expression that had greeted her. 'Good. Excellent. I had a feeling that you were more intelligent than the usual servant. Now....'

Becky flinched and sat back on the hard chair, but his long fingers were spreading over the page, stopping at various names and amounts, and she realized her feelings might be hurt but to him they couldn't matter less. She concentrated hard.

'These accounts,' said Rupert Fielding, frowning, 'go back several years. Years in which I have to admit I let things go. I didn't scrutinize them sufficiently. And now I realize I must make amends.' He sat back in his chair, grimacing with pain as he did so, but looked at her with new interest. 'Or at least, you will do it for me. I will teach you what needs doing – it won't be hard. You see, I shall have enough to do getting the house into better shape before Mrs Richards and I marry so you will oblige me by sorting out these accounts. And if you find any deficiencies, or suchlike, then you must tell me and I'll do something about it. I suggest you come up here every morning to do the paperwork – we'll do it together, to start – and then continue with the household duties after that. You understand?'

Becky drew in a strengthening breath before she replied, meeting his eyes fearlessly and raising her chin. 'Yes, sir.' She hesitated. 'May I ask a question?'

He frowned. 'Well?'

'Forgive me, sir, but surely Mr Briggs, your bailiff, could do this for you? Isn't it part of his job to handle your estate finances?'

Silence. Rupert slowly stretched out his legs, put a hand to his back and rubbed it, still staring at her. Becky was suddenly afraid. She had been insolent and could well be sent off without any reference. She knew that, all her life, this rebellious feeling had been her great difficulty, and now, she had probably spoiled everything.

'A good question, Rebecca.' He shifted again, the pain bringing a rictus of anguish across his long, grey face. 'And one I wouldn't have expected. But I'll answer it because I can see your intelligence is enough to understand and do what I am asking. Well, Mr Briggs certainly does deal with the tenancy fees and suchlike, but I don't intend to let him loose on them any more.'

They stared at each other and she had a sudden flash of knowledge that was warm and reassuring. Nat was in trouble. Which meant he could have no power over her. She smiled.

'I'll do what you say, sir. I'll try hard to learn. But, please, may I have an hour or two off every day to go home and see that my mother is well? She – she worries about me.' Their gazes remained locked until he nodded, and gave her a freer smile than she had ever received before.

'Does she?' He looked back at the papers in front of him. 'You're an astute girl, Rebecca.' A moment's pause, and then, 'Briggs refers to you as Becky – so that's what I'll call you.' He looked at her, direct and demanding. 'Yes, you may go home for a short while in the evenings, but now, I'd like you to start straight away. Here's pen and paper and the files dealing with all the farms are over there in that cabinet. I'll explain as we go along. I'll take a short walk – tell Nellie you'll be here until dinner time.' Slowly and painfully he rose, put a hand on the back of his chair and looked down at her. She saw the hint of a smile touch his thin mouth.

He looked at her in silence and then, 'I thought I heard you singing to me, when I was just becoming conscious again,' he said slowly. 'You have a sweet voice. Something about a sprig of thyme, wasn't it?'

'Yes.' Becky was amazed. She would have liked to ask then about his mentioning of the girl Grace, but already he was limping towards the door, looking back at her and saying, 'When you've finished for the day put the book back in the top drawer, lock it and always bring me the key. I'll be up here again very soon. In the meantime, just read through the pages and make what you can of them.'

The door closed behind him and she was left looking at the figures on the pages before her. But instead of feeling resentful, Becky instinctively knew she was being drawn towards a new step of her life's journey. Where might it take her, she wondered, but then she looked down at the figures in the book, switched her thoughts, preparing to try and recall all the knowledge she had gained at school.

She was helping Nellie dish up the midday meal when Nat Briggs rode into the courtyard, tied up his cob and then marched through the kitchen without saying anything. Becky thought he looked important and wondered what message he was carrying to the maister. They soon found out.

Ten minutes later Rupert Fielding hobbled downstairs and stood, leaning against the door jamb, Nat Briggs a shadow behind him. In a cold, rapid voice, he said, 'You had all better know that my hopes of bringing Mrs Richards here soon are delayed for a while. She tells me that she has had to accompany her sick sister who is going abroad for a month. Well, perhaps this is just as well. It will give us more time to get the house into better shape. But I shall need someone to organize things.' Dark eyes rested on Becky. 'Come to my study after dinner. I want to talk to you.' Clumsily he turned, leaning against the door for a few seconds, and then as Nat Briggs stepped away, slowly limped towards the hall.

Nat Briggs swaggered into the kitchen, sat down in the chair Nellie always used, and said enjoyably, 'Bad news, it were. She don't wanna come, clear as daylight. Went white as a sheet when I told her 'bout the accident. Reckon she don't fancy an injured husband.' He laughed coarsely. 'Wouldn't be up to much, would he?'

Nellie and Becky exchanged glances. Then, 'You got proper nasty thoughts, Mr Briggs,' said Nellie acidly. 'If the pore lady got to take her sister abroad for health reasons, then it makes sense that she can't come here, surely. And now, if you wants your dinner, get yourself cleaned up first, if you please. I don't like nothing dirty round my kitchen table.'

The meal was eaten in silence and Becky's thoughts, for once, avoided Nat Brigg's presence, although he sat opposite her. She was sorry for the maister who must have hoped so much to see his lady. Indeed, must have needed her here while he was so weak. And whether the excuse was a valid one or not, she felt that Mr Fielding deserved some sympathy. And then, suddenly, why did he want to see her again? She hurried Nellie through the washing of the dishes, and was thankful to see the back of Nat Briggs, who had tried to get a quiet word with her and then flung off in a flurry of temper when she said shortly, 'Not now, Mr Briggs. Mr Fielding said he wants to see me, so I must go.'

He sat in the study, his dinner tray pushed aside on the table and an open letter in front of him. As Becky knocked and was bidden to enter he looked at her and nodded at the chair beside him. 'Sit down. We have to make plans.'

She sat, watched him draw a paper towards him and read through what was written, his pencil moving from one item to the next. And, although she guiltily berated herself for doing so, she slid her glance towards Mrs Richards' letter, open and seemingly forgotten, in front of her.

...Amazed that you expect me to come while you are in such a state. Surely you have servants who can nurse you through this foolish accident? And meanwhile, I am taking Maria to Italy because her poor lungs need the warmer winter air. I will write when I expect to come home again....

Such an unkind, unloving message was enough to instantly push Becky's quick emotions into a depth of new compassion. She had already felt that the maister needed her help and now, whatever else he asked her to do, she knew she would at once respond with cheerfulness. Even with some odd and unasked for sense of fondness, perhaps. The idea was strange, but she accepted it.

Looking at his lined, creased face, occasionally tensing with spasms of pain as he moved in his chair, she told herself that she would be helpful and obedient. And perhaps, as they got to know each other better, he might tell her how he came to know her song, *The Sprig of Thyme*.

CHAPTER 9

R upert Fielding looked at her across the desk and she saw how fast he was ageing now. Some of the brightness had gone from his dark eyes, and as he spoke, she thought that his voice was no longer so demanding, as he said slowly, 'Things have got on top of me. And now, with this back – well, there's so much to do.' He pulled Felicity Richards' letter towards him, gave it one glance and then sighed, pushing it into a drawer in the desk.

Becky didn't know what to say, but her sympathy for him made her suggest the first thing that came into her mind. 'I'm sure Mr Briggs will do all he can to help.'

He looked at her with a curious half smile. 'I'm sure he will. But even Briggs won't know about cleaning up the house. We need more help, another girl from the village, perhaps.' He stopped, nodded, face full of thoughts. 'A man to do the other work, see to the beams, the window frames that need mending, all that sort of thing.'

Wondering if she was speaking out of turn, she said, 'I could find someone to help with the housework, sir. She and I could do all that's needed with the cleaning. Would you like me to – to....' The expression on his face made her stop. Had she gone too far?

No. Indeed, she thought she saw a brief look of relief. 'A good idea. Yes, see who you can find – someone reliable, young, who won't mind hard work. We shan't need an interview if you find the right girl. Not as if she'll be responsible for anything if she's working with you. And Nellie Mudge can still give a few orders. Although—' Abruptly he stopped, narrowed his eyes, continued to stare at her.

'What I need,' he said very slowly, measuring his words, 'is a woman in charge of all the work. Not fair to ask Nellie to have to do it as well as the cooking and the rest of the kitchen work.' A pause and he still looked at her. Then, slowly, 'What about you? Think you could take on the housekeeping duties?' A wry smile briefly softened his face. 'You seem to know what you're about – you're not stupid, are you?'

Becky wasn't sure exactly what she was. Kitchen skivvy, accounts keeper, and now – housekeeper? It was all happening too quickly for her confused mind to know where to turn. She sucked in a deep breath, thought hard, and then said quietly, 'No, sir, I'm not stupid. But I'm not sure if I can deal with all the things you're asking me to do. I mean, you engaged me to work in the kitchen, didn't you?' She paused, but it must be said. 'And now you're asking me to look at your accounts, still help Nellie, and then tell a new girl how to clean the house. I – I don't know whether I can do all that.'

He sat up straighter, began moving papers on his desk and looked down at them. 'Of course you can. You're intelligent, and,' he glanced at her and she saw that for once he was smiling as if he meant it, 'there's something about you. You'll do it all. And I'll give you a good wage.'

She met his eyes and felt herself returning the smile. This was all very strange and she felt as if she was becoming closer to Rupert Fielding. Could she believe what was happening? And could she do it? Still confused, she kept looking at him, saw the smile grow.

He nodded. 'You'll do, Becky Yeo. I'm a good judge of people's capabilities, and I have no doubt that you'll not only clean up the house but put my accounts right and make a thorough job of it. I think you're an ambitious girl, so give me your answer, and then we'll get down to making plans. Yes or no as housekeeper?'

She said 'yes' without further deliberation, and felt that their exchange of smiles signified another shift in their odd relationship. And then she added the final, important part of the bargain. 'Sir, please will you explain to Mrs Mudge? Before I go back to the kitchen?'

He seemed amused. 'Kitchen politics, eh? Very well. Ask her to come up and see me when you go down. Don't worry, she's a sensible woman. She knows a thing or two. I'm sure she'll understand that this is a good move for her.'

Joseph Freeman was contented, working on the new set of pews in Manaton church. The Reverend Mr Broadland, who had engaged him, left him alone without too many visits to inspect the work. As usual, he felt at one with his woodworking tools; his long hard fingers enclosed chisels and knives, saws and hammers, and he knew he was working on something important to his being. Not just a job of work, but a piece of craft that meant more than the week's pay and the hot meal at night. It meant he was slowly discovering what his life held. Sometimes, as he worked in the silent church, old images filled his head; the first job after leaving the workhouse with farmer Eli and his beaknosed wife Lizzie. The beatings, the coldness of the attic bed, the ever lasting hunger. Until he ran. And that brought more images: sleeping between rocks out on the moor, with bracken piled into a mattress and a blanket; eating berries when he could find them; copying the ponies and sheep and nibbling leaves and stems; stealing fruit from a farm orchard. And then the Reverend Mr Gosling, elderly antiquarian and folklore collector, and the first kind person in his life, had found him, one day, at the end of his small tether, taken him back to the vicarage, washed, fed and clothed him and then discovered that this bony little imp showed intelligence as well as a lot of curiosity. So he had learned as he grew into adolescence; so many things. The old songs the reverend collected. The pleasure of learning to read and write. To speak clearly. To treat other people with manners. And finally, to be himself. No longer the wretched little Jack Adams from the union, but a new person with a new name. Joseph Freeman. He gave himself the stimulation of this new name, knowing that

Freeman would help him to find the freedom he craved. Free to discover where his life would take him. Free to travel and eventually find his future.

So, accompanied by many snatches of songs remembered from Mr Gosling's collection, the carvings grew slowly but with pleasure and great craft. Sometimes he thought about Becky Yeo and smiled. Yes, he would find her again. Miss Freckles. Becky Yeo with the determined mind and thick chestnut hair. The girl who wanted to be kissed, and who would be, again, sometime soon. At the moment he was too occupied to make plans. He sang a couple of snatches of the *Sprig of Thyme* and settled more deeply into the carving. He was content.

Until one morning, Nat Briggs came into the church and stood behind him and he saw a shadow fall across the rose he was carving. Turning, he looked into closely set, sly eyes and at once recognized the threat that puffed out Briggs like a territorial bird fighting its corner.

Deliberately, he put down his chisel and hammer and leaned against the pew, straightening his back. 'And what can I do for you, Mr Briggs?' There was cynical note in the words and Nat instantly picked it up.

'More what can I do for you, Freeman, 'cos you an' me must have words. That message you brought the other night – not so important after all, I found, going to the Reverend. He said it would've done next morning, he did. So why did you think to get me out at night? An' if you got a reason it'd better be a good one.'

Joseph studied the small man standing a few inches too close to him. Saw sweat on his leathery face, smelt rankness in his breath, and knew that if he cared to do so, he could floor Briggs as easily as if he were a small annoying mouse in the flour bin. But he wouldn't do so. The man was irritating, that was all. So, raising an eyebrow and smiling, he turned back to his work, picked up the chisel and said casually, 'Don't make so much of it, Briggs. Seemed a good idea at the time – free supper and a look at the pretty maid we've both got our eye on.'

Nat grunted, snatched at his arm, raised in the act of completing one small rose petal, and tried to pull him around. Joseph turned, said tightly, 'Leave me be. I don't want to hurt you, so get out of here and take your foul thoughts with you.'

'You're fooling with that maid!' Nat burst out. 'You leave her be, she's mine and she knows it. And now you know it. too. An' I'll see that you gets a bad name, Freeman. What I say goes round here. I can get you out of work just as easily as I got you that harvest work on the Yeo farm – remember that.' He was breathing fast, his eyes dilated and the words spitting as he spoke.

Joseph frowned. 'Get out,' he said very quietly, and raised the hand holding the chisel. 'Get out and leave that maid alone. She's not for the likes of you, or me, probably, but I don't want you sniffing round her any more. You hear me? And if you do bother her, I'll deal with you and by God, if it comes to that you'll be no use to anybody afterwards.'

They stared at each other for a few seconds, and then Nat took a step back. His mouth lifted and he showed yellow teeth in a snarling grimace. 'Just wait,' he growled. 'Just wait. I'll get you, see if I don't.'

Joseph waited, smiled tightly, and watched Briggs march away, leave the church and bang shut the door. No backward look. Just the sound of horse hoofs trotting off, and then the old peaceful silence returning. He rested against the pew for a long moment, breathed in a huge breath and then looked at the chisel, still in his left hand. Sharp enough to maim or even kill. But only a threat. He would never use it – never desecrate its magical use – to do anything other than carve wood. But if Briggs had taken it as a threat, then all to the good. And now – just wait and see what would happen next.

He continued with the carving, completing the rose flower, and then started on the first leaf, and while he worked he thought of Becky Yeo and slowly he knew that he must see her again, very soon. She was in his life, in his dreams and that little trouble maker Briggs must never be allowed to take her away from him. Because

– and here he paused in the middle of veining the leaf – he wanted her himself. Longed for her in a way that he had never felt before. Because she was important in some way that had only just begun to make itself clear.

Yes, he must go and find Miss Freckles again – soon.

Nat Briggs cornered Becky, late in the afternoon, as the light faded and the old house became shadowy. She was coming upstairs after going to the village and asking young Ruth Hext to come and start work the next morning. The Hext family was poor, father Nathan suffering with his chest and not permanently in work, so Ruth had been pleased. 'Workin' at the big house? Yes, I'd like that, Becky.' Then she'd stopped. 'I mean, I s'pose as you're Miss Yeo now – housekeeper, are you?'

Becky had nodded, smiled. 'Yes, I am, Ruth, but no need to think anything's different. Becky'll do.' But even as she walked home, she had known that everything was suddenly different. And of course the village would be the first to know and talk about it.

'Becky!' Now Nat had his hand on her arm, swinging her round to face him. She saw the gleam in his narrowed eyes and flinched, stepping away from him. But he came after her, this time pulling her by the waist so that she couldn't move and found herself facing him, too close, too tightly held to escape.

'Let me go. What d'you want?' As if she didn't know.

He grinned, showing his teeth. 'They've told you? That I wants to marry you?'

Becky struggled. No use. He was holding her in a vice of tight arms, his rank breath warm on her half turned away face. 'If you let me go we can talk. I won't be treated like this. Just let me go, Nat.'

Slowly he released her. 'Tell me as you will. Tell me *now*.'

She strengthened herself for what she knew must come as she said fiercely, 'No, I won't marry you.'

' You got to! It's only sense, see – me the estate bailiff and now you the one in charge here in the Manor – we can make a good pair.' His grin sent a shiver down her back. 'Good pickings to be had, my maid. An' we'll be happy, together, you an' me in my little ole cottage. Just the two of us, warm an snug, an' I'll give you babies.' He sniggered and again pulled her close. 'Cos I'll love you proper, Becky.'

Footsteps approaching and she jerked herself away from him, turning and running in the opposite direction while Rupert Fielding's sharp voice echoed down the passage. 'Briggs? What're you doing here?'

In the distance she heard obsequious, muffled words from Nat. She reached the kitchen in a flurry of quick breaths and was thankful to shut the door behind her. Things had happened far too fast today and although she had told Nat she wouldn't marry him, she knew that he would keep pestering her. It was a thought that created shadows at the back of her mind. She saw Nellie Mudge standing by the hearth, thoughts flying across her lined face and Becky knew at once that Nellie had talked to the maister and now looked ready to confront the new housekeeper.

Becky went up to her, saying quietly, 'I hope you understand that the idea is to take a lot of extra work off your back, Mrs Mudge. And it's just that I'm younger – perhaps a bit stronger – and there's so much to be done.'

They looked at each other, and then Nellie sighed as she sat down heavily in the chair beside the fire. 'Aye, I understand. And you're bringing in another girl, he said. Well, that'll leave me to do the cooking. Not what I expected, but there.' Slowly she smiled and then added, in a lower voice, almost as if she spoke to herself, 'O' course, I'm not surprised. You belong to the house. Right that you should give the orders.'

Becky pulled a stool from under the table and slowly lowered herself on to it. She frowned. 'What do you mean, Mrs Mudge? How can I belong to the house? I don't understand.' But, even as she spoke, she heard Thirza's voice going on about something bad happening. Was it to do with the Manor? With Mr Fielding? A name whispered? With Grace?

Nellie fidgeted and bent her head. 'No, no, I'm just speakin' out of turn. I don't mean nothing.' Her eyes, shadowed but sharp, met Becky's. She nodded and then smiled more easily. 'You been busy today, maid. Time for a sup o' tea. An' you can tell me all the plans now that you got a new girl to help you. Bedrooms are finished, so it'll be the morning room and the drawing room, I dessay. An' you'll have to get in a man to deal with those window frames.'

Drinking tea all was quiet, Nellie going on about the plaster that was wet in the dairy, and how that Briggs never helped, just made trouble. She eyed Becky warily. 'Keep away from him, maid. He's no good. And one of these days the maister'll learn just how bad he is....'

Becky nodded, thinking that Rupert Fielding already had knowledge of some bad accounting – she began to wonder what else might turn up in the days ahead.

Every day seemed shorter than its predecessor. Cleaning, turning out, taking down curtains and tapestries and pictures, searching in corners and cupboards and finding filth and spiders and even vermin, took time and stamina. Ruth Hext was a strong girl and worked well, but even so, Becky found it all tiring and thought provoking. But to keep the work up to a high standard, she reminded herself that, when the maister's parents lived here in the Manor, it must have been a beautifully kept home. Then the thoughts developed: how could he have borne the following years when decay and dirt masked all the wonders of the old structure and its magnificent decorations? And, slowly, she came to realize that many of his old ways of neglect and loose living had changed since the accident, and then wondered if the blow on the head had liberated some old, forgotten ideas. But what with checking on his accounts, first of all with his help, and now on her own – and finding many cases of deficiencies – she was thankful each night when, candle in hand, she traipsed up the old stairs and fell on the iron bedstead.

All her thoughts, it seemed, were of work and what must be

done today. So it was a surprise when Ruth arrived one morning with the latest piece of news spreading around the village. 'That Joseph Freeman been put off from the church over to Manaton.' The girl's eyes were sharp with enjoyment, gossip always bringing pleasure into dull lives.

Becky, on her way upstairs, paused in the open doorway and looked back. 'Why? What happened?' For a moment she was elsewhere; out in the dusky evening, held close in a warm, strong embrace that had comforted her, thrilled her, taken her into new worlds. His name brought it all back, and she waited for Ruth's answer with an uneasy feeling of urgency.

'Reverend Mr Broadland found the Poor Box gone. Reckoned only that Freeman could ha' done it. So Reverend put him off right away. Left the carving unfinished, so that's a pity, 'cos we heard as it were good.'

The Poor Box stolen? But that was absurd. Joseph wasn't a thief. Becky said quickly, 'But why was he suspected of taking the money? Could have been anybody – the church is never locked.'

Ruth tied her apron around her waist and said happily, 'Course it were him – Mr Briggs said as how he knew Joseph Freeman for a bad one and wouldn't never let him near such as the Poor Box if he'd had his way.'

Nat Briggs. Becky sucked in a great breath and tried to control her rage. 'That's a load of rubbish,' she snapped over her shoulder, and ran up stairs before Ruth said any more.

In the study, taking the account book out of the locked cupboard and setting it on the table, Becky saw only Joseph's face before her. He was smiling, looking at her with that smile that eased all her anger and pain. She almost heard him say, laughing in that deep voice, 'Don't take on so, Miss Freckles. Briggs and me have got a big sort out coming one day. But for now I'll go on my way.'

Standing motionless at the table, she thought she heard him as she stared blindly out of the window and wondered what was happening to her. Of course he and Nat had to sort things out –

one day. And of course Joseph was going on his way. That was how he lived. Away from her.

Very slowly, she let out her held breath and sat down, trying to look at the black figures on the pages in front of her. But she still heard him, deep inside her head, and she was able to weakly smile as she imagined him saying, 'I'll be back, Becky. One day.'

CHAPTER 10

Dinah came calling after the evening meal, shyly sitting in the kitchen near the fire and looking first at Nellie and then at Becky. She sipped the small ale offered and Becky had to be the first to speak, wondering what this visit was about.

'How's things at the farm, then, Dinah? Mother and Will all right? Did he do any good at the market with that calf?'

Dinah looked over the rim of the cup and nodded. 'Good price he got. He's all right but Mrs Yeo's took bad.'

Becky's heart missed a beat. 'How bad? Why didn't you come and tell me before this?' One question crowded into the next. 'What's wrong with her?'

'Coughing,' said Dinah. 'Made her go to bed, though she didn't want to. Will ses she's no good unless she's fit for work, so off to bed he took her.'

'I must go and see her. Mrs Mudge—'

She turned to the older woman who shook her head and smiled wryly. 'You're in charge now, maid. No need to ask if you can go.'

Becky nodded. 'No. So I'll walk back with Dinah. I'll take Ma something hot. Mrs Mudge, is there any chicken broth left?'

'In the pantry. I'll put it in a bowl.'

They walked quickly towards the farm, Becky with a basket on her arm and Dinah for once inclined to chatter on about Will. 'He do order me about, but I'm learnin' fast. Ses as I'm a good worker, an' he's glad to have me.' A smile lifted the small mouth and broadened the dumpling cheeks.

Becky said warmly, 'That's good, Dinah. And I'm glad you're there, too.'

The lane brought them into the farmyard where Prince barked and the kitchen door slowly opened. Will stood in the doorway. 'What you come for then, Becks?' He stood back, letting them enter.

Becky put her basket on the table. 'To see Ma, of course. How is she? What are you giving her for her cough? That coltsfoot medicine is the best – did you find it?'

'Stop fussing. My lord, how you women do fuss.' But Will smiled as he went back to his fireside chair. 'She's just got a cough, nothin' to worry about. But we needs her down here so I ses, off to bed, Ma, I ses. Course, she didn't want to go.'

'I'll go up and see her. Dinah, warm this up, will you?' She stayed long enough to see the broth poured into the pan on top of the range and then went quickly up the narrow, steep stairs into the bedroom where she heard Thirza coughing and wheezing.

'Ma, I'm here. How are you? What can I get you? Shall I ask the doctor to come out?'

Thirza lay very still in the narrow bed, huge eyes in her pale face following Becky's every movement as she tidied the old patchwork quilt slipping to one side, covering the thin arms resting on it and then pulling up the one chair in the room to sit down beside the bed. 'Ma, I'm sorry I'm not here – I ought to be here.' She felt a huge pang of guilt. Of course she should be here, nursing her mother, taking over all the kitchen duties. She shouldn't be up there at the Manor, being paid a wage that exceeded all her dreams, and telling Ruth and Nellie Mudge how to go about their businesses. Mr Fielding should never have made so many demands on her. He knew she was just a farm girl, needed at home. She began to blame him for everything, until a final thought reminded her that, if necessary, her wage could pay the doctor to come out and see to Ma. And Dinah was obviously proving herself, *so don't worry so much. Don't blame yourself. Just try and cheer her up and see what she needs.*

It was clear what Thirza needed beside the coltsfoot medicine – warmth, rest and good food. Becky found an old blanket long ago consigned to the chest under the window and lovingly tucked it around her mother's thin frame. 'I've got some broth for you,' she said cheerily. 'That'll give you some strength. And if you don't feel better tomorrow I'll get the groom from the Manor to ride into Moreton and ask Dr Gale to come and see you.' As Thirza shook her head, Becky added, as lightly as she could manage, 'Don't worry, I can ask all sorts of favours from the maister, 'cos I'm his housekeeper now.'

Thirza's eyes were saucers. 'Housekeeper?' she croaked. 'But—'

'Don't try and talk, Ma. I'll sit with you a bit and maybe then you'll sleep.' Footsteps outside and then Dinah came in, her smile warm. 'Here's the broth, Mrs Yeo. Sit up a bit, eh?'

Between them they raised Thirza into a sitting position, bolstered with pillows, and helped her sip the broth. Then, with a hint of colour in her cheeks, she sank down again, smiling at them as she said breathlessly, 'Lucky, aren't I? Two maids to look after me.'

Becky sat by the bed until her mother's eyes closed and her breathing grew quiet. Then she went downstairs, to find Dinah sitting opposite Will and mending the collar of a shirt, a domestic scene which surprised and pleased her. Warmly, she said, 'I'll come again tomorrow. But if Ma's worse, then, Dinah, come and tell me.'

Dinah nodded, suddenly got up and then hesitated, looking first at Becky and than at the door. 'Going, are you?'

'Yes. It's late, I must get back.'

Dinah went to the door and opened it, looking at Becky over her shoulder, almost as if she wanted to say something, then followed her out into the darkness. Becky shut the door behind her and stopped. 'What is it? What's wrong?' Not something else, she thought anxiously.

But she saw Dinah's eyes shining as she fumbled in her apron pocket. 'He came today, wants you to have this.'

'He?' A flash of hope spun through her. She took the offering and felt her pulse quicken.

Dinah's voice was low. 'That Freeman, he came when Will was out. Said as how he hasn't got time to go to the Manor. Left this for you. Just an ole weed, I'd say, but there – he said it were important.'

Becky took the small, wizened twig and stared at it. A faint fragrance rose, something she knew well, and not just the fragrance, but the words naming it. A sprig of thyme.

Instantly, the world cleared of all its threatening shadows. A shaft of brilliant light suddenly shone down into her circling mind and she heaved in a huge breath of relief and joy. So he hadn't forgotten her. So Joseph Freeman still held her in his thoughts, whereever he was, what ever he was doing.

She thanked Dinah, said goodbye, then walked home in the darkness feeling that nothing could ever again disturb her mind. The moon shone, the shadows were forgotten. Never mind the problems – Nat Briggs, Ma being ill, Joseph not being here. She knew that she could deal with whatever was asked of her, now and in the future.

Humming a snatch of her song, she quickly walked back to the Manor. She had never felt so happy as she did at that moment in her life.

The work at the Manor continued: dust arose, carpets and curtains were cleaned; the amount of washing and ironing increased. A labourer, Jimmy Browning from the village, came and made even worse messes mending broken window frames and replastering damp walls. Ruth laboured well and long, and Becky was thankful for the girl's strength and stamina.

And slowly she found herself settling into the daily routine; the planning of duties over breakfast in the kitchen, with Nellie Mudge adding small snippets of useful information from the old days, and then the hours upstairs going over the accounts with the maister. And in the evenings slipping down to the farm to see how Ma was getting on.

The happiness she had felt when the sprig of thyme lay in her hand slowly faded away, but she knew it was stored at the back of her mind. One day it would come back. Just like Joseph. Her thoughts of him, all the time, were busier than ever, shining into her daily routine like tiny stitches of gold brightening a dark canvas.

Joseph loved her. And of course he would come back.

Even so, it was helpful to immerse herself in the work, trying to push aside small and painful fears that still persisted despite her hopes; when a cupboard in Rupert Fielding's study revealed a broken latch, the half-open door falling out and throwing a pile of papers on to the floor, she was almost grateful – more work. Something to fill her mind and let Joseph go. She picked them up and then put them in a tidy pile on his desk. Mr Fielding could sort them out in his own time. Now she could get the latch repaired and the cupboard properly cleaned before the papers went back. She went downstairs for the midday meal with a quiet mind.

Nellie Mudge put spoons and bowls on the long scrubbed table. 'Mr Briggs's gone over Hameldon to see farmer Worth about his pigsties. Falling down, need repair, Briggs'll have to see what the maister ses. Quite a journey.' She looked at Becky and smiled broadly. 'Have your dinner in peace, he won't be here.'

He returned late in the afternoon, cursing the roads and the summer dust that covered them, complaining about having to ride up over the great shoulder of Hameldon: 'Time we got a proper track without that hill making the horse blow. Where's me meal, Mrs Mudge? I'm starvin' hungry.'

Becky watched him gulp down the dried up plate of stew that Nellie produced, wash it down with ale, and then get up, heading for the door and the maister's study. 'I gotta tell him about the sties – need brickin' up. That farmer Worth, he don't know nothin' about repairs. Get him to pay, I ses.'

Becky stood well away from him as he left the room, but, as he passed her, she said, 'Mr Fielding's not in his study. He's resting in his bedroom. Wait, can't you, till he's up again?'

He glowered at her. 'Don't tell me what to do – I'm the bailiff and I'm runnin' the estate for him while he takes it easy.' She watched him climb the stairs and then disappear down the long passage. She hoped that Mr Fielding would soon be up again – Nat Briggs alone in his study somehow seemed to be a danger. But then Ruth came out of the morning room with a pile of old newspapers and magazines. 'Burn 'em, shall I, then?'

Becky nodded. Nothing important there, she thought, and then her mind turned to the pleasure of slipping away to visit Ma. The afternoon work finished, she had a word with Nellie who nodded, and she was out in the warm fresh air, almost running along the rough track leading to the farm. Enjoyment grew. She spent too much time in the house, overseeing, working, counting up figures. This short hour or two of freedom saved her from any of the sad thoughts that still came. Thoughts of, Where is Joseph? And when shall I see him again?

She looked around her on the brief journey, suddenly newly aware of billowing white clouds travelling the brilliant blue sky, of the beauty of grey sunlit stone and drifting colours of moor grass, heather and gorse. Old Bowerman's Nose stood tall, looking down at the surrounding moorland with what Becky liked to think was a sort of blessing. No shadows today. Passing the wayside grave she dropped a heather bell on it and wondered, had there been mourners for the poor woman who had taken her own life? And what had happened to make her do it? Was it true, or just an old story? Folklore, thought Becky, shaking her head and then allowing Joseph to ease her mind into serenity as she came into sight of the farm and quickened her pace.

Thirza was recovering slowly from the cough and was up, sitting by the hearth, watching Dinah cutting up a rabbit and preparing the evening meal. Their voices came to a stop as Becky entered the kitchen, and she at once looked anxiously at her mother. 'You look better, Ma – a bit of colour in your cheeks. I hope you're not working too hard.' She turned to Dinah. 'What a good thing you're here to help out. Will treating you all right?'

Dinah chopped at the carcass in front of her. All she said was a quiet, 'Yes', but Becky saw the small mouth lift into the semblance of a smile and began to wonder what thoughts it was concealing. And then Will himself appeared, muddy boots at once kicked off into the hearth. Dinah smiled a greeting, her knife still in her hand. He stared at Becky. 'You here again? Village knows 'bout you bein' the maister's housekeeper. Grand title – but what do you do all day?'

Becky heaved a deep sigh. Nothing new here, then – Will, as always, going on at her. And yet – she saw him glance at Dinah and grin, the sort of grin she remembered from his youth, and had not seen since. Was it possible that Dinah was working some sort of miracle on bad tempered Will? And that idea made it possible to merely smile at his provocative words, and say quietly, as she pulled a stool from under the table and sat down, 'I work, Will. I work hard. Simple as that. And you wouldn't be interested to know exactly what I do. So give me your news. What's happening on the farm?'

Will sank down into his chair and looked at her. She saw thoughts slide over his tanned face and waited; never any good to try and hurry him. Then he said unexpectedly, 'Farm's all right. But village is full o' that Freeman chap pinching the Poor Box from the church and then being put off by the vicar.'

Inside Becky a knot formed and she sat up straighter. 'He didn't take it, he's not that sort. Not a thief.'

Will's blue eyes glinted at her. 'How do you know? You been seein' him again?'

With infinite control she said quietly, 'No, I haven't. But he didn't take that Box. I could never believe that he did.'

'Well,' a yawn, then the hint of a grin, 'mebbe you're right. Village ses it were Briggs took it – just his sort of nasty trick. Wanted to get back at Freeman, see, so showed it to vicar and vicar fell fer the story. Only now....' Will rose, found his pipe on the mantel, sat down again, intent on filling it, but his eyes slid round to watch Becky's reactions.

'Now what?' She tensed.

Will puffed hard and smoke drifted around him. 'Now vicar wants to make it good for Freeman, so he's workin' over to Hound Tor fer another vicar who wants to find out about the ole stones all over the hillside behind the tor.'

Silence while the smoke circled and then wafted away. Becky felt her knot untying slowly while her thoughts rushed and circled around one fact: Joseph had been cleared of the theft and was now working again. Her heart leaped. After a pause she asked casually, 'So what's this vicar doing with the old stones?'

Will stared at her. 'I dunno. He's just one of the reverend maisters on the moor these days, lookin' at all the ole stones, diggin' them up and writin' things about them. That's all I know.'

A word arrived in Becky's mind from – was it school days, or had she heard it somewhere? *Antiquarians.* These men who were trying to set up fallen stones and discover what they could about them. Stones that they believed were so old they couldn't be dated. And Joseph was working with them. She knew somehow that he would be interested in doing this. Joseph was a craftsman so he would care for old things like stones with forgotten stories attached to them.

She felt lighter, excited, relieved and so wasn't ready for Will's next words. 'You decided 'bout marryin' Nat Briggs, then, have you? He's waitin' fer an answer. What'll it be, Becks?'

A rush of disappointment and fast growing rage filled her. Her voice was loud, words erupting without thought. 'I'll never marry him! I hate the sight of him – his filthy clothes, that ragged hair, the way he looks at me, always trying to touch me – of course I won't marry him! You must be mad to even think I would.'

Silence. Will sucked at his pipe. Behind her Becky sensed Ma fidgeting in her seat, heard Dinah dropping rabbit pieces into a cauldron then turning to swing it onto the fire. Becky's thoughts ran around in circles. Here were familiar sounds, scents, memories, and people she loved. She must make amends for that outburst. Ma would be upset, Will angry, Dinah resenting the trouble she was bringing into the cottage.

She moved to Ma's chair, taking her hands, smiling into her anxious face. Her voice quietened as she said, 'Sorry, Ma. I know you want me to think well of him, but I can't.'

Thirza nodded very slowly and sighed. 'Would have been a good thing, but no, you ses. So what'll happen to you, maid?'

Becky thought hard before answering. Mustn't mention Joseph. Must keep Ma happy and without further worries. She said brightly, 'I shall stay on at the Manor, helping Mr Fielding. And when he marries and doesn't need me any more I'll find another situation. He'll give me a good reference, I know.'

Dinah stirred the pot vigorously. Will shifted in his chair, reaching out for the newspaper and Becky felt everything change. Her words had brought a kind of hopefulness and although she knew they were only fantasy words, she breathed deeply with relief. It was important to keep her loved ones happy and unaware of all her secret thoughts and longings. A great realization came then, listening to Ma telling another choice bit of village gossip, and Dinah laughing, a strong, almost hurtful knowledge that living at High Cross Manor had changed her completely.

The Manor provided comfort, warmth, work that she enjoyed; and above all, her hopes and longings for Joseph had made her a new person, unable any longer to feel at home in this small, shabby cottage. No matter how she loved them all, Ma, Will and even Dinah, she knew she was no longer part of them. Her words, just now, fantasy though they seemed, were merely emphasizing her new life.

So it was with a feeling of hidden guilt she refused the offer of a meal, kissed Ma and told her she was enjoying being at High Cross Manor, and that she would come again another evening; touched Will's shoulder as she passed him and left the cottage, walking home slowly down the shadow-laden track, and wondering, with a new sense of expectancy, what sort of future awaited her.

CHAPTER 11

A cloud moved slowly overhead, masking the sun, and Joseph paused in his digging to stand upright, wipe his face of sweat and look around him. The stones littered the hillside below the weathered rocks of Hound Tor, the valley sheltered from winter winds and sloping down towards the Becka Brook. Gorse and heather rampaged down the hill, with a windswept mountain ash tree standing alone in its midst.

He savoured the beauty and the solitude, allowing himself a moment of stillness before turning and going to his bag, looking for the bottle of water, filled this morning when the digging began. It was empty. He would have to go all the way down to the brook to refill it. And the Reverend Mr Gould might have something to say if he asked for a break. For a moment he thought about the brook, narrow but vigorous, bubbling over stones and coursing beneath its clapper bridge, journeying on towards a larger river and then merging with the sea. Becka or Becky – Joseph smiled. Becky was certainly a local name.

Her image came to him then in a flash of memory. Tall, well formed, thick, rich hair tied in a knot; a smile that welcomed and bestowed pleasure. He needed to see her again, to hold her, to kiss her, to tell her that she was the one. But would she wait for him? A girl like Becky must have admirers other than Nat Briggs. That name forced Becky's image to fade and he frowned. He and Nat had things to sort out – one day. But now, turning, he saw Reverend Gould approaching and so once more bent to the spade which, since early morning, had been moving turf and heather, bracken and gorse, to reveal the stones.

'I think this was a village, a community.' Reverend Gould's well spoken voice made Joseph deposit his spadeful of peaty earth on one side and look up.

'Yes, sir, there's certainly a lot of stones – could well be a village, I dare say.'

The tall man, clad in priestly black with a shallow hat on his sparse light brown hair nodded. 'Possibly. If you and the other men keep removing the turf, I feel sure we shall find evidence of past life. Tell me if you dig up any shards of pottery.'

'Yes, sir.' Joseph returned to his digging, ignoring his thirst and waiting for the day to finish, when he would drop into the Hound Tor Inn nearby before going with the other men to the farm where a hot meal would await them, and then retiring to the barn and their hayfilled beds, provided by the Reverend.

They were a small gang, three of them and Joseph. When Reverend Gould's back was turned the men talked – about the heat, the pay, their women at home, the need to get to the inn and have a tankard of frothing ale. Jim, Ed and Davy were tough men who worked hard, and Joseph found himself enjoying their company. He was surprised at this, for much of his life was lived alone and in lonely places. Perhaps he had something to learn from this job of digging out the old stones.

'Reverend Gould said as how it might be a village, what we're digging up. So folks lived here all those years ago. Wonder what they ate?' Jim was working beside Joseph, keeping up an easy chatter as he bent and dug.

Joseph said, 'Same as us, I expect. Meat if they were lucky, vegetables, water from the brook.'

'Hard life, carrying it up 'ere. And where did they grow their crops, then?'

'You must ask Reverend Gould. He'll know. Perhaps—' Joseph stopped abruptly, bent down and picked something out of the soil he had just dug.

'What's that, then?' Jim peered over his shoulder.

'Looks like a bit of broken pottery. I'll show it to Reverend Gould.'

Joseph put down his spade, crossed the turf to where Davy was digging, with Reverend Gould beside him. He held out his find. 'Is it a piece of a pot, sir?'

The vicar looked at it for a long moment. 'Yes, it is. A cooking pot, perhaps. Well, excellent, so now we know that they cooked food in their little stone houses.'

He glanced at Joseph and smiled. 'Now, Freeman, next thing we want to find is the hearth where they burned bits of timber, gorse roots and bracken to cook the food, where they sat around to get warm. Keep digging.'

The small find encouraged the men to continue excavating, and by the end of the afternoon, when the sun was already starting to sink towards the horizon, Joseph had unearthed what Reverend Gould insisted was a hearth.

'This is splendid,' he said excitedly. 'Now we can imagine a family sitting within these stone circles, these small houses, talking, eating, telling stories....'

Joseph and the other men crowded around as he went on to give a history lesson, about the weather being warmer in earlier days, and how these men chose a sheltered site in which to drag the moor stones into circles, using timber posts to prop up the roof which was thatched with gorse and heather to keep out the Dartmoor storms.

But Joseph wasn't listening. Finding the remains of the old hearth had started new thoughts in his mind. Now his imagination took flight and he suddenly realized that what he had always missed in his life was a proper home. Of course he had lived in various houses – the institution, then Eli's farm, and finally the Reverend Mr Gosling's big country house with all its comforts, but he had never been able to say, 'this is my home.' And now, this untidy circle of stones was telling him that it had once been the hub of life for a family. Despite all the privations, all the lack of comfort, the hard work to survive, it had been their home.

It was a revelation; he knew now that a home was the one thing he lacked in life, and from that moment on he felt himself become stronger and more imbued with a purpose. No more roaming, no more searching for freedom, for surely in one's own home that sense of freedom would settle down and end the search on which he had been engaged for so long.

He must find – create – his own home. And he must tell Becky what he was doing.

Becky mounted the stairs, ready for her morning work with the accounts. Mr Fielding was still in his room but she heard something in the study. Opening the door she saw Nat Briggs sitting in the maister's chair, papers piled on the table in front of him. Their eyes met and she sensed his excitement as he said roughly, 'I been writing a report 'bout they ole pigsties over to Worth farm. Maister'll be pleased to see this.' He picked up a scrappy bit of paper covered in rough writing and grinned at her.

Becky looked at it, frowned and then turned away. The key to the accounts cupboard was hidden in its usual place where Mr Fielding had left it after yesterday's session of explaining how the ledgers worked. She said nothing, but went to the cupboard, unlocked it and took out the heavy ledger, returning to the table and putting it down, opening it at the correct page and then looking at Nat. 'You can leave that with me, Mr Briggs. I'll see that Mr Fielding gets it.'

Nat got up, hovered beside the table, looking over her shoulder at the open pages. 'Where is he, then?'

'Resting. I think he did too much yesterday. His back still pains him.'

'Hmm.' Nat's voice was scornful and Becky turned to glare at him.

'So you can get on with all your other work, Mr Briggs. I'm sure you've got enough to keep you busy.' She wouldn't look at him, just wanted him to disappear. She picked up a pencil and tried to concentrate on the figures in front of her.

'Housekeeper, now, eh? That's a lift up for a maid like you.' She heard his voice change from a sneer into something more threatening and waited, tensely for what she sensed was another demand. 'That's as maybe,' he went on. 'But don't think you can give me orders. I know too much about you, see.'

Becky felt the sudden silence crowding in on her. He was standing behind her chair and she knew he was grinning again. Slowly she turned and looked at him. She felt afraid, knowing that, since Mr Fielding's accident, Nat had grabbed a certain measure of power and now, clearly, he was ready to use it. 'I don't understand you, Mr Briggs.'

They stared at each other, and she added, 'I have to get on with my work, even if you don't. So please, just leave me alone.'

He laid a heavy hand on the back of her chair and leaned over her. 'Don't talk like that, Becky Yeo. I'll do what I like. And you must listen to me.... If you don't think more about taking up my offer ....' He paused, sharp eyes intent on her face.

'Your ... offer?' Fear ran down her spine. Playing for time, she edged away from his bad breath and sweating face.

'Don't play with me, maid. Asked you to marry me, I did. And I'm still waiting for your answer.' His voice was harsh, his expression full of hard excitement and a flush of temper.

Becky swallowed a lump in her throat and felt her pulses race. She had known that this confrontation had to happen, but now it was here she still wasn't ready to give in. Her voice shook but was still clear. 'I need more time, Mr Briggs. I have to think about it ... I mean, all this work keeps me so busy that I haven't—'

'If you got any sense, you'll make time, Becky Yeo. Or else....' He laughed. She heard the note of triumph and felt an instant stab of apprehension. What did he mean? Was it something to do with Joseph? Or Will? Or even Ma?

Taking a huge intake of breath she turned away from him, forcing herself to look back at the ledger. Behind her, Nat put a hand on her shoulder, pulling her around to meet his eyes. From his pocket he pulled out a crumpled piece of paper and waved it in front of her face. She saw the triumph in his narrowed eyes, and at once felt the fear grow.

'This 'ere,' said Nat, almost whispering, and bending closer to her, 'tells me something 'bout you, Becky Yeo, that you wouldn't want folks to know, 'specially your Ma and your brother. So you'll do just what I tell you and it'll be all right. But if not, then, well, I'm warning you, see.' He stepped back and folded the paper, putting it back in his pocket, an unpleasant grin spreading all over his face.

Becky said nothing but her stomach knotted and her breathing quickened. She pushed back the chair, stood up and faced him. Her voice was unsteady. 'Let me see that—'

He laughed. 'Course not. This bit o' paper's my hold over you, maid. I'm keepin' it safe.'

Their eyes met and held, his gleaming and hers wide with unease. Then, as if nothing had happened, he grinned, and walked to the door. 'I'll be around, just make up your mind, Becky, an' let me know when you decide to say yes. No hurry – not while I got this paper.' He left the room and she sat down again, not knowing what to think or to do.

Slowly, then, she started to make sense of Nat and his bit of paper. The pile of papers that had fallen out of the broken cupboard remained where she had put them, in front of Mr Fielding's chair. Clearly, someone had gone through them. The tidy pile was now in small heaps and it dawned on her that Nat had taken one of them. The paper that in some way concerned her.

The afternoon work was done, Ruth had gone home and Nellie Mudge was busily preparing the evening meal when Becky sat down in the kitchen, her mind awhirl with thoughts. She needed to tell someone about Nat Briggs's sly trickery; needed someone to advise her what to do next. She had no wish to tell Ma and Will what had happened. She knew that a secret hung about all that Nat had said. A secret about her? Her mind was busy but it held no direction. She wondered if Grace was part of this secret; if Mr Fielding, too, was part of it. Who could help her?

Carefully, she said, 'Mrs Mudge, did you know that Mr Briggs wants to marry me?'

Nellie turned slowly, spoon in her hand, and met her eyes. 'No,' she said shortly. 'Have you told him yes or no?'

Becky tried to smile. 'I'll never say yes. But he keeps asking me. And now....'

'Now? What's he up to then? Another of his nasty tricks I dessay.'

It was a relief to think she could tell someone. 'He has a paper which he says concerns me and if I don't say yes he'll show it to my family.' She swallowed the dryness in her mouth. 'From what he says, Ma and Will would be shocked.'

Mrs Mudge put down the spoon, lowered herself into the cane chair by the fire and shook her head. 'That man – evil, I reckon. So what are you gonna do, maid?'

'That's just it, Mrs Mudge. I don't know what to do. Or who to tell. I feel so helpless.' Becky watched the old face slide from disapproval to thoughtfulness, and added unsteadily, 'Can you help me – please?'

'I wish I could.' Nellie was silent for a long moment. Then she sighed. 'But secrets are nasty ole things – hurting people who don't deserve to be hurt. I don't think I know enough to help you, maid. Why not tell the maister? He should know how Mr Briggs is treating you.'

'Yes, I suppose he should. Perhaps tomorrow I'll tell him.'

Mrs Mudge pushed herself out of her chair and turned again to the hearth and its simmering cauldron. 'Nothin' like the present. Why not now? He'll be resting, waiting for his dinner, in a good mood.'

Becky sighed. She supposed that Nellie was right. Mr Fielding ought to know that Nat said he had some sort of hold over her. What was the word? *Blackmail.* The thought made a shiver trickle down her spine, but she managed a smile. 'Thank you, Mrs Mudge. I'll do that. I'll go up and find him now.'

The house was shadowy with the day ending, its half-darkness filling her mind with even more disturbance. Becky went up the sweeping staircase slowly, trying to think what she should say to Mr Fielding. Would he be impatient with her, saying it was nothing to do with him, and not to bother him any further? But something urged her on. She stood outside the study door, smelling a faint fragrance of cigar smoke, and knew that he was there. She knocked and was bidden enter.

'Becky? You want something?' He sat in his usual chair, glass beside him and a cigar in one hand. She thought he looked tired and again wondered at her presumption. But something kept her, standing before him, trying to find the right words.

They came suddenly, and were out before she even knew what she said. 'It's Nat Briggs, sir. He wants to marry me and I can't do that. He says he knows a secret about me. He's – he's blackmailing me.'

The words hung in the scented air and she watched Mr Fielding's eyes narrow. He leaned forward, pain showing as he moved his body. 'He's doing – *what?*'

Becky trembled, but knew she must go on. 'He says he knows a secret that he will tell my family if I don't marry him.'

Rupert Fielding was silent for a long moment. Then he said, 'Sit down. Tell me more.' He picked up his glass, drained it, and then said, almost to himself, Becky thought, 'That damned knave. I'm not surprised – everything he does is underhand.' Then he looked at Becky, sitting opposite him, and said quietly, 'And where did Briggs get this idea of a secret from, do you know?'

She thought quickly. 'I found a pile of old papers when they fell out of that cupboard,' she gestured to it. 'The latch is broken. I put them on the table for you to see when you next came in. But when I came up this morning he was here, sitting in your place, and looking through them.'

Another long pause and the cigar remained in Rupert Fielding's hand. Then he said carefully, and in a clipped, angry tone Becky had never heard before, 'Those papers were presumably private ones. My father kept a daily journal, recording everything that happened within the estate. And you're telling me that Briggs read them?'

She nodded. 'I didn't see him reading, but I knew the papers had been disturbed, and he had one of them in his hand. He put it in his pocket when he went.'

'The devil.' His voice was very quiet, his body still while he thought. And then, abruptly, he pushed himself out of the chair, stiffly, painfully, and came a step towards her. 'You don't want to marry him? Why not?'

She looked at the floor, embarrassed. 'He's sly, he's too full of himself, he treats me so badly….'

'How does he treat you, Becky?'

She closed her eyes as the memories flashed. 'Always trying to touch me. To – kiss me.'

He grunted. And then, 'Something I have to ask you.' His voice was almost apologetic. 'Are you sure you've never given him any hope of marriage? Have you – forgive me – flirted with him?'

'No. *No.*' She tried to control her emotions. 'I have never given him any encouragement, sir. I can swear that.'

'Very well, Becky.' He looked at his watch and returned to the chair. 'Isn't this the time when you usually go home for a couple of hours? Well, go then. And leave a message with Mrs Mudge to tell Briggs I want to see him the moment he arrives.'

She left the study, gave Mrs Mudge the message, and then, putting a shawl around her shoulders and carrying her hat, left the house, knowing only that she must find Joseph. Her mind circling with confused thoughts, she walked quickly down the lane, ignoring the shadows that reached out to envelope her. His name sang in her head. Joseph was the only one who could calm her, help her in this frantic panic that was eating her up.

CHAPTER 12

He was working at Hound Tor, someone had told her. Was it Ruth? That was where she must go. But would he be there? Not at this time of the evening, surely. Well then, perhaps in the Inn. He liked his pint of ale, she knew that. She would be almost sure to find him there. But if not? Her mind refused to think any further. She walked rapidly down the lane, knowing by instinct where the potholes were and turning left where the path climbed up towards Swallerton Gate and the grave, all still and dark in the shadow of great Bowerman's Nose.

The evening was warm and she pushed her shawl off her shoulders. Small noises rustled and crept in the hedges as she walked but she paid no attention. Her mind was fixed on just one thing – finding Joseph and telling him about what had happened today.

Perhaps he would just laugh it off. Men thought women were too emotional, she knew. Will, for example, always said that. But Joseph was different and would understand – wouldn't he? She was uncertain what he could do to help her, but just to talk to him, to tell someone of her worries, seemed to be the only way she could go.

Now the grave loomed up in front of her and she paused for a second, running her hand over the small headstone and allowing her mind to fly back to the girl who was buried here. Life was unpredictable, often cruel, even though it also brought immense joy and hope. Passing the mound, she spared a thought for the girl and her unborn child. She must have known great unhappiness.

And then she heard raised voices and faint laughter and knew the inn was only a short distance up the road. She ran then, leaving behind the great misty outlines of Hound Tor's rocks and behind them the tall pile of Bowerman's Nose. Nothing mattered except finding Joseph.

The inn was crowded with men standing and sitting, men who worked all day and whose clothes reflected their work. Miners, stone masons, labourers, farmers. The inn smelt of bodies, damp coats and worn boots. Pipe smoke warmed the rank air, and for a moment she hesitated inside the door. This was not the place for a woman, she knew; only girls who earned their living in bad ways came here, to find a man likely to pay for an hour's warmth and intimacy. She shouldn't be here – what would Ma say? How Will would shout at her … and then, what would Mr Fielding say if he knew his housekeeper was here, in this common place? But then such thoughts vanished, for above the rough talk and laughter she heard the one voice she sought.

Joseph had his back to the fire, a tankard of ale in his hand, and was talking to someone whom she couldn't quite see. Suddenly, her strength failed her. What would he say when he saw her? She shouldn't be here. She must go … but she didn't. Instead she willed him to look across at her, and he did so, his smiling face suddenly sharp with surprise. She saw him mouthing words which didn't reach her through all the other voices, but knew what he said. 'Becky. Miss Freckles….'

Relief filled her and she leaned against the closed door, feeling her legs tremble and her body weaken as she watched him push his way across the room. He took no notice of voices asking where was he going. He was at her side, looking into her distraught eyes and saying rapidly, 'Come outside. Here, take my hand.' And then they were out in the quiet evening air, smelling the welcome freshness of moorland, hearing only small night sounds, her hand remaining in his, bringing new strength and a welcome feeling of rightness.

He drew her away from the inn, slowly walking down the dark lane and into the shelter of a covert of trees sloping down towards the valley. They pressed close, warm and silent, and Becky felt her panic subside, her thoughts slow down, the sense of relief making her body lighter, stronger.

At last he stopped, put his arms around her and drew her close. 'What are you doing here, Becky? I can see something's wrong – tell me.'

She leaned her head against his chest, heard the slow beat of his heart, and whispered, 'Nat Briggs says he knows a secret about me. He won't tell me, just says I must marry him if I don't want him to tell Ma and Will about it.'

For a moment she heard the heartbeat leap, then his arms were tighter, his voice speaking into her hair, as he said gruffly, with an edge to his voice, 'I'll deal with that little flyblow. He's not going to make you unhappy and afraid – I'll see to him. And you just keep out of his way. I've got you safe, I'll never let you be hurt. You mean so much to me, Becky love.'

She lifted her head, looking into his shadowed eyes and knew she had been right to come and find him. Slowly, her fear vanished, leaving in its place a feeling of relief that swamped her with new hope. Whatever Nat Briggs had in mind would never happen if Joseph had his way. She was safe.

But could the secret be forgotten? A flicker of anxiety stabbed. She put her arms around his neck and whispered, 'But the secret, what about the secret? I must find out what it is, and then I can face Nat.'

His lips were close to hers, and she relished the sweetness of his breath behind the hint of tobacco and ale. She wanted him to kiss her, but he was still too enraged. 'You must tell Mr Fielding that he's threatening you. And he can demand to know whatever it is that the little ratbag has in mind. Then you'll be free of him and his threats. And if he still wants to play games, then leave him to me.' His voice lowered, sinking into a tone of deep felt anger. 'Don't worry, I'll see that nothing harms you. I can deal with him. Don't let that little flyblow upset you. He's all talk – of course you can't marry him. Oh Becky....'And then he was kissing her, her eyes, her nose, her throat and the peep of warm flesh half hidden beneath her shawl, then finding her lips. They kissed and kissed until breath ran out. And then he kissed her again, light kisses this time, travelling over her face, ending up on her closed eyes.

Seconds later, but surely longer than that, with the joy of her love sending all other thoughts spiraling away, she opened them and smiled. 'I think I love you,' she whispered, still knowing the excitement and wonder of his lips on hers. 'Stay with me, Joseph.'

He didn't answer, just sighed as his arms dropped by his side, leaving her alone and lonely in a way she had never felt before. 'Becky,' he said, very low. 'If you want me, Becky, then you must wait. Wait a little longer.' He put his arms around her again, looked into her wide, hurt eyes, and said slowly, 'I wouldn't make a good husband, Becky. I'm not good enough for you. There's things I have to do – to find out – before I can settle down in one place.' He stopped and a wry smile flashed out, 'With one woman.'

'But—' She didn't understand. 'Just now, when you kissed me, I thought—'

'I do love you, of course I do, but my life isn't worked out. Not yet. I have to make my way first. Can you understand?'

'No.' She was near tears because it had all seemed so perfect. And now it was finished. She pulled away from him, fumbled for a kerchief in her pocket and wiped her eyes. They stood in silence, looking at each other, lost in the moment until he reached out, stroked her hair and ran a finger down her cheek. 'I don't think I have the right to ask you to wait. You're a lovely girl, other men must find you so. Others will want you, you could be married and settled in your own home before I come back to you. I don't want to spoil your life, Becky.'

'But you're spoiling it by going away.' Her voice rose, because the hurt was too deep to control. 'Why can't you stay? Why can't we marry and live like other people do? You can find work – we'll rent a cottage, I expect Mr Fielding would let us have one—'

'No.' An uncompromising word which made her catch her breath.

'But you said you love me.'

Joseph sighed. His voice deepened. 'I do. Always believe that. And I'll ask you to marry me one day. But not now. Try and understand, sweetheart. My name is Freeman, and that's how I have to live – freely – for now.'

'I don't understand.' Her mind was running in circles and nothing was clear. 'You say you love me but you don't want to be with me. It doesn't make sense.'

His arms tightened around her. 'Of course I want to be with you. Now and always. But you have to let me go. Wait a little longer, Becky, and I'll come back to you.'

Very slowly she drew away from him, taking in sharp intakes of breath, making herself stand straight and strong, regardless of all the emotions filling her. 'I see. Your life is more important than us being together. Well, don't think I'll wait forever. Maybe I'll find my own life while I'm waiting – what would you think of that?'

His voice grew steely. 'I wouldn't blame you, Becky. But I just hope you'll wait a little longer for me. You see, you're the only one, and there will never be anyone else. But I have to live my life.'

Silence for a moment that stretched endlessly.

Then pain struck even deeper and anger seemed the only way out. She pulled away, tears in her eyes, voice tremulous but sure of itself. 'I don't believe anything you say! You're just like all the others. Ma told me men only want kisses and soft words, and then they're off somewhere else and now I know she's right.'

'It's not like that. I swear.'

'Don't bother! I'm not waiting for you, Joseph Freeman, I've got better things to do, other people to love and work for. So don't come back, 'cos I'll have no more to do with you.' She ran, heart racing, eyes swimming, tripping over stones in her haste, but nothing could stop her. Get back to High Cross Manor, hide herself away, think about something – anything – other than Joseph.

It was with enormous relief that she reached the Manor, locked the door behind her and went up to the small bedroom where she collapsed, lying there with all her dreams shattered and, in spite of all her strong resolution to forget, Joseph's voice ringing in her ears. *I'll be back, Becky. Just wait for me.*

In the morning there were raised voices, and an atmosphere of disturbance spreading throughout the house. Nat Briggs had been closeted with the maister since very early, and Becky heard his footsteps pounding down the stairs with a feeling of relief. He was going. She waited in the scullery until he had left, thundering through the kitchen with a hard, unpleasant look on his face and slamming the door behind him.

Nellie Mudge got on with her cooking, but looked at Becky as she came back into the kitchen. 'Sounds like maister told him off,' she said. 'An' not before time. Now we can all get on with our work and forget his nastiness.'

Becky nodded. His absence was a blessing, but she still felt anxious. What had the maister said to him? How had Nat Briggs answered? The business of the secret weighed heavily on her mind, and she went up towards the study to deal with the accounts with a feeling of unease. And Joseph was still in the background of her mind, their confrontation last night a shadow which refused to move away.

Rupert Fielding didn't hear her first knock on the door, and when she repeated it he answered in a slow, quiet voice, which made her wonder even more what had happened between him and Nat Briggs.

She crossed the room, immediately aware that he was looking at her in a different way from usual. Generally he quickly said good morning and then started talking about invoices and accounts. But now he was sitting well back in his chair, one hand at his back, rubbing the still painful muscles. He gestured towards the chair facing him and, instead of at once pulling the account book towards him and explaining something to her as she expected, merely sat there, eyes fixed on her face.

Becky felt uncomfortable under his unblinking gaze. She

thought perhaps he was blaming her. Had Nat told enough lies to make her seem as guilty as he was? Did Mr Fielding think that, between them, they were planning something to their advantage, and at a cost to the maister and the estate?

She saw on the table a piece of crumpled paper and realized this was the scrap that Nat had waved in front of her face as he told her that he knew her secret. And now it was in front of the maister…. Suddenly words erupted from her. 'Has he given it back to you? Can I forget all about it? Is he still trying to make me give in?'

Rupert Fielding picked up the paper, looked at it, folded it and then put it into his waistcoat pocket. He didn't reply at once, but his eyes never left her face. Eventually, he broke the silence. 'Becky, I think you should take some time off. Tom will drive you into Moreton and you can buy yourself a more suitable dress. You don't look like a housekeeper and you should. And another thing – you are to move into one of the guest bedrooms. That attic is not suitable for your situation.'

She was astounded. 'I don't understand.'

He sighed, moved painfully in the chair. ' It's quite simple. A kitchen maid can wear shabby clothes, but a housekeeper has a certain position to keep up and must dress accordingly.' He waited but she said nothing, and then he smiled, chuckling slightly as he said drily, 'I thought you'd be pleased. Young girls love dresses, don't they?'

'Why yes, of course. And I know my clothes are shabby and old. So, well, thank you, Mr Fielding.' Her uneasiness vanished and she returned his smile, even as her thoughts circled. Why should he do this for her? What did it mean?

He sat up, reached for the account book and said, in his usual sharp voice, 'You can go this afternoon. Tell Tom to come and see me when you finish here. He can also post a letter for me.' He stopped, looked at her, frowned, and then added slowly, 'I am hoping that Mrs Richards will be returning to England in a week or so. I am asking her to come and visit as soon as she can.'

Becky nodded, tried to return the conversation to more normal matters and said, 'She'll notice a change in the house, sir. It's really looking very good now, except, of course, for the repairs in the library.' She paused as a wonderful idea flashed through her mind. 'I don't think Jim Browning has much idea about working with wood. But there is a local man who is a real craftsman.'

Rupert Fielding pursed his lips. 'Yes, I remember – the man who repaired the bed panel? What was his name?'

She held her breath for a second. Then 'Joseph Freeman. He's working at Hound Tor at the moment, digging up the old stones. I – I could get a message to him.'

'A good idea. Do that, please. It's important to get the library shelves repaired and back to their old appearance. Tell him to come as soon as he can.'

Becky said a quiet, 'Yes' and waited for a moment. The secret was still in her mind, but he hadn't said anything about it. She saw him scrutinize the account book and then push it over the table towards her.

'You're doing a good job on these, Becky. In fact, you're working very well. I shall see that your wage is increased.'

They looked at each other and then she said quietly, 'Thank you, sir. And I'm grateful to you for giving me the chance to better myself. It's always been my dream.'

'Has it? You're ambitious, then? You've always wanted to get on in life?' His eyes were narrowed and stared at her. His fingers began drumming on the table and he said slowly, 'Becky, we must talk about the paper that Briggs stole, and which he was threatening you with. The secret he has discovered.'

Her heart began to race. She sat a little straighter and tried to prepare herself for – what?

Rupert Fielding moved painfully in his chair and slowly got to his feet. He stretched, grimaced, then turned to the window, his back to her. For a long moment he was silent. Then abruptly he turned, looking down at her.

'Becky, the secret was once forgotten, but now it's come alive again. It concerns me, mostly, but your family are part of it and all I'm prepared to tell you is that you have nothing to fear now from Briggs. I confronted him with all the deceit that has come to light in the accounts ledger, and also threatened him with losing his position as estate bailiff if he continues to harass you. I hope that will make you feel better. No need to allow him to frighten you, because I don't think he will trouble you any more.'

It seemed as if a weight had dropped off her shoulders. She took in a huge breath and felt her whole body soften. 'Thank you,' she said unsteadily. 'Does that mean that he – Mr Briggs – won't tell anyone about the secret?'

'He's given me his oath, for what it's worth.' Rupert Fielding's voice was dry and his face reflected his thoughts. Then his expression changed. 'One other thing, Becky, I want your promise that you will never tell anyone about this matter. Not your mother, your brother, or anyone else. It happened in the past and nothing can change it, but it's better to let it lie there – forgotten. So, have I your word?'

She stared at him, uncertain. 'But you said it concerns us – so why can't I know?'

'Because it's unnecessary for you to know.' His voice was hard. 'It would possibly distress you, and I don't want that. Be patient, Becky, be patient and forget all this trouble. You have your life before you – a good situation here, and everything is going well for you. So why worry about past events?' He smiled.

Becky thought hard. To do as he asked, and forget a secret had ever existed – it sounded sensible. And he was right. Her life was jogging along serenely. She enjoyed her work at the Manor; she was able to give some of her wages to Ma, and she thought Will was more kindly disposed towards her than he had ever been.

But – *Joseph.*

The one shadow that was always there, and perhaps would never go away.

Determinedly, she raised her head, met Rupert Fielding's questioning eyes, and said, 'Yes, sir, I give you my word. I won't think any more of that secret.'

He nodded, smiled with a happier expression than she had seen before, and said, 'Good. So now let us get on with the accounts. And you must tell Tom to get the trap ready for your afternoon outing. Oh, and don't forget to send a message to the man about the library repairs. What did you say his name was?'

'Joseph Freeman.' Her voice was tightly controlled, and she bent her head as she opened the ledger and prepared to listen to the morning's instructions about credit and loss. She felt proud of herself, sitting there, a housekeeper who was to dress suitably and have a comfortable bedroom here at High Cross Manor.

Her mind focused then on the accounts ledger, and the morning sped by without any more disturbing thoughts.

CHAPTER 13

A new feeling of authority came into Becky's mind now. Mr Fielding wanted her to look like a housekeeper as well as acting as one. She wouldn't argue about that. When the accounting was finished for the morning, she went downstairs and found Tom in the yard.

'Mr Fielding said that you are to drive me into Moretonhampstead this afternoon.'

A look of surprise crossed his face. 'Drive you?'

'Yes, Tom. I have some shopping to do.' Brief amusement swept through her. She was the housekeeper and he must know his place. 'Where's Eddie? I have a job for him.'

The boy came out of the stable. 'Eddie, the maister wants you to go to Hound Tor and find the men who are digging up the stones in the valley beyond the Tor. Tell one of them, Joseph Freeman, that he should come here to the Manor as soon as he can. Mr Fielding has work for him.'

They were both wide-eyed.

'I'll be ready after dinner, Tom,' she said firmly. 'And there will be a letter for you to post in Moreton, please.' Not waiting for his answer, she went back into the kitchen.

Nellie Mudge gave her a long, thoughtful look. 'Something happened? Briggs charged out like a randy bull.'

'Mr Fielding had words with him. He's got to stop all his little tricks with money and repay it. And he's not to worry me any more.' Her voice was lighter and she knew that her smile was unbounded. 'Mrs Mudge, I'm to go into Moreton this afternoon and buy a dress that's more suitable for a housekeeper. And I can move into one of the guest rooms!'

She felt like dancing around the room, but a housekeeper would never do such a thing. Instead she went to look in the cracked little mirror hanging on the far wall. Her face was bright, her smile easy. No worry clouded her eyes. Everything suddenly seemed wonderful; the secret was forgotten, Nat was out of the way and Joseph was coming to work here at the Manor. She would see him every day. She couldn't help turning to Nellie and saying, with a laugh, 'I'm so happy! Things are going right at last....'

Nellie stirred the pot on the fire, not looking at her. She said thoughtfully, 'Sounds as if the maister likes having you around. You've done well. Just be careful, that's all.'

Becky stood quite still. 'Careful? What do you mean?'

Nellie pursed her lips and looked away. 'Nothing. Just – well, don't ask for too much.'

'But I haven't asked for anything. Mr Fielding has done it all – made me housekeeper, said I must have a new dress and a better bedroom.' Some of her joy slipped away. What was Nellie going on about? She walked over to the range and looked into Nellie's suddenly veiled eyes.

'What do you mean? Tell me, please....'

There was a long moment's silence while Nellie straightened her slumped shoulders and thought. Then, turning to the pot on the fire, she said tightly, 'I don't mean nothing. But others might wonder at the maister taking such a fancy to you.'

Becky felt something inside her knot and a growing uneasiness made her remember Ma saying that Mr Fielding was a bad man. And now Nellie was hinting at something unpleasant. She said slowly, and with a tremor in her voice, 'It's not like that. I'm just a servant. Like you. Like Tom and Eddie.'

Nellie looked over her shoulder and their eyes met. She nodded her head and said, very quickly, 'Like Grace.' Then she bit her lip and shook her head, as if knowing she had said too much.

Heart starting to pump, Becky asked unsteadily, 'So tell me about Grace. Please.'

'I'm not sayin' any more. I've said too much as it is. But I don't want you hurt, maid.'

'Why should I be hurt?' Becky couldn't leave it, watching as Nellie went back to stirring the pot and not saying any more.

The meal was a silent one with thoughts flying around but no words expressing them, and Becky was glad when Tom came to the door and said the trap was ready.

The small dressmaker's shop in Moretonhampstead had little stock, but Becky chose a dark green worsted frock, long sleeved and high necked, that would be warm in the winter, its dark colour not showing too much wear. She tried it on, looked in the long glass, and wondered at the change she saw. No longer an untidy young girl, now she was neatly, almost elegantly dressed, her hair knotted at the back of her neck, and a new felt hat which she couldn't resist, dipping over her eyes.

Mrs Best, the dressmaker, smiled at the reflection. 'Suits you, Miss Yeo. And it'll wear well. Send the account to Mr Fielding, shall I?'

'Yes, please.' Becky kept the frock on and watched while the old one was packed up.

She felt different, now; more sure of herself, capable of meeting Mr Fielding's friends when they called, and able to push aside foolish remarks from old Nellie and concentrate on her new status in life.

When Mrs Best asked obsequiously, 'I do hope you'll keep my name in mind, Miss Yeo. Your recommendation would be most helpful,' she felt a touch of power and abruptly understood how Nat Briggs had felt when Mr Fielding had been unable to deal with matters. and he had found himself in an unexpected position of authority. Perhaps it was difficult to blame him.

Driving home in the trap, she hardly noticed the colours of the countryside. Dying bronze bracken sheeted the hillside, and heather bushes on wiry stems had turned brown. The sun shone on the rocks littering the green turf, and bleached moorland grass waved in great pale drifts, but her mind was on her new situation, and on the prospect of having Joseph working at High Cross Manor.

Eddie came back with a message from the Reverend Mr Gould that he would be sorry to lose Joseph Freeman, who was a good worker, but understood Mr Fielding's need. Freeman would report to High Cross Manor at the end of the week. And in the meantime he hoped that Mr Fielding was recovering from his unfortunate accident.

Rupert said roughly, 'Typical of a parson, no sense of urgency – all these idle antiquarians can think of is the old stones and what they were once used for. Repairing a dwelling means nothing to them. Still, if Freeman comes at the end of the week that'll be something.' He looked at Becky, who had brought the message and now stood in the study, wondering if her new dress was approved of.

'You look different – ah, the dress. Yes.' He smiled as if amused and she blushed, her thoughts abruptly circling. Had Mr Fielding treated Grace in the same away as he was treating her? But who had Grace been? A village girl, like her?

'Very nice.' He got to his feet, pain evident in every slow movement, and limped towards her. 'And what about the bedroom? Have you moved in? Which room have you chosen?'

'The second guest room – Mrs Mudge said it would be the best one for me. And no, I haven't taken my things there, not yet. The day has gone so fast.' They were close, so close that she smelled cigars and whisky and saw a new light in his hooded, dark eyes. Alarm touched her and she stepped backwards.

At once the light vanished, replaced by what she read as irritation. 'Not afraid of me, are you, Becky?' His voice was quick and hard.

' I – no, no, of course not, sir.' She fought to get control of her feelings and managed a tight smile.

He stood there, looking at her and slowly she felt the uneasiness die. He was just the maister, admiring the new dress and making sure that she was moving into a better bedroom, one that was her due now she was promoted to housekeeper. He held no fear for her. Indeed, she enjoyed his smile, as he limped towards the door.

'Go and move into your bedroom, then, Becky. And no doubt you want to go and see your mother and brother after dinner to tell them your good news, eh?'

'Yes,' she said. 'Yes, sir, thank you.'

In the open doorway he stopped, looked over his shoulder at her and said quietly, in a warmer tone of voice than the one she was used to, 'Don't call me that, Becky. Mr Fielding will do.' He nodded, smiled briefly, then disappeared down the passage.

She stood in the middle of the study and waited until his uneven footsteps faded, then she breathed in deeply and went out of the room, closing the door behind her.

Upstairs in the attic room, she gathered her few belongings and carried them down to the guest room at the back of the house, where she sat on the bed thinking for a long time and trying to work out just what was happening in her life now.

So many changes; and the most extraordinary one was surely that Mr Fielding was being so kind to her. What had she done to deserve this? Had her work, both with the accounts and the cleaning of the house, struck him as exceptional? Yet she had to admit to herself that his regard seemed more personal. That he saw her as Becky Yeo, and not just another servant working in his house. Perplexed, she got up from the bed and walked across to the window, pulling back the newly washed curtains and then staring out at the moorland, stretching away into the distance.

For a moment her thoughts ceased worrying her and a sense of peace came instead. From this window at the back of the house she saw the age old beauty of Dartmoor reaching out, full of approaching autumnal colours, and thought back to the years that she had spent in this valley below the high hills and tors and knew, once again, that she would never want to leave it.

She knew, too, that certain things had changed her – made her suddenly grow up and become more perceptive about life. Finding Joseph – she smiled, remembering their early encounters – had been the most important of the strange events now affecting her life. Understanding Nat Briggs's unwanted and frightening pursuit of her was another. And now this almost unbelievable feeling of sympathy and something even warmer – was it friendship? – that Mr Fielding had instilled in her. This was the most extraordinary.

She sighed, turned back from the window and looked around the room. So this was her new bedroom, her own place where she could be alone when she needed to be, resting or thinking and planning – dreaming, perhaps. As the second guest room it didn't have the elegance of the more superior room next door, but even so the decorations were splendid and pleasing. Rugs, softening the old highly polished floorboards. Flowered wallpaper. Dark, heavy oak furniture in which to store her few clothes and belongings. A bed with a softer mattress than she had ever lain on before, pillows and warm blankets covered with an embroidered counterpane and pictures on two of the walls. It was almost the room of a fine lady, someone more used to living in comfort than herself, she thought, wryly smiling.

In the long pier mirror that stood beside the large wardrobe, she caught sight of her reflection: a tall girl in a dark green dress, tight at the wrists and high at the neck, falling into a full skirt with just the hint of a bustle at the back. Did Mr Fielding think she looked a proper housekeeper? What would Joseph say if he saw her now? Would Nat Briggs pursue her even further? And Ma and Will – here her thoughts homed in on the farm and she knew she must go and see them. Mr Fielding had said she should go and tell them her good news. Yes, she would do so, but she would keep to herself the strange business of the secret which still cast a shadow into her thoughts. It was as if she were keeping secrets herself now; another peculiar turn in life and one she wasn't sure she enjoyed. Sighing, she tidied her hair, picked up her shawl and went out of the room, closing the door behind her with a firm hand and walking down the sweeping staircase with a step that was infinitely more confident than usual.

Trudging back to the Reverend Mr Gould's homely barn at the end of the day, leaving his work mates at the inn, Joseph Freeman mulled over the fact that Rupert Fielding wished to employ him. Good. He would enjoy working in the old house, using all his craft and skill. The pay would be useful, for he was saving for the future. His future, wherever it might take him. Already he had a small pouch containing the remains of his small inheritance from the Reverend Mr Gosling and to this he added whatever could be spared after an occasional draught of ale at the inn and what was needed to renew tools and clothes. Food came with the weekly wage and was sufficient to keep him in good working trim.

His thoughts moved forward. At High Cross Manor he would be in daily contact with Becky. Here he found himself smiling in anticipation. Yes, they would be able to meet quietly and without anyone knowing; he could tell her again how he loved her. He would prove it, loving her warmly, passionately too, if the chance came and she was willing. Yet he knew, at the same time as his pulses raced, that he was being too forward, too quick, too foolish.

For to fulfill his ambitions, and to woo Becky and win her, he must have a home to offer her, with regular work in some capacity that suited him. Then, very slowly, he made a hard decision; he frowned but knew it was the right one – it must be no to High Cross Manor. No to seeing Becky and enjoying their possible meetings. Could he accept it? He must. Yet one thought lingered. If Becky thought he was just walking away from her she might well look for another suitor. Which would not be hard. An image of Nat Briggs flashed into his mind and he scowled as he walked up the track to the Reverend's house with its outbuildings and hayfilled barn.

Somewhere in the future – his and Becky's joint futures – Joseph knew that he and Briggs would confront one another. There would be an explosion of rage on his part, and the seeking for sly revenge on Briggs's part. His thoughts turned dark; he welcomed them, but forced them away. Leave them for another day. One more part of his life to be settled.

For the meantime he must work. A plan came into his mind. Find employment somewhere further away from the temptation of seeing Becky, work which would forward his ambitions. Learning how to work with stones – for stones would build a house and a house would end his wandering. And perhaps Becky would wait until it happened. He must see her for a last time and explain. But his face, as he washed at the pump in the yard before presenting himself in the kitchen ready for the evening meal, was tight with unease.

Suppose Becky decided not to wait for him? What would life hold then? It was a thought that haunted him when, later, he returned to the barn and pulled his hay bed around him, shutting off the noisy voices of his friends sharing the barn, the idea lingering unhappily in his mind until he quelled the dark thoughts by singing a few bars of her song.

'*O'er the wall came a lad, he took all that I had....*'

When sleep overtook him he dreamed of Becky, and of taking her into a new life where they would be always together.

Becky opened the farm door and went into the familiar warmth and nostalgic scent of her old home. She found Dinah stoking the fire and pushing the black cauldron to one side as the flames roared. A smell of turnips and bacon told of the meal to come and Becky smiled. The girl was proving herself, it seemed, darning Will's clothes and making hot meals for him.

'Smells good, Dinah.'

She looked across the room to the settle at the side of the fire and saw Ma sitting there, knitting in her hands, smiling a welcome. 'Ma – are you better? You look much more like yourself.' She bent and kissed the warm cheeks.

Thirza's eyes were wide. 'My soul! Don't you look smart! Why, that's a new dress – how did you get that, maid?'

Becky sat down beside her mother. 'Mr Fielding said I must dress more like his housekeeper, which I am now, Ma. So much has happened lately. Where can I start? Well, Mr Briggs has been found out to be a cheating rogue, which didn't surprise me. Apparently he's been taking money for years, bits and pieces from farm rents, and that sort of thing. Mr Fielding has found out now and has threatened to dismiss him.'

Thirza's smile died. 'Cheating? Dismiss him? Oh no, but we thought he'd make you a good husband, and now—'

'Now,' said Becky firmly, 'he has to repay the money and behave himself or he'll be put off.'

Silence for a moment. Dinah stirred the pot and Thirza stared at Becky. And then the door pushed open and Will came in. He looked at Becky and grunted, 'So who's this fine maid, then?'

She lifted her head. 'Mr Fielding's housekeeper, that's who. And I'm dressed to suit the position.' She smiled saucily. 'What do you think, then?'

Will came to the fire and sank into his usual chair, Dinah standing aside to make room for him. 'You looks like a lady, but you aren't,' he said shortly. 'Never right, is it? Was it the blow on the head that's made the maister a bit funny?' He pursed his mouth. 'Village ses as how he's changed a lot. There's gossip, I can tell you.'

'Gossip?' Becky's heart sank.

'An' mostly 'bout you, Becks. They ses as you've charmed the old man, that he likes you too much so makes you his housekeeper. An' something 'bout a bedroom, too.' Will's voice was hard, his eyes narrowed as he stared at her.

'That's wrong!' Becky said rapidly, hands forming fists. 'Whoever says such wicked things? Tell me who?'

'Just gossip. You know how it is. Young Ruth chatters, I dessay, now she works at High Cross, and o' course Mr Briggs, too. I hear as he's full of fury 'gainst the maister, and, so they ses, 'bout that Joseph Freeman. Wants to get back at him for whatever he reckons he's done. Tells everyone he'll get him and give him a good hiding.'

Becky felt her stomach turn over as horror and anxiety filled her. She knew that village gossip only ever had a grain of truth in it, but the idea of Nat seeking revenge on Joseph made her feel sick. Must it end in violence? What would Joseph feel about this hateful business of being hunted down and challenged? Would he, in his turn, fight Nat to the extent of physically harming him? Would such hatred, like secrets, go on forever?

She sat there quietly, hands round her mother's shoulders, wondering how to deal with all this unexpected wretchedness.

And then Thirza said, very quietly, so that her words were only just audible, 'Has the maister said anything to you, maid? About his feelings? I mean – what does he want of you? Is it just the housekeeping, or something....' She stopped, blinked, and seemed to shrink on the settle, 'Something more? Something – deeper, p'raps. Has he, well – touched you?' The words died, and she shook her head unhappily as she added, 'I'm sure you know what I mean.'

CHAPTER 14

Had Mr Fielding touched her?

No, of course he hadn't. But oh, yes, she knew just what Ma was trying so wretchedly to say. Becky's mind was suddenly a whirlwind of flashing images. She saw hot, lusting eyes, felt possessive strong hands, heard Nat's hoarse voice and knew instantly that this was what so often happened with needy men and vulnerable women. And then the grave beneath Bowerman's Nose flashed behind her eyes and new knowledge surged, for this was what must have happened to that poor woman who became pregnant and then hanged herself, because life in those unforgiving days would have been unbearable if she hadn't. Someone had touched her – loved her, then left her with the baby.

Men, thought Becky, with a surge of red hot hate. And then thought instead of Joseph, who had loved her sweetly and gently, had never scared her, never – what had Ma said? – taken advantage of her. Joseph would never force her. She could refuse him and he would just nod and smile and hope she might change her mind later. And, of course, it was just possible that she might, because she knew, deep down, that she loved him.

But Mr Fielding? No, he hadn't touched her. Whatever feelings there were between them – and yes, she felt something for him, a sort of warmth, but not like that sensual excitement she felt for Joseph – everything was different. She liked him, felt sorry for him. That was all there was to it, and she guessed that, strangely, he liked her, too. Just – liked her. Not – wanted her in his bed.

She stared at Ma and broke the silence that tightened the small room. 'Of course he hasn't! It's nothing like that between us. Why ever do you think he might be like that?'

Thirza sucked in her lips and looked down at her clasped hands. 'I dunno....'

Becky felt stirrings of anger resolve all the shock that had filled her mind. Now thoughts came and went, and new ideas became certainty. Village gossip. Mrs Mudge knowing something. Mr Fielding thinking she was Grace.... she stared at her mother.

'But you do know! It's something to do with Grace, isn't it? That name he said when he saw me at his bedside. And I suppose that's who he was bad with. That's what you were thinking about. Wondering if he treated me like he did Grace. Well, who was she? Just another village girl, I suppose. Like the one in the grave up the lane. So tell me, who was she? Come on, Ma, you have to tell me.'

Thirza shook her head. Will got up from his chair and went to the sink to wash his hands. Over his shoulder he said gruffly, 'What's all this about, then? If you got to tell her something, Ma, than for the Lord's sake tell it. You're makin' out that Becky's no more than a whore, and that's never right. Up in the air she may be, but all right, she's not a bad girl.'

'Grace was a girl working at the Manor.' Thirza's words rushed out as if they had been waiting to be released for a long time. 'The maister took her, made her pregnant and then she went away. That's all I know.' She looked across the room. 'I just didn't want him to do that with our Becky, Will. So don't shout at me. I didn't say she was bad – just that he was then an' so he might still be, for all I know.' She had a red patch on each cheek and her voice was higher than usual.

Will dried his hands, grunted and pulled out the chair at the top of the table. 'So let's forget it all,' he said firmly. 'I'm hungry, I want me tea. Got it ready, Dinah, have you?'

Becky let out her breath and nodded her head. He was right. This was a muddle about nothing that mattered. Now she knew about Grace she felt better. Just another girl treated badly, but nothing new in that. And she could assure Ma that nothing like that was happening between Mr Fielding and herself. She even managed a smile. What a thought! She said warmly, 'Well, now that's all done with I'd better be getting back. Ma, you can stop worrying about what's going on, because nothing is. I'm just working for him, and he's treating me well.'

She looked into Thirza's eyes and smiled fondly, thinking her mother looked better, with more colour and an extra bit of flesh on her. 'Stop worrying. You're a proper old worry, you are. And no need. Just think of the money I'm earning now – I'll give you something nice, Ma, to make you feel better. Have a think about what you'd like, and we'll go into Moreton one day soon.'

Thirza smiled weakly and took her hand. 'That'll be nice, maid. Why don't we get some dress stuff an' I'll make it up for you? You don't want to wear that one all the time, it'll get real spoiled if you do.'

'That would be lovely, Ma. Thank you. One day next week. I'll ask Mr Fielding if Tom can drive us.'

The room seemed lighter, happier. Becky looked at Dinah, spooning turnip stew onto the plates on the table, went towards her and said quietly, 'You've looked after Ma so well, Dinah, thank you. So maybe there'll be a present for you, too. Something pretty to wear at the fair next month?'

Dinah pouted as she sat down and pulled her plate towards her. 'That ole fair, it's nothing but men dressin' up, makin' a lot o' noise and getting drunk.' She slid a sly glance at Will, next to her and grinned. 'But we'll go, eh, Will? You did said yes....'

Becky caught the exchange of friendly teasing and saw her brother's usually tight face relax into a simpler expression of good humour. 'Get on with you,' he said between mouthfuls. 'You maids don't know nothing 'bout the proper business of the fair, selling stock and horses. Course we'll go.'

Thirza sighed, Dinah smiled and Becky felt an uplift of her spirits. Things were better. No more troubles. Ma looking much better and healthier, and Dinah somehow charming Will into a different, nicer person. She got up, kissed her mother, put a hand on Dinah's arm and smiled at Will as she passed. 'We'll all be there, can't miss old Uncle Tom Cobley and all that fun, can we? Never missed Widecombe Fair before, so no reason to miss it this year.'

At the door she looked back at the three most important people in her life and felt a great warmth spreading through her. 'I'll be back again in a day or so.' Closing the door behind her, she walked back to the Manor with her mind full of extraordinary thoughts.

The ghost of poor unknown Grace was there, Mr Fielding too, and then Joseph, who would be coming here very soon. She knew she would be glad to see him, so glad, indeed, that she would welcome him with kisses – if that was what he wanted.

He came very soon, knocking at the kitchen door as Becky sat down in the early evening, resting after the day's work. Ruth opened it, looked back at Becky and grinned. 'Joseph Freeman to see the maister. Tell un to come in, shall I?'

'Yes – well, yes, of course, ask him in.' Becky was surprised, yet she'd been waiting for him every day. She got up, slowly walking towards the door, making sure she didn't show the excitement building inside her, and smiling coolly at Joseph who wiped his boots, removed his hat and stood just inside the kitchen doorway. 'Mr Fielding's in his study. I'll take you up. This way.'

She knew Mrs Mudge and Ruth were watching, wondering, guessing, and was glad to walk into the hall and up the stairs, Joseph just behind her. Only when she reached the top of the staircase did she turn and allow her smile to show her feelings. She waited until he stood beside her. 'You'll be here. We'll see each other often ...' she murmured. Now she was close to him she looked into his grey eyes and then saw something there that took away her smile. 'What is it? Something's wrong....' Her voice was low because the study door was only a few steps away.

Joseph narrowed his eyes and kept his distance. 'I'm not coming, Becky. I need different work, not here, but somewhere else, out on the moor.'

'What? But why? I thought you'd be pleased. . . I told him you were a good worker. It's such a chance.' She couldn't believe it. All her hopes and dreams were being thrown back at her. A black pit of self pity and anger filled her mind and her voice rose. 'I don't understand you! Sounds like you don't want to be here, with me. So you don't care, after all. Like Briggs said, you're just one of those men who pick up a girl and then leave her.' Tears swam and her voice wavered. 'Got another one, have you? Somewhere else where it'll be easier to kiss her and take what you want?'

He lunged forward, arms on her shoulders, shaking her, so that she felt the strength of his hard body and knew how she would miss his presence, his touch. His voice roughened. 'Don't say that! You know it's not true! I'm going because I know it'll be better than being here. It's part of what I've got to do. It's for us, Becky, for us. Can't you understand that? It's because I want you to be with me that I have to go.'

Behind them the study door opened and Rupert Fielding stared out, frowning, eyebrows raised. 'What's all this about?' he rasped, looking at Joseph. 'Who the hell are you and what are you doing here? Becky, explain, please.'

She swallowed her threatening tears, took a deep breath and met his accusing eyes.

'I'm sorry, Mr Fielding. This is Joseph Freeman. You wanted him to come and work, you said, but—'

Joseph's deep voice cut in, polite but determined. 'I'm sorry, sir. I was glad to hear that you were offering me employment, but I have other work so can't do as you want.'

Becky looked at the floor but knew Rupert Fielding was inspecting Joseph from head to toe. He probably thought this was a wild man, one of the travelling labourers always up to tricks to earn a penny or two. He would most likely be glad that Joseph had refused the offer of work. 'I see,' he said coldly. 'Very well then, go and do your other work. But why are you here in my house with Miss Yeo, making such a row?'

Becky stole a glance at Joseph who bowed his head for a moment, and then looked at Rupert Fielding and said quietly, 'All my fault, sir. I just came up to apologize to you.' He stopped for a second. 'And then Miss Yeo didn't like what I told her.' His lips set tightly together. 'I'm sorry, sir. I'll go now.' He made a rough bow, turned and went quickly down the stairs, disappearing through the door into the kitchen, while Becky stared, only half believing what was happening. Suddenly her rage evaporated and she knew she had treated him badly, impossibly. She must go, find him, explain, make it up, not let him go like this with everything wrong between them. She was on the first step down when Rupert Fielding's strong voice stopped her.

'I think we need to talk. Come in here.'

He held the door, frowning, and she entered. Her mind was in chaos, still reeling from Joseph's excuses, feeling anger and the piercing pain of a love that was being rejected. She sat down when Rupert Fielding nodded to the chair opposite him and simply stared at him. What he wanted to talk about she had no idea and wasn't interested, for all her raging thoughts were of her loss and her anguish.

He brought out an extra glass, poured whisky into it and refilled his own glass. She looked at the golden liquid he watered down and then placed on the table next to her, and, as in a dream, heard him say, 'I think you could do with a sip of this, Becky.'

Slowly she put her lips to the glass, felt the fiery spirit burn her throat, warm her stomach and almost without knowing, felt her emotions fall back into place. It dawned on her that he was looking at her rather anxiously. She managed a weak smile. 'Thank you, Mr Fielding.'

He nodded, put down his own glass and then, slowly, as if searching for words, said, 'Becky, you're still a child, despite your undoubted abilities. You told me about the trouble with Briggs. Now it appears this man, Freeman, is also upsetting you. Can I help in any way?' Becky stared. Why should he care? And indeed, what could he do to help? No one could help. Joseph had gone and it was the end of all her dreams and hopes. She took another sip of whisky and felt self confidence return. But what could she, a servant, say? He wasn't really interested in her life. She thought hard and then said slowly, 'Thank you, sir. I mean Mr Fielding. No, I don't think you can help. No one can. Joseph has gone and I must forget him.'

'I see. So that's how it is.' His smile was easier, different from his customary forced expression. 'You and Joseph Freeman, eh? But you're very young, Becky – you'll find someone else before long. Just forget him, that's the best thing.'

She looked at him, a long stare, thinking how little he knew about love, and then words started to pour out, startling her and clearly surprising him. 'I won't forget. I love Joseph and he loves me, he told me so, I thought we would marry one day. But now he's gone off and so I must think about other things.' She paused. Images ran before her eyes. Hope had died, reality was hard and she felt lost.

Rupert Fielding narrowed his dark eyes, then said quietly, 'I think you need someone to advise you. Why not ask …' he paused for a second, 'Mrs Yeo? She will help, I'm sure.' He paused, smiled and added, 'And remember, there are plenty of respectable young men about who might suit you. I know quite a few—'

'I don't want anyone else! Joseph may not be what you call respectable but I love him! He's strong, and has a good mind, and he knows what he wants.' Suddenly she felt tears on her cheeks and bowed her head, fumbling for a handkerchief.

And then one was pushed into her hand. It smelt of whisky and cigars and she mopped her face, staring across at the man who looked so anxiously at her. 'Go home, Becky,' said Rupert Fielding almost tenderly. 'Go home and see Mrs Yeo. Have some time off – try and get over this lover's tiff. And then you'll feel better.'

Stiffly she got to her feet, looked down at him, saw how his face was warm and caring, and wondered why. But her own feelings swamped his. 'Thank you, Mr Fielding,' she said in a choked voice. 'I'll be all right. But yes, I'll go home now.' She nodded at him, went to the door and opened it. Suddenly she couldn't wait to find

Ma, tell her, cry on her shoulder, hear words that would comfort and advise.

Closing the door, her mind fixed on going home, she missed what he was saying, almost to himself, as she left the room. 'Poor child. Poor little Becky. What must I do?'

Joseph left the Manor without meeting the curious eyes of the women in the kitchen, or answering the greeting Tom threw at him as he crossed the darkening yard. Inside him something pounded and surged as Becky's furious words stayed in his mind and he knew wretchedly that he must get just get on with his life. She hadn't understood but slowly he began to realize that he couldn't really expect her to because he hadn't explained everything properly. But then came the defiant thought, if she loved him, wouldn't she have tried to do so? Understood that a different, more instructive job would help him along his life's journey? Help him to arrive at the point where he could return and ask her to marry him? She must know that he loved her, desperately and passionately; but how could she understand, when he hadn't told her in more detail just why he was leaving? Questions rampaged through his mind – but he knew that he still had to go. If she loved him she would wait. The thought overpowered all else as he walked on.

As he neared the inn familiar voices lured him in. Warmth, rough friendship, the persuasive forgetfulness of a few pints of ale – that was what he needed. Much later, as he and Jim and Davy lurched out into the darkness, Joseph knew where he was heading: Monday morning, out to Hexworthy. An overheard stray remark that old farmer Narracott needed men to repair his newtake walls was all that he needed.

Joseph slept deeply and without dreams and on Sunday, his muzzy head ordered him to remember the Reverend Mr Gosling's disciplines and attend church. The service soothed him, he joined in the familiar hymns and enjoyed Nat Briggs's glowering scowl from the end of the pew. When the Yeo family came in his heart lurched. He looked across at Becky, saw how, after the initial surprise of meeting his gaze, she turned her head away and looked into her prayer book. He heard her sweet voice soar above the others as they sang and had to force his thoughts into his future. He watched her leave the church without another glance. So that's how it was.

Well, he didn't blame her.

Early on Monday morning, gathering his bag of tools and bundle of clothes, he started on the long journey to Hexworthy, trudging determinedly over moorland, along green lanes heavy with climbing shadow from the overhanging trees, then on into rough farm tracks, all the while trying to forget Becky and telling himself he was doing the right thing. If farmer Narracott took him on he would be working on the damaged newtake walls; working with stones, and instinct told him this was the right thing to do, the next step along the journey his life was ordering him to take.

Reaching the farm he paused for a moment in the autumn sunlight, feeling it warm his body and even lighten his thoughts. Hope clamoured and brightened the day – he could be on the way to going back to Becky.

CHAPTER 15

Becky didn't go home. She was too confused, too hurt, and also felt all her love for Joseph changing to resentfulness. How could he just go off and leave her? All that talk about doing it for her – what on earth did that mean? And it was no help when she felt like this – sad, angry, at odds with life. Nothing seemed to make sense and so she changed her mind about going to the farm. To trouble Ma with all this stuff about Joseph would make matters worse. And, anyway, how could she explain when she didn't understand it herself?

So she went to bed, hoping for sleep, which eluded her into the small hours. Images of Joseph and their loving embraces raced through her mind, and even into her dreams. But when, next morning, she awoke, she knew a certain new calmness and feeling of hope. Perhaps he would, after all, return. Perhaps she might try and work out why he had gone. Perhaps....

As it was Sunday, she walked to the farm and joined Ma and Will in the familiar journey to Manaton Church. Dinah and her family came behind them, and along the rough track trotted Nat Briggs, his face a picture of thunder. Becky bent her head and refused to look up as Will and Ma responded to his rough greeting.

The church, with its age old sense of peace and quiet, calmed her a little more. She noticed the half finished pew end on the new installation and thought about Joseph bending over his work, chisel in hand, mallet lifted, and found herself saying a quick prayer for him, where ever he might be.

When the first hymn was announced and the choristers began to sing, she heard the deep baritone voice that she knew so well swelling the sound, and felt her heart start to race. Impossible, then, to stop herself turning slightly, looking back over the pews and finding him, a big man with bright, untidy hair, singing heartily and meeting her impetuous gaze.

Just for a second, that last look, and then she turned back, burying her head in the book she held and willing herself to stop remembering, for all the new hopeful thoughts had long gone. He had left her and yet he was still here…. At the end of the service she found an excuse to hurry Ma out of the church and away, hoping desperately that Joseph would understand and not follow.

'You're in a hurry, maid,' said Thirza, a frown on her pale face. 'Must be that ole duck I got stewing – smell it, can you?'

Becky saw how her mother's usual smile was lacking, despite the jolly words. And that palor seemed to emphasize the lines and wrinkles about the unhappy eyes. Ma looked older. Ice touched Becky and she took her mother's arm, hearing her voice grow taut and high and hoping no one saw Joseph and started wondering. She couldn't talk about him. Rapidly, she said, 'Just that I got to get back to High Cross Manor soon after we've eaten – lots of things to do.'

'On a Sunday?' Will was in step with her. 'Not right, that. Day off, is Sunday – what's maister thinkin' of, then?'

Becky thought hard. 'He has to rest. So I have extra to see to.'

She was thankful when the meal was finished, enabling her to make her excuses to leave. 'I'll be over another evening, Ma.'

She sensed that Thirza fought to produce a smile as she watched her leave the yard, and she felt disturbed because after all Ma didn't seem to be getting any better. But mostly she was uneasy because of that worried look which didn't go away. As if Ma had a secret. And now she had secrets from her mother, which was surely wrong, but she knew for certain that for the moment things must be left as they were. Ma would be troubled to hear about Joseph leaving, and Will would probably rekindle his anger about the man whom he suspected of playing with his sister.

At the Manor, the rest of the day was somehow filled. Of course, there was little work to do – Sunday was a day set apart from the rest of the busy week. Ruth had gone back to her family in the village and Nellie Mudge sat in the sun in the yard with a mug of tea, closing her eyes and occasionally dozing. Only Tom and Eddie remained, their voices soft and slow in the stables and linhay, mingling with the horses' snorts and nickering.

Becky found enough to do to pass the afternoon, but by time dusk started to fall she was at a loss to fill the remaining long hours. Until suddenly, the moor called her. Looking out into the oncoming night a new feeling spread through her, coupled with an instinctive knowledge that she was beginning to find out who she really was. No longer the young, unthinking girl from the farm with no cares. No longer the entranced Becky who had fallen so quickly for strong, rough, Joseph Freeman. Now she was older – if not in countable years, then certainly in experience. She was a housekeeper who gave orders. Someone who understood accounts and household expenses. A young woman who was thought highly of by her employer. She recalled Mr Fielding praising her abilities and lifted her head a little higher. Well, now she must act for herself. Decide what she must do about Joseph, about Nat Briggs and his threats, about finding her own way through life, just as Joseph had said he must do, and those new thoughts brought new understanding.

This comforting knowledge was warm as she wrapped a shawl around her shoulders and left the house, gladly stepping out into the approaching dimpsey. She felt a fierce need to be among the moorland valleys and hills, breathing their fragrance, rejoicing in the peace and stillness, finding her way ahead.

As it darkened, a waning moon shone patchily through steepling clouds, but she knew her way. Up the lane, into the rough track, past the grave, beneath Bowerman's immense grey pile, then out of the shadows and onto the moor itself, strong, bunchy heather beneath her feet, bracken reaching for her hands as she passed; ponies suddenly whickering as she came upon them. She walked steadily to Hound Tor, passed the huge, black rocks, wondering for a moment about the black hound said to haunt the place, then smiled to herself as she started going down the valley. Here, she knew, among these stones, was where Joseph had been working. She wished he was here, but knew that for a foolish, impossible thought. He was on his way, just as, now, she was on hers.

When a heavy, upright shape appeared through the half-darkness she stopped to examine it. A rough stone circle, with an opening at one end. Something suggested this might have been a shelter with tall stones to keep out the wind and the rain when it was perhaps thatched and cosy, but now it was open to the stars. Intuition sent a word flashing through her busy mind – *home* – and she smiled, knowing this to be so. Someone's old home, now ruined but in the process of renovation. There were signs of digging, of footmarks and a forgotten earthenware bottle of water. Joseph's perhaps? No, for she knew enough of him to be aware of his care of his tools. Joseph would never leave anything necessary and important behind him. His tools were part of his life.

Warmth slowly crept through her body as she stood, looking at the stones, and wondering what was happening to her. She walked further down the valley until she heard the singing waters of the Becka Brook and then turned back. There was a peace here among the thick heather stems and the foxy coloured dying bracken, the last sunset colours slowly leaving the vast sky, and she felt it spread through her body and mind. The peace that is necessary to help one live. This is what she needed – not advice from Ma or Mr Fielding, but a sense of the age old living in this calm, still land. Birth and death, tragedies and joys, problems and resolutions – had all been lived out here.

She felt the truth filling her mind as, slowly, she went homeward, and wondered if Joseph, digging here, had discovered the same thoughts as she now had. Perhaps it had started him on a new line of thinking: Was it these old stones which had made him refuse the offer of work at High Cross Manor? So where had he gone now? And was he thinking of her, as she thought of him?

Able now to smile, and feeling a wonderful new sense of understanding, she returned to High Cross, feeling more secure; telling herself that tomorrow was a new day and who knew what might happen then?

Farmer Narracott, elderly and bent, nodded at Joseph, small, deep-set brown eyes inspecting him warily. 'You used to workin' with stones?' he asked in a high pitched, hoarse voice.

'I've been working with the Reverend Mr Gould on stone circles in the valley below Hound Tor. But I'm keen to do more.' Joseph waited. He must get the job. 'Walls, is it?' he asked and the old man nodded.

'Newtake walls built long time ago. An' now fallin' down. Repairs, they need. Plenty more stones in the field, an my man'll show you what to do. He'll make a waller of you if anyone can.'

They looked at each other for a moment and Joseph felt his face grow taut. Yes or no?

'Start right away, can you?'

Relief softened Joseph's voice. He smiled. 'Today if you want. Can I lodge here? And what do you pay?'

The money wasn't much but it would do. 'Sleep in the tallat,' Bill Narracott told him. 'Plenty of straw up there. An' Missus'll feed you two meals a day. Agreed?'

Joseph held out his hand. 'Thank you, Mr Narracott.' They slapped and the bargain was made. 'Tomorrer,' said Bill Narracott, turning away and walking his lopsided way back to the farmhouse. 'Seven-thirty sharp. Dan'l will be here. I'll tell him to instruct you.'

Joseph climbed down from the tallat, washed at the pump in the yard, and then waited for Dan'l to appear. He came quickly, stocky and heavily built, striding through the yard, staff in his hand, eyes inspecting the new hand and the expression on his weatherbeaten face stern. 'Joseph Freeman?'

'That's me.' Joseph waited. He hoped they would get on.

'Farmer ses you're not a newtake waller by trade.' There was doubt in the strong voice.

'No. A general labourer. But I can work with stones.'

'We'll see. Let's get on then.' Dan'l led the way out of the yard, collecting tools before leaving the outhouses, and then strode rapidly into the open moorland opening up before them. He didn't speak until they had crossed two pasture fields where the sheep stared and began to move away, and then, looking at Joseph by his side, he said, 'You'll find it hard, I dessay. These ole walls should have been repaired long ago, but Farmer, he lets things go. Now it's made the job more difficult. You ready for work?'

Joseph nodded, aware that he was being tried out. 'I'll match you,' he said, and met the other man's speculative gaze. 'Where do we start, then?'

'Right here.' They stopped beside a ruined wall, the stones covered with moss and ferns and needing only a push to drop out. 'I'll clear the rubbish off, you collect all the moorstone you can find. Any size'll do to keep the stock safe.'

Joseph realized in a few minutes that the work was, indeed, hard. Moorstone lay in small heaps and clitters at the edges of the field and it took all his strength to haul the granite blocks towards the wall where Dan'l waited, eyes sharp and assessing. But he nodded. 'That's good. Now we'll start building.'

They worked on as the sun rose and warmth began to build sweat on their labouring bodies. In places the old walls were five feet high and strength was needed to reach up and fix the repairing material into the right spaces. Joseph soon learned how to sort out the stones so that they balanced without the use of mortar, but it was a tricky job and Dan'l was critical. 'We mustn't let too much daylight through,' he said, as he and Joseph regained their breath after heaving a large stone into place. 'Just try and make a network o'stones.'

At midmorning they stopped for crib which Dan'l took out of his satchel and shared. Sitting with their backs to the wall, they ate bread with chunks of fat bacon and onion and drank cold tea and Joseph felt himself glowing with the sense of work and satisfaction. He looked sideways at his companion and saw the strong face showing a hint of a smile.

'Well,' he said, between mouthfuls, 'will I do?'

'You'll do,' said Dan'l and handed over another onion on the end of his knife.

Breakfast in the kitchen and a knock at the door. Nellie nodded to Ruth, who got up and went to open it. Becky, glancing around, saw Will standing in the doorway, his face dark with anger and his fists tight by his side.

She got to her feet, alarmed, thinking at once of Ma. 'What is it, Will? What's the matter?'

He stepped inside, removed his hat and scowled. 'I got to see the maister. Now. Go and tell him.'

'But he's still in his bedroom—'

'I don't care, I gotta see him. Go on, tell him, now. *Now.*'

Her mind in a whirl she led him up the stairs. 'Stay there, while I knock and see—'

Roughly he handled her aside and threw open the door, pushing his way in. She saw his narrowed eyes, blue as steel, staring into the room. He stopped just inside. 'I gotta talk to you, Mr Fielding. You gotta tell me what you've done, and why, and what you're gonna do 'bout it now we knows the truth.'

A taut silence shot through the maister's room, seemingly catching her in it, cold and sinister, spreading throughout the house. They were all listening, she thought wildly, down there in the kitchen, Tom and Eddie coming out of the stables, probably Nat Briggs too, just arriving in the yard. She felt a shiver run though her whole body and without knowing what she did took a step forward into the room, standing just behind Will, and looking over his shoulder.

She saw Mr Fielding standing at the wash basin, soap on his face, holding his razor as he turned at the interruption. He wore riding breeches and a white shirt, open at the neck. His expression, meeting Will's glare, was tight and aggressive, his voice quiet, but cold.

'What the hell do you want, coming here like this, Yeo? What are you talking about?'

Suddenly Will turned, found Becky just behind him, took her arm and yanked her forward. 'This,' he shouted, breaking the silence and raising an echo down the stairs. 'My sister, that's what. That's who. Only she's not – this maid you've taken in and made a fuss of – well, now we knows why you done it. My poor old mother told me just now 'bout you and Grace. Said she couldn't keep it to herself any longer, poor soul. Cryin', she is, ses you must do some'at to help.' Suddenly he stopped and looked into Becky's wide, unbelieving eyes.

He wiped his mouth on his sleeve, thrust his falling hair back over his head, and Becky realized that he had abruptly found himself in an unmanageable situation. He had said his bit, and now – what? Even as her mind swayed and circled, she knew she must help him. If he was any ruder to the maister the tenancy would be ended; they would have to get out of High Cross Cottage, find another job, another cottage…. She must put aside the business of Grace and the maister until Will could be made to go home.

Quickly she looked at Rupert Fielding, standing there brandishing his open razor, eyes like a hawk about to pounce on its prey, and said, somehow making herself smile, 'What a fuss! I'm sure he doesn't know what he's saying, Mr Fielding. I'll take him downstairs.'

The silence again, only different this time. She felt it was full of strange thoughts and ideas. Facts that must be told. She watched Rupert put down his razor on the washstand, use the towel to wipe his face, and then walk slowly, still limping, across the room to where his jacket hung on a chair. He put it on carefully, brushed a speck from a sleeve, and then looked back at her.

'No,' he said at last, the word clipped. 'Take him into my study. We have to talk.'

'But Mr Fielding—' She didn't want them to talk. She needed

Will to go home, to where Ma was crying, to where the work waited.

He stepped closer to her, looked into her anxious eyes. 'Do as you're told, Becky.'

She heard something in his voice, something unexpected, raw, almost uncertain, and then felt an answering emotion. Of course she would do what he wanted. Nodding her head, she turned and walked out of the room, looking at Will and silently ordering him to follow.

The study was waiting for them, empty and quiet, with the morning sun filtering through drawn back, faded curtains. They filed in, automatically waiting until Rupert sat down in his big swivel chair at the head of the table, gesturing them to also sit.

Will sprawled, Becky sat upright, her body tense, eyes fixed on Rupert, waiting for him to start. She felt in a dream, a bad one, where nasty things were slyly creeping all around her, making her flesh creep. She wanted this talk, whatever it was about, to be over, for life to return to normal: the accounts; the ordering of the household; the thoughts about Joseph; she and Ma going into Moreton to buy dress material....

'Go on, then, Yeo, tell me what you know about Grace. What your mother told you.' Rupert's voice was short and sharp. He stared at Will who coloured and fidgeted, looking at Becky as if asking for help. But no help came. She was watching Rupert, seeing his eyes slowly shadowing, becoming even darker than normal. Wretchedly, she wondered why the colour in his thin face had died. What on earth was all this about?

Will waited for what seemed a minute or so, and then said, haltingly, 'Ma ses that Grace worked here in the kitchen, and you took her out one night and she got with child.'

Rupert made a rough noise and then cleared his throat. 'And what if I did? That sort of thing happens with girls and young men. You know as well as I do—'

'But this one's different. She went off to Newton 'cos your dad said she must, an' she had the baby. Only then she died.'

That terrible silence again. Becky heard it making her heart beat too quickly. It beat like a pump in her ears. *Go on, Will … what happened then?*

They were staring at each other like dogs in a brawl. Will's colour returned and he leaned across the table. 'That baby was Becky,' he said gruffly. 'My Ma took her in and brought her up. What I'm saying, Mr Fielding, is that this maid is yours. You an' Grace's daughter.'

Breath sucked in, emotions numbed, Becky half rose and then sank back into her chair. She met her father's dark eyes across the table and saw him sadly smiling at her. 'I'll make it up to you, Becky,' he said, half whispering, holding out a hand towards her. 'You'll be my daughter from now on. I promise you....'

CHAPTER 16

Becky didn't want to hear any of this. Mr Fielding, her father? Grace – the invisible woman he'd once taken her for, her mother? No! Ma was her mother, had brought her up, was still her mother. And what else had Will said? Not his sister? Then who was she? Yes, she was Becky Yeo all right. Then a new thought sliced in painfully, was she now Rebecca Fielding? But who were they, Ma and Will? The lump in her throat stopped any words coming out, but anyway she had no idea what to say.

She stared at Rupert's offered hand and very slowly shook her head. In her mind she began to rage. *You're not my father. You're the squire here. You own everything, even our little farm. You can't possibly be my father.*

His voice firm and steady, he said the incredible words again, each one an assault that set her trembling. 'I'm your father, Becky. I'll see that you live a good life from now on. You'll be my heir. The estate will come to you when I go. Your mother – Mrs Yeo – can take on her true relationship to you; she's your grandmother, you see. Grace was your real mother.'

Grace. Her mother. Becky stopped breathing for a long moment and watched how her new father smiled at her. He looked as if something wonderful had happened. Perhaps it had, for him. But for her? Her thoughts flew. For Ma? For Will?

Very carefully, she rose from her chair, hand still on the table to quell her trembling, and said, 'Thank you, but I don't want to be your daughter, Mr Fielding. Ma has always been my mother, and she still is. I must go and find her. Tell her what you say, tell her that it makes no difference because she's still my ma and always will be.' She looked at him, saw impatience narrow his eyes and felt a welcome rush of quick anger. Anger was better than misery. Anger could get you living again.

'Don't try to stop me,' she said, her voice quicker and firmer now, her hand leaving the table. 'I'm going. You must just do without me. I'm going back to the farm.' She turned, looked down at Will's wide-eyed face. 'And you're coming with me. Don't stay here any longer, work's waiting back there. So come on.' She grabbed his arm, pulled at him so that, clumsily, he got to his feet and followed her through the door.

They went down the stairs in silence, not looking back when Rupert Fielding came to the door of his study and called after them. 'Becky. Don't go. I need you here. We'll talk it all out. I'll explain … we'll make arrangements—'

Outside the kitchen door Becky turned and looked at Will. 'We're going home,' she said brokenly and felt the first tears fill her eyes. 'Ma's waiting for us. Come on.'

At the farm they fell into each other's arms and wept. Dinah stared while Will grunted and harumphed around the kitchen until Becky turned to him, heaved in a huge breath, dried her eyes and said, 'We'll be all right here. Go and work, Will. You'll feel better when you're doing something. And take Dinah with you. Tell her what's happened.' She managed a stiff smile, nodding at him. 'I'll help Ma get some broth going.'

When the kitchen was empty she sat beside Thirza on the settle. She saw her face full of anguish and offered a handkerchief to help wipe the tears away, realizing abruptly that Ma must be afraid she had lost her daughter. Something must be done, or said, thought Becky, trying to line up her flying thoughts. Ma must understand that nothing had changed and would never do so.

But it was Thirza who spoke first. 'I'm glad you know at last, maid,' she said unsteadily. 'It's been haunting me for so long. Now we can go and see your mother's grave in the Newton churchyard.

You'll know then that it's all true an' you'll have to think of me as your ole gran. 'Cos that's what I am. I was Grace's ma, you see.'

'Grace's mother.' Becky's thoughts slowed down. 'She must have had a sweet voice, for Mr Fielding to remember her singing.' A long pause before she could correct herself. '*My father* said so. He heard me sing and that must have been what reminded him of Grace. Of Mother.' She smiled at Thirza, watching so intently. '*The Sprig of Thyme*, it was. My favourite song.'

Thirza nodded, eyes calmer, breathing slower. She laid a hand on Becky's arm. And her voice was quiet. 'Sing it now, maid.'

Becky breathed in, raised her head and stared around the kitchen. She sang the old song lovingly, feeling that this was a moment of reunion between Grace and herself, who had been a young girl in this same cottage. The only connection they had. And then thoughts of Joseph slipped into the words as she sang,

'*O'er the wall came a lad, he took all that I had, and stole my thyme away.*'

As her voice died away, she felt Thirza's hand press hers, saw the swimming eyes lovingly smiling at her, and knew that even if Joseph had stolen a part of her away, at least she had this part. She was a grandchild, a daughter, a sister. She was loved.

Suddenly she said, 'Ma, is Will still my brother? Was he Grace's child, too?'

Thirza shook her head. 'No, maid. He is my Roger's child, born two years before Grace had you. So he's,' they looked at each other and then smiles banished the sadness as Thirza laughed, 'he's your uncle, maid!'

'My Uncle Will! That's lovely! I shall call him Uncle from now on!'

'Yes.' Thirza still smiled. 'So I'm your gran and he's your uncle.' The smile left her face. 'An' the maister? What'll you call him, child?'

Becky got to her feet, went to the basket on the floor under the kitchen cupboard, picked out onions and turnips, put them on the table, found the knife and began peeling and chopping. She was glad to have something to do. Lard in the pan on the fire, a trip into the dairy to find some stock left over from the last bit of bacon, and then everything put into the pan to cook for the midday meal. Will and Dinah would be hungry and it would help to return to ordinary, every day events. Perhaps the strange happening of the morning would gradually disappear into the past. Perhaps they would all get used to the new names and titles.

But would she ever get used to calling Mr Fielding Father?

As she helped Thirza cut bread and put plates on the table, she wondered, too, about Joseph. Would her status as daughter of the local squire make any difference to him?

She stirred the bubbling broth slowly, and found herself hoping that they would meet again very soon. As Will returned with Dinah and the conversation slanted towards farm work, Becky knew that, somehow, she had to go and find Joseph and tell him. She had to find out if, as Mr Fielding's daughter, he could still love her.

'Know 'bout the devil, do you, then, Joe?'

Dan'l Hunt and his wife Mollie sat around the glowing peat fire, the men smoking pipes and Mollie stitching away at a new shirt. Over a week now since Joseph had been taken on by farmer Narracott, and he and Dan'l had become friendly. Mollie had offered liniment for aching shoulders, and now evenings were often spent at their cottage, with Dan'l enjoying having a new audience for what he called, ' Havin' a good ole tell.'

'Devil's been around Dartmoor over the years, you see. Down to the Dewerstone, oh yes, they all know he be there, and then that ole business at Widecombe church, when the devil rode his horse up to the tower with a boy he found sleeping and then horse and all and pinnacle came crashing down.'

'I've heard about it. A good story.' Joseph was enjoying the warmth, the company, Mollie's excellent cooking, and the passion in Dan'l's heavy voice. He took another swallow of cider. 'Go on,' he said amiably, and waited for the next tale. He was interested in the old folktales but more so in the warmth of Mollie and Dan'l's very clear love of each other. This was a home, he thought, to be envied. A small dwelling with enough warmth, food and understanding, a home to be lived in for the rest of one's life, should one be lucky enough to make it. As Dan'l had.

Would that he, too, could do the same. And this brought his thoughts back to Becky whom he had last seen at church, that brief glimpse of her, the shocked stare, her head instantly turned away and then nothing more. The work on the newtake walls had taken most of his mind since he'd been at Narracott's, but now the daily labour had built a routine of its own, he had space to consider his love for Becky.

Dan'l was going on. 'Well, there's the whisht hounds baying 'cross the moor on wild nights – an' the black dog with fiery red eyes at Okehampton. Oh, I could tell you all sorts. But mebbe we should talk 'bout the fair coming up. Widecombe fair.'

Joseph thought on about Becky and something leaped inside him. Surely she would be there? And if he was, too, then they could meet – just an unexpected meeting with a chance to tell her what he was doing. What he hoped to do. 'Yes,' he said, nodding at Dan'l. 'I'll be there.'

And then something nagged at the back of his brain. Something he'd heard the Reverend Mr Gosling talking about when he was working at his folk tales and songs and the fun at Widecombe Fair. 'Pony racing and tug o' war – and do they wrestle nowadays? I've heard about Devon wrestling – different from Cornish, they say. No kicking. Is that right?'

'It's frowned on these days,' Dan'l said soberly. 'Brutal stuff, that is. But it goes on – in places where no one can see and find out. When there's a need for fighting someone and it gets outta hand – then they'll wrestle. Why? You thinkin' of having a go, boy?' He guffawed, making Mollie frown. 'I got a pair of my ole dad's skillibegs somewhere – haystuffed pads for your legs. Want me to sort 'em out, do you?'

Joseph laughed and thought of Nat Briggs who needed a good trouncing, if anyone did.

'Maybe.' He put down the cider mug and smiled at Mollie, sitting there stitching away just as he could imagine Becky doing when they had their own home. If they ever did. His smile died and Dan'l said heartily, "Ere, have a fill up afore you go back to that cold old tallat.'

The fire shifted and a flicker of red flame made them look down. Dan'l picked up the iron bar and poked the half burned turf of peat. Blazing warmth brought a new glow of companionship and he smiled at Joseph as he said, 'There's tales I could go on tellin' you, but you're probably ready for your bed. But before you go, here's a last good 'un. Ever heard of ole man Satterley building his own cottage while the revellers were all drinkin' theirselves silly at Holne?'

'Building his own cottage?' Joseph was caught. 'What with?'

'Moorstones, all the loose stuff turned off the field an' lyin' in the hedges.'

Joseph settled down more firmly in his chair and grinned across at his host. 'Go on,' he said. 'Sounds like a proper bedtime story.'

Becky spent the day at the farm, sitting with Thirza and hearing about her mother, Grace.

'You look just like her, maid – that glossy thick hair and the way you walk. Yes, just like my Grace.' Thirza seemed to find consolation in at last talking about her daughter and the shocking behaviour of the young maister. 'He were han'some in those days – had lots o' girls, so we heard. But Grace was his special one. But she didn't want to go with him. Came runnin' home often, sayin' he was chasin' her. But what could we do? Can't tell your landlord to stop his boy from makin' a nuisance of himself. And so she did as he wanted.' Thirza sighed and Becky saw how suddenly her grandmother was looking her age. No longer the age of a mother, but now the lines on her thin face were deeper, the streak of grey in her hair reaching out over the whole of her head. Yes, Ma had become Grandma in every way. Becky wondered how she had ever thought of her as Ma when obviously she was older and more experienced in living than a mother might be. But there, she had been a naïve child, not questioning anything or anyone. And now life had taught her many things. Grandma, Mr Fielding, even Will and Dinah, had all brought lessons into her simple way of life. And especially Joseph.

Thirza slowly continued, recounting the sad day when Grace discovered she was pregnant and went to see the young maister about it. 'Told him how she were and what would he do about it, but he just laughed, and told his dad who said Grace must leave home and have the baby somewhere else. Didn't want neighbours to know, see. Gave her some money, he did, and suggested a place she could go to in Newton. Made her sign a piece of paper sayin' she'd had the money an' wouldn't come back. So she left us. I mind the day....'

Thirza's eyes swam and Becky said quickly, 'Don't tell me any more, you're upsetting yourself.'

'But I must. Must tell you how it happened. Once you were born, she came home here. Said she wasn't well, and would I look after you for a day or so. Course I said yes an' wanted her to stay, but she'd signed Mr Fielding's piece of paper and he'd said he'd want the money back if she didn't stay in Newton. Said he'd threatened to end our tenancy, too, so off she goes and we didn't see her no more.'

Becky saw it all in her mind; the young mother parting with the new baby; Thirza worrying even as she cared for the child, and then the awful news that Grace had died. How terrible that must have been, for everybody. Her mother, dying in lonely surroundings with no one to care for her; Thirza and Roger, still alive at the time, deciding to keep the baby, but not letting anyone know it was Grace's child. Making the secret....

'We were glad to have you, maid. But we knew that we mustn't let maister know that you were Grace's child case he turned us out. So that's how it happened an' all of us told you I was your Ma. When Roger died, you were too young to care very much, an by then Will was treating you like you was his sister. So we went along with it – and so did all the village and everybody.' Another painful sigh. 'The Lord knows what they'll all say now.'

Becky put an arm around the thin shoulders and hugged her grandma. 'It doesn't matter what anyone says. I bet some of them suspected and I think Nellie Mudge knew. Well, now Mr Fielding has got to be open about it and let the truth be known, so they can talk as much as they like.'

They were still discussing the matter when Will and Dinah returned at the end of the day. Dinah smiled shyly at Becky and said, 'Doesn't make any difference, do it?' Will frowned as he kicked off his boots. 'Course it does.' He looked across at Becky. 'You gotta sort it out with the maister. You're his daughter, so he has to treat you like his own. What you gonna say to him when you go back? That is, if you do go back.'

Becky met his gaze and nodded. 'I'll go back,' she said slowly. 'You're right, of course, he's got to treat me properly. But I don't know what I'll say – not yet.'

When she reached High Cross Manor she saw that Tom had the trap ready, with the cob already in the shafts. He nodded his head towards the house. 'Maister's waitin' for you, Miss Yeo. He said you'd be going out this afternoon.'

Becky saw curiosity in his eyes and turned away. 'Thank you, Tom. I'll go and tell Mr Fielding that I'm back.'

Walking through the kitchen she met Nellie's direct stare and knew she must explain her absence. 'All that bother this morning,' she said, as casually as she could manage, ' Meant I had to go home and talk to Will and Ma.' The name seemed to lodge in her throat – *not Ma, but Grandma now* – and she coughed it away. 'Has Mr Fielding been asking for me?'

'Yes,' said Nellie, curiosity plain on her lined face. 'Came down in a rage – said where were you. We said we didn't know and then he went out to see Tom. Going out when you comes back, Tom ses.'

Becky nodded, said nothing more and went upstairs to the study. She knocked, feeling nervous but determined to have the matter out. Told to enter, she did so, and met Rupert Fielding's dark gaze as she closed the door behind her. Standing quietly in the centre of the room she sucked in her breath. 'I'm sorry I went off this morning. I knew I had to go and see my mother—' She stopped abruptly. Now was the terrible moment. 'To see my grandma and tell her I knew about you and Grace – my mother.' It was out. She felt the air around her clear.

They stared at each other and for a long moment neither said anything. Until Rupert eased himself out of his chair and limped across to stand beside her. He looked into her wide, expectant eyes and slowly nodded. 'You're a good girl, Becky. Your heart is in the right place. And I have to confess that I have grown fond of you – even without knowing, until the other day, that you are actually my daughter. Indeed, Briggs did us a good turn, using my father's journal to bring daylight into what was an unhappy little business, but which has now had a wonderful result.'

His smile was one she had never seen before, lighting up his drawn face and lifting straight lips.

'A wonderful result …' she repeated his words bitterly, seeing a new, happier light in his eyes and feeling an instant sense of resent-ment about his unthinking selfishness. 'For you, perhaps.' Her emotions overflowed. 'But for my mother it was a lonely and shameful death. And for my grandmother a life of keeping a terrible secret, until today, when she is having to go back into all that pain and hurt, which you, and you alone, caused. I see nothing wonderful in any of it.'

She watched his expression change from ease to tense surprise. His voice, when he replied, was stiff, words coming out in small jerks of automatic defiance. 'But you're my daughter. I can give you a new life. We'll go to the solicitor, I'll make a new will. You'll come and live here, of course. You'll never need to worry about your future, about money....'

Seeing his selfish pleasure, she felt only mounting anger. 'Your daughter, yes, Father, that is who I have to admit I am. But it will make no difference to my life. You see, I know what I want to do, and where I want to be.' The words were shrill and fast. 'One day,' she told him vehemently, 'I shall marry a good man. But none of it will have anything to do with you. No money, no inheritance, thank you. I'm going to leave this house and never come back. I – I never want to see you again.'

He was speechless. She saw the light fade from his eyes, making them darker and narrower. He cleared his throat, rubbed his back with one hand and held the other out to her. 'But Becky, you can't just walk away – you're my daughter, you belong here, with me....'

Against her will, she recognized his feelings, and then, like a shaft of blinding light, suddenly felt them herself. Father and daughter – what was she doing? Surely she should accept what he said and stay here – live a life of comfort and social happiness?

But suddenly Joseph's deep voice rang in her ears and she remembered that he found it vital to live his own life, to find whatever it was that his ongoing journey through life demanded of him. Now she knew she must do the same, so, ignoring the outstretched, unsteady hand, she shook her head, and gave her father a last hard look before turning away. In the doorway she paused, but only for a few seconds; and then closed it behind her with the knowledge that she was acting in a way she might well come to regret.

As she walked down the wide staircase she was more than ever aware of the portraits of past Fieldings watching her. She paused on the last step, looked at them and wondered if anything like this had ever happened before in this family. An illegimate child was common enough among the labourers who lived and worked on the moor, but if a girl in the gentry fell for some handsome lad's charms and persuasions, what had happened to the poor child? Still gazing at the painted faces, she wished she knew; wished someone would help her, advise her how to behave. For now, after all the drama of knowing the secret was unfurled, after sharing Thirza's distress and Will's anger, she knew she was at a turning point in her life. She had refused her father's offer to take her into his own easy upper class community. And Joseph had left her, intent on living finding his own path.

She stood in the marble floored hall, hearing her heart race, and wishing desperately that she knew what to do next.

CHAPTER 17

A nd then it flashed into her mind like a streak of lightning, releasing all the fury and misery she was feeling. She knew exactly what to do.

Upstairs again, in her bedroom, she took off the green dress and slipped into the old brown checked cotton she used for work. Firmly she told herself that the green one had never belonged to her; along with the smart hat it was all part of Mr Fielding's – Father's – gift. It took a moment of very strong decision to lay both garments on the bed, and she indulged in one last lingering look. She liked the dress very much and knew it suited her and that she would probably never have another one so elegant and well made – but, no, it wasn't hers and so must be returned.

She turned back to the mirror, tidied her hair and made sure she looked neat and presentable before gathering her few remaining belongings and wrapping them in her shawl. Foolishly imagining that the room seemed to have a feeling of reluctance at her departure, she gave it a last appraisal, picked up the bundle and went downstairs, this time ignoring the painted, intolerant stares that she imagined followed every step, then returning to the study, knocking lightly and then, without waiting to be invited, opening the door and stepping inside.

She put down the bundle and looked at her father.

He stood by the window, staring out onto the stretching vista of sun-burnished browny green moorland, then, turning as she came in, he caught his breath. 'Becky – thank goodness you haven't

gone. I've been thinking what I can do for you, for your family ...
to try and make up for all the bother and unhappiness.'

'Yes?' Her voice was cool and she wondered at this new feeling
of maturity. 'So what are you suggesting, Father?'

He raised a brow at the unfamiliar word and then smiled,
reaching out to take her hand and leading her to the chair by the
table. He stood at her side as she sat, and nodded. 'Well, first
things first. You are no longer just a housekeeper but will live here
with me as my daughter, in charge of all the household duties and
ordering the servants to perform them. I shall open a bank account
for you and you can drive into town to buy what ever you want.
And as for your family....'

Becky waited.

'I've thought about how I can compensate them for what has
happened.' His voice was easy now, his smile warm. 'I shall call on
your brother – I mean, of course, your uncle –' the smile slid into
amusement '– and offer him a different cottage – a better one – on
a larger acreage of land. And a means of paying labour to help run
it. What do you think of that?'

Becky's mind flashed to High Cross Cottage, the farm she had
been brought up in, with all its discomforts of damp walls and
leaking, weedy thatch, and she said very certainly, 'He won't want
anything different. Just some repairs to our home as it is now. New
thatch on the roof, the walls shored up where necessary and
perhaps a pump installed for well water.' She felt a surge of power
as she added casually, 'And you don't need to ask Will, for I know
what he'll want and it won't be anything new.'

'But surely—'

'And as for Grandma – Mrs Yeo – just pay her the wages due to
me, perhaps install a modern range to cook on, and get a girl in
the kitchen to do the rough work.'

They looked at each other and the seconds hummed by. Then
slowly he sat down, easing painfully into the big chair, still looking
at her. She watched a slight frown mar the easiness of his previous
smile. 'I said it once before, didn't I?' His voice held a wry tone,

'when first we met – that you had it all worked out. Well, so you have now, it seems.'

She nodded. 'Yes. And I don't want anything for myself, thank you. No bank account, no new clothes. Indeed, no Father. Because I'm not staying here.'

She saw amazement and a growing expression of anger on the taut face.

'I don't believe you. You're just trying to pay me back, to get your revenge.'

Instantly she snapped. 'Your word, Father, not mine. I just want to go and get on with my life. Revenge isn't something I know about. And perhaps you should forget it, too – simply do what you can for my family, and then live your own life.'

His good humour had vanished. He sat up stiffly, staring at her with hard, narrowed eyes. 'I don't need advice about how to live, thank you – just remember, will you, that you're still a tenant of mine – and, yes, you're my bastard.' His voice was harsh, and the word hung in the air. He frowned. 'And must I remind you that your mother was nothing more than an uneducated peasant? Indeed, you're not much better yourself.'

'Oh, but I am!' Something was sparking alight in her mind; confidence, awareness and a certainty that life was beckoning her on. 'I have learned so much being here, doing your accounts, running the house and learning how to get on with servants.' She nodded, got to her feet and looked down at him. 'I'll thank you for all that, Father, but please understand that I want nothing more from you.'

A long pause while they looked at each other, his face ugly with what she sensed was not just disappointment but also a lack of understanding, while she knew that her own must reflect the calm satisfaction she now felt. For a second she wondered where the sympathy she had once felt for him had gone, but then that brief thought, too, vanished as her own needs took charge. She picked up the bundle and walked to the door. 'Goodbye,' she said, without looking back, and left the room.

The door closed behind her and if the loud click cut into her new feelings, perhaps even momentarily reminding her of the loneliness of the man she had left behind, it didn't stop her leaving the house. Outside the moor was waiting, and somewhere Joseph would be working, timing the day as it ended and an evening of rest awaited him. She hurried down the lane towards the farm, smiling as she went, and knowing with all her heart that she was taking the right path.

They looked at her with amazement, Thirza saying brokenly, 'But your position – your place there at the Manor – and your father …' and Will's brow creasing as he cut in with, 'Why you doin' this? Comin' back here – you don't have to do this, Becks.' Even Dinah's smile died and she turned her head away as if to distance herself from the family argument.

Becky had expected recriminations. She took Thirza's hand, sitting by her on the settle, and said forcefully to Will, 'I'm doing what's best for all of us. Mr Fielding will do repairs to the cottage, make it warmer and drier – I told him you need a new range, and Grandma must have a girl to help with the rough, and you must tell him you need help with new stock and feed. It's what you deserve, Will, so don't argue about it.'

Sharp blue eyes met hers as he reached up to the mantel for the tobacco jar. 'You done all this, then? Told him what to do, eh?'

'Yes.' She watched him sit down and fill his pipe. 'He knows just what I feel, he understands.' But – did he? Did he not perhaps think her a selfish creature who just wanted something to quieten her family, before disappearing to find her own freedom? She cast away the thought. It didn't matter what Father thought. All that mattered was her family, here, and Joseph, wherever he might be.

Will was looking at her and she knew what he was thinking. She said the words before he did. 'I'm here for a purpose, to try and find Joseph Freeman. If you have any news of him, then tell me, please, Will.' When he made no reply, she forced a smile. 'Uncle Will, if you want.'

He grunted, but the narrowed eyes lost their hardness. 'Soft on him, are you? I knew it from the start. Think he's the one for you, then?'

She nodded. 'I know it. We knew it soon as we met. He's working somewhere on the moor, and I want to find him, to tell him about all this muddle with Mr Fielding. I don't want him to hear talk and start wondering.'

Another grunt. 'Think that'll bring him to your side, do you? Maister's daughter wantin' the man she fancies?'

Becky tensed. 'No, I don't. He's not like that. He's different from all the others. He's—' How could she explain? 'He's trying to make a way for himself before he can ask me to marry him.'

'Huh. Better get some reg'lar work then, he must.'

'Perhaps he has.' She leaned forward, smiled at him as sweetly as she could, despite her irritation. 'But I have to find him. Will, help me, please.'

Will looked away. 'I don't know nothin' 'bout him.'

But Thirza had half turned, was looking at her with glowing eyes. 'So you'll stay here, maid, with us while you're looking? Come home, have you? Oh, that's lovely.'

'Let's say I'm home till I find Joseph, Ma.' She pulled Thirza's thin body closer and was thankful to see more colour in her cheeks and a look approaching happiness in her eyes.

Her spirits rose. Perhaps things were working out. Perhaps, now she had taken this step along her new path, everything would come about as she hoped and prayed it would.

Dinah's quiet voice broke into her thoughts. 'Village knows, Becky. Lots o' talk 'bout you an' the maister.'

Becky turned to her. 'I expect so.' She looked at the small girl sitting on a stool at Will's side and wondered what the Meldon family had said. 'And you – what do you think?'

'I mind how he looked for you at the harvest supper. That big man. Lovely, 'e were. You're lucky, that's all I think.' Dinah bent her head and poked at the ash in the hearth.

Quietness then while the fire hummed, until Thirza fidgeted

beside Becky and cleared her throat. Then, half questioning, half nervous, 'An' what 'bout Mr Briggs, then, maid? Still wants to marry you, I dessay?'

Becky took a steady, deep breath, meeting another, almost forgotten, part of the problem, now edging back into her mind. 'I don't know,' she said slowly. 'And I don't care. Nat Briggs has no hold on me any more now everyone knows. I shall try and forget him.'

But she knew, and guessed that her family sitting there in the quiet, warm kitchen also knew, that Nat Briggs wouldn't forget her. And wondered if he could make any more trouble.

Strange to be back in the attic on the small truckle bed after the comfort of her new room at the Manor. Even stranger to awaken to the cow lowing and the boasting, noisy cockerel, but she got up at once, eager to start her search. Never mind breakfast – a word of reassurance to Thirza that she would be back during the day, and please keep a bit of a meal for her, and then she was ready to leave the cottage. Thirza came after her, a small package in her hand. 'Bread and a lump o' cheese, maid – keep your strength up as you go.'

Becky paused, stowed it in her pocket, kissed her grandma and then went quickly out of the yard, down the lane, pausing briefly as she decided which way to go. A moment's hesitation and then she turned into the Manaton road, arriving soon at Easdon Farm. Smiles and easy talk, but no one there had heard of Joseph. She nodded, smiled back and continued walking. The morning was overcast with an edge of chilliness forecasting autumn. She wrapped her shawl closer around her shoulders and took time to look at the country as she walked.

This narrow lane meandered through small pasture fields with the heights of moorland enclosing them. Even with autumn on the way, still so much colour. Fiery bracken on the verges, dying leaves and here and there a persistent flower or two; purple sheeps' bit, golden hawkweed, tiny emerald ferns of feathery spleenwort.

Becky thought as she walked and new certainties came into her mind. This was the place she loved and it was no unhappy task to just walk and walk. When she reached the end of the lane, where it crossed the road leading to Princetown, she stopped, went into a field, found a stream trickling down the valley, and drank from it. Then she went back to the lane and sat on the verge beside the old cross.

Beetor Cross was known as the Watching Place. No one knew who, but someone in the long ago had watched here. Now, eating her bread and hard cheese, she felt she was in the right place. She would watch for a while, and then surely someone would come into sight and perhaps give her news of Joseph.

But the man who came along the lane, trotting steadily towards the Cross, was Nat Briggs.

He saw her at once, even although she was trying to hide away behind the hedgerow saplings that grew around the cross. Didn't want him to see her, eh? But here they were together. Hot pleasure flooded him. So it had been worth all the fuss of hacking off some of his untidy hair, even washing and changing his clothes, after listening silently and seemingly obediently to the maister's strict tirade earlier this morning.

The study had been airless and hot, the maister still in pain as he edged down into his chair, face grey and more lined than usual, and there had been an unusually hard note in his voice. 'Briggs, I know you for what you are – a good bailiff in many ways, but a man who can't stop pilfering and cheating, as well as blustering and upsetting people. After years of trusting you I now realize you've made a fool out of me by taking advantage of the authority I gave you – I mean, of course, taking money which is due to the estate and keeping it yourself. Even accepting the occasional bribe without consulting me about the matter. All of which has to be repaid, don't forget.'

Pride had made him open his mouth at that point, words of excuse ready on his tongue, but the maister had been too quick.

'No, don't bother to deny it, Briggs. I have proof in the ledgers, and there have been complaints from several tenant farmers about your overbearing behaviour. But I'm giving you a final chance, so just listen to me.'

He had listened, forcing back the hot anger rising through him. The job was a good one, and he could still make it worth his while to keep it, for surely when the maister married, he would be too caught up in his new found happiness to look at the ledgers every day, or even to believe what those lying farmers told him? So he bowed his head, nodded and stood silent at the opposite side of the maister's table.

And then had come the important news. The secret about Grace Yeo and her bastard was out; that young pup, Will Yeo, having found the nerve to come and face the maister. Nat had heaved in a big breath when he heard that Becky had gone off after the row and was no longer here at the Manor. Where had she gone? Was this his big chance to make her marry him? His mind whirled. Could he find her? Offer sympathy? It had been hard to keep his face straight as he listened to what the maister so threateningly had said was his last chance.

'I want a complete survey of the estate. Farms and their occupants, acreage, stock, sales and purchases and so on. It'll keep you busy and I want it before the end of the month. So get going, Briggs, and don't be tempted by any more of your wretched little cheating thoughts. Just remember that there are plenty of likely men ready to jump into your shoes as estate bailiff.'

That had made him swallow rapidly, forcing down the gnawing anger that grew so rapidly inside him, but seeing the sense of the job ahead. Someone else to become bailiff? Not if he could help it – and he could. So, a tone of apology in his chastened voice. 'Yes, sir, I understand. And I'm—' It hurt to force out the words but they had to be said. 'I'm sorry 'bout the things you mention. Won't happen again.'

A hard look on the maister's thin face. 'They certainly won't. All right, Briggs, on your way.'

And now here, at Beetor Cross, with Becky sitting down again on the rough grass, not looking at him. Nat smiled gently, something he had never done before.

'Morning, Miss Fielding.' The new name hung in the air and he watched her frown. 'What you doing here, I wonder? Maister said as 'ow you'd gone from the Manor, but I didn't reckon on seeing you so far from home.' He dismounted, tethered the cob to a handy branch and went over the grass, to sit beside her. He thought she looked worried, not the bright, sometimes too self confident Becky he thought he knew. Something had happened to make her look like this. Well, her unhappiness could be a help as he tried to tell her that he still intended to marry her. For a moment he couldn't stop his smile; marry Miss Fielding? Go up in the maister's estimation? Almost be in his world? Certainly a better pay, better living.

'Becky,' he said quietly, 'you look sad, maid. Anything I can do to help?'

Her head lifted, tawny, gold-flecked eyes met his and he felt himself stir with longing. 'No, thank you, Mr Briggs. I can manage by myself.'

What could she manage? He softened his voice even further. 'Course you can, a bright maid like you can do anything. But I wants to help, 'cos I know you've just heard 'bout your mother and well, I did warn you, didn't I? So try me – there might be something I can do to help.'

He waited while she looked at him, thoughts clearly chasing across her peachy, suntanned face, freckles decorating the soft cheeks and making him breathe more rapidly.

She thought for what seemed too long. Then, unevenly, as if coming to some big decision, she said, 'You know everybody around here, don't you?'

He nodded.

'Well, I'm trying to find Joseph. Joseph Freeman. You know, the man who—'

'I know him.' He heard his voice harden, but tried to keep looking sympathetic.

For a few seconds he paused, thoughts suddenly racing. Then, with delight, he knew how to answer. Leaning forwards, he put a hand on hers, and sadly, almost apologetically, shook his head. 'So you haven't heard? An' I thought it was all about…. It's real bad news for you, Becky, maid.'

'What?' Her voice was sharp, her face tight with alarm.

Imagination flashed. 'Why, he been stealing again – like the Poor Box in the church, only now from his maister's pockets when he weren't looking, so they ses. And so he got the push – sent on his way.' He paused, assessing how much further he could go. A last idea sprang into life.

'Seems he been seen takin' the sailors' path up north – goin' to take a ship, I dessay, to get away.' Another pause while he watched her face settle into disbelief, and then into contorted pain.

'Sad, maid, but that's what he done.'

She said nothing, just buried her head in her hands and for the first time Nat Briggs felt a touch of guilt; but it had been needed. He'd got rid of Freeman and now, for sure, she'd be his for the taking.

CHAPTER 18

'Look,' he said, 'I know you're upset, but see, the man's a bad 'un, and you must forget him.' A pause while he watched her face, saw her look up at him, eyes swimming. 'And there's others around, Becky, who can offer you better things. Like me – oh yes, I know—'

Her mouth opened as if to argue but he shook his head smiled, and went on rapidly, 'I've been bad at times, I know it. But only 'cos I were mad for you.' He let the words float away, watched her surprise and then added very softly, 'An' still am, maid. So p'raps you an' me could be together now?'

Becky stared. The face she had always hated had softened, become almost appealing and she thought about what he'd just said. Nat Briggs, offering for her, again. And this time with what sounded like real feeling. But she would always love Joseph. Yet Joseph had gone away – and from what Nat had said, he wouldn't be coming back.

Her head pounded. *What to do? What to do?*

She saw Nat's hand reaching out for her, and instinctively denied the urge to move away. *Where is my strength?* The message came like a shaft of blazing light, invigorating her mind and refreshing her body. *Strength, that's what I need. So think hard.* Reality flowered. He was probably lying about Joseph. Nat Briggs would always lie if he thought it would benefit him. And she knew Joseph Freeman well enough to recognize the lie. He wouldn't steal. He wouldn't run away. He wouldn't leave her. Yes, he had gone away, but he had said he would return. Sometime.

Becky took a deep breath and shook off Nat's hand. She looked into his small, scheming eyes, recognized his duplicity, and slowly got to her feet. The problems were fading. 'I don't believe you, Mr Briggs,' she said, her voice steady and her face composed. 'So you can go on your way, and leave me to mine.' Carefully she left the hedge and regained the road.

'But—' His voice followed her but she didn't respond, didn't even turn, simply started walking back towards High Cross Farm and home. As she walked, taking no notice of his abusive shouts, she sorted out all the churning thoughts in her head. No good continuing searching for Joseph, for, even if Nat had lied, which she was sure he had, no tenant farmer on the maister's estate would care to argue with him, for Nat had a hidden measure of sly, underhand power which would bully them into silence.

Stepping out down the lane, back towards High Cross Manor, she thought of what she must do next. She had bridges to build with her father. She was hurt, but must she hurt him even more? There was pride to push away, compassion to find. And then, from the farm, there was a last duty she and her grandma must perform. As she walked, she felt a wind sneaking around the bend in the lane, ruffling her skirt, but she welcomed it. She felt new and positive. Her life had taken a different turning, and she was able to deal with it.

Nellie Mudge stared as she entered the kitchen but Becky merely smiled a little stiffly, and then walked through to the hall, shutting the door behind her. In her head she told herself she should have demanded entrance through the front door. After all, she was Rupert Fielding's daughter with a position to keep up. Then, smiling wryly at such ideas, she went upstairs to her room and saw the green dress still lying on the bed. Quickly and without further thought she changed into it, tidying her hair and looking into the mirror, seeing a new Becky there; a more mature girl who stood very straight and had a calm expression. She felt ready for the business of apologizing to her father.

The study door was ajar and, although she paused for a second, she entered without knocking. Rupert was standing by the high crowded shelves at the far end, his hand poised to take out a book.

'Father,' she said and watched him glance back, his expression suddenly changing from tight concentration to a slight, almost apprehensive smile.

'Becky.' His voice was warm, no longer the harsh crispness she was used to. She saw how the skin crinkled beside his eyes, knew him for an ageing man and felt herself soften towards him.

'I'm sorry for all I said. It must have hurt you. But I was hurt, too, and worried about Ma. I mean Grandma. I've thought about it ever since. Please – forgive me.'

He limped to her side, arms outstretched. He looked into her eyes and his smile grew. When he spoke his voice was soft, almost husky. 'I'm the one to be forgiven, not you.'

His arms rested warmly on her shoulders and she relaxed beneath them. This was a moment she had never dreamed about, but it seemed to be right. She returned his smile, nodded and said very quietly, 'I accept that I'm your daughter – but I must go my own way. Can you understand that, Father?'

He dropped his arms, stood a little straighter, and gestured to the leather chairs beside the window. 'Let's talk about it, shall we?'

Seated opposite him, the light falling on his lined face and making him screw up his eyes, she tried to collect her thoughts. She must tell him about Nat Briggs and his lies. Convince him that Joseph Freeman was her true love, and that somehow she must find him.

And, finally, offer her father the caring love a daughter should feel.

Standing up, she twitched a curtain aside to filter the sunlight, then sat down again, feeling herself to be a part of this old house, this old family; after the storm of initial shock, a growing understanding and family feeling came. Perhaps new happiness?

She sat down again. 'Father, in spite of what I said yesterday, I have to ask your help over something.' Watching his change of expression, she wondered uneasily how he would react and hoped that the anger had worked itself out.

'Whatever I can do, I will. Just tell me what you want.'

Thirza leaned on Becky's arm as they left the cottage and climbed into the High Cross Manor carriage. Tom Butler smiled as he closed the door behind them. 'Won't take long, Mrs Yeo. And I see you got your flowers ready.'

Becky watched her grandma's weak smile as she nodded and looked down at the posy of pot marigolds picked from her small garden, edged with dying heather and a couple of still green harts' tongue ferns. 'They're lovely,' she said reassuringly, and then sat close to Thirza as they left the yard, rattled along the lane, before turning into the road leading to town.

Thirza had no words and Becky was too full of thoughts to talk, so the journey was a silent one, broken only as they stopped outside Wolborough Churchyard and Tom helped Thirza out of the carriage. Becky followed, taking her arm and saying gently, 'Do you know where it is, Grandma?'

Thirza nodded. 'Up there. In the corner. Just behind that big stone angel.'

Just a grassy mound, forgotten and unloved. Becky felt a pang of anguish sweep through her as imagination flowered. Grace, her lonely, sick mother, who had left the baby behind and must have known she was dying. But Becky pushed away the sadness, knowing it was Thirza who needed the sympathy and love now, for Grace – Mother – was long gone.

Together they stood by the neglected grave, Thirza looking down at the posy of flowers lying on it, and Becky saying quietly, 'Almost looks like a bit of moorland – the turf and those few flowers. I think Mother would have liked them.'

Thirza nodded, wiped her eyes and then, with surprising strength, said, 'I'm glad to be here, maid. Time and again I've wanted to come, to say it's all over, let's forget it, but couldn't do so without tellin' you why. And now, well,' she turned to Becky and managed a smile, 'Now I can go home and know she's all right.'

Becky felt a huge lump in her throat. 'And we're all right, too, Grandma – I mean Ma. I'll always call you that, for that's who you still are.'

In silence they walked back down through the churchyard to the waiting carriage and then Becky said, 'Now we're here in town, why don't we go and buy that dress material we talked about, Ma? I'll put it on Mr—' she stopped, looked at Thurza, and then went on, 'on Father's account.'

They smiled into each other's eyes and Becky knew that something had ended, but something else, old and loving, was still continuing. 'I'd like that,' Thirza said quietly, and accepted Tom's help in climbing into the carriage.

Back at the farm, Thirza offered tea, but Becky resisted. 'I must go back and see what's happening at the Manor. Remember, I'm in charge now.' They laughed together and Thirza watched and waved as the carriage rattled out of the yard and down the lane. When she went back into the cottage, she put the length of pale mauve, flower-patterned material on the table and smiled to herself. A long shadow had passed and life was happier. Now she could get back to work.

Rupert Fielding watched his daughter walk into the drawing room, followed by Ruth carrying a tea tray. He thought how Becky had changed since her first appearance in the kitchen that night of the harvest supper. She had grown up. More determined and efficient, more aware of life. She would make a good wife for the right man. She had told him she had given her heart to Freeman, but where was he? Hardly a keen suitor, if he kept disappearing. But there were plenty of suitable young man around who might fill the bill. The Master of the Hunt's eldest son was heir to a big estate and popular with tenants and friends, and not yet spoken for. Perhaps a word in the right ear might be a good thing.

Rupert accepted a cup of tea and thought about Widecombe

Fair; yes, a useful meeting place. He watched Becky drinking her tea, smiling at him with those tawny eyes, and then sitting back, quite at ease, looking for all the world what she had become, the daughter of the Manor. He said casually, 'Widecombe Fair next Tuesday. I hope you'll allow me to take you – and Mrs Yeo, if she cares to come. Of course your brother—'

'Uncle.' Her smile was full of amusement. No resentment any longer, he noticed.

'Your uncle,' he returned the smile, 'will go on his own – taking stock to sell, I shouldn't be surprised. And perhaps buying. Sales are usually good at this time of the year. What do you think, my dear?'

Becky bit into one of Mrs Mudge's cut throughs and let the cream and jam fill her with quick pleasure. Swallowing the mouthful, she thought for a minute. Widecombe Fair. Everybody would be there. Perhaps news of Joseph. For a second bleakness filled her, but then she wiped her mouth and said, 'Thank you, I should like to come with you, Father. And I know Ma will be grateful not to have to go in the rickety old trap. I'll make sure we're both ready – Tuesday, isn't it? Let's hope for a fine day.'

It was a day of sharp winds and shifting clouds, but as the carriage arrived in Widecombe a slant of bright sun shafted into the gathering crowds of people, wagons and traps making their way to the Green and the adjoining fields. Sheep and cattle were being driven into hurdled pens and a general noise of wellbeing and excitement spread over the whole village. Children raced and shouted and dogs barked. Every household had someone there, for the fair was the great occasion of the whole year.

Becky had gone to much trouble over her dress. The green one was the only suitable garment for such an occasion, but with Thirza's help she had decorated it with a lighter green braid, and put a cockade of green and blue feathers in the small, matching hat. She felt well dressed, and hoped that her father would think so too. His tweed jacket and highly polished boots showed off his position as estate owner, and she thought he had more colour in his thin face as he escorted them through the gathering groups of farmers towards the tent where refreshments were being organized by the village wives.

'I suggest you and Mrs Yeo stay around here, Becky – I need to meet my tenants, so I can't be with you all the time. But there are seats here, and perhaps your brother – 'that amused little smile, 'uncle will come and find you. Will you be all right?'

'Yes, of course, Father. Don't worry about us. I can look after Ma and take her to see the stalls.'

There was so much to see and enjoy. Not just cattle and moor-land sheep for sale, but ponies driven down from the moor, nervous and fidgety as prospecting farmers looked them over. And then, of course, all the fun of the fair. Stalls of hoopla, coconut shies, two-headed sheep, fat ladies, and men with big muscles charging a shilling for a fight which they would surely win. Becky smiled, looking around her, for she had been here every year as a child. She recognized many faces of drovers who had brought the cattle in, and dealers looking for new stock, but some were older than she remembered.

Thirza, too, was enjoying herself. Now that the awful secret of Grace's shame, her tragic death and Becky's birth had been faced and dealt with, she felt herself to be stronger and able to think happier thoughts. Looking at Becky, walking beside her, smiling at familiar faces, she hoped with all her heart that her granddaughter would marry a good man and settle down. That there would be no more problems.

As usual, the towering sun-burnished hills enclosing the village caught her, making her stand still for a long moment, looking around. She had been born here and the tors and valleys were home, wild and savage as they were. The quick wind was driving the clouds to cast moving shadows over the high ground and, lower down, the small pasture fields of village farmers stretched as far up the slopes of Hameldon as they could, ending before reaching the skyline, as if the high moor, isolated and primitive, denied further entry. A gleam of sunlight caught a patch of faded heather and green scrub and Thirza smiled. She knew it all, loved it. Grace flitted through her mind, but now she had built the power to release the memory. For a moment her smile faded; but then she told herself, *no reason to fear any more shadows, please Lord.*

Rupert Fielding walked slowly, using his cane to ease his aching back and moving from the Green to the fields where sheep and cattle were penned. He caught the eye of one of his tenants, Walter Worth, from the north of the valley, on whose pigsties Nat Briggs had filed a report saying a larger amount than he had expected needed to be spent on rebricking and reflooring. Walter Worth came up to him, touched his hat, and asked after his health.

'Improving, thanks,' Rupert said. And then, 'About your pigsties, Worth – seems a lot of money you reckon must be spent on repairing them.'

The man, short and middle aged, with a furrowed brow that shadowed his suntanned face, frowned even more as he said, 'Oh no, sir, I reckoned it cheap as possible. Gave Mr Briggs the figures, but haven't heard nought from him yet.'

Rupert considered. He recalled the figure on the scrap of paper Briggs had left on his desk. 'What do you call as cheap as possible, then, Worth?'

The answer didn't surprise him. There was a difference of just over three pounds and this, he realized, would go into Brigg's deep pocket once the work was done. He pursed his mouth and looked at his tenant. 'Briggs get on all right with your men, Worth? Polite to your wife and family, is he?'

A moment's awkward pause while the farmer shuffled his boots. And then, 'Well, not what you'd call real perlite, sir, if you gets my meaning. More likely to give orders and say jump to it.'

Rupert nodded, and Worth, encouraged by his silence, added, 'Makes my ole cow man feel bad, sir. An the 'prentice lad ready to lash out—'

'I see. Thank you, Worth, for being so open about things. I'll see to the pigsties next week. My regards to Mrs Worth – and, in future, come to me rather than Briggs, will you?'

'Yessir. Thank you, sir.' The furrowed brow relented half an inch and what passed for a smile flitted across Walter Worth's fleshy face. Rupert nodded again, proceeded on his way to the pony sales, thinking of finding a suitable mount for Becky, and then, leaning on his cane beside the penned enclosure, stood still, ordering his plans.

Arrangements had been made for the thatcher to repair the Yeo farmhouse, for Will Yeo to buy stock and feed and for Mrs Mudge to look around for a girl to help in the farm kitchen. Yes, reparation was being made, but what could he do for Becky? There must be something else, more important than just money and position. But what?

So many people, so much noise as they walked around the fairground, and Becky saw Thirza visibly tiring. It was becoming clear that the secret of Becky's true birth had spread through the village. There were several stares, some polite, 'Morning, Miss Fielding's, and just a few frowns and shakes of the head. But in general there were kind words and gestures, and she was touched and surprised by the warmth of the greetings showered on her and Thirza as they went from one stall to the next.

As they walked, her eyes wandered over the sea of faces. Would there be, somewhere here, the tall, golden haired figure of Joseph? She hoped desperately, but saw only the usual villagers and farmers, their wives and their families.

Then she saw Thirza's weary expression and said, 'Ma, I'm going to find you a chair in the tent and get you a cup of tea. You can rest for a while – I want to go around and ask a few questions.'

Thirza sank gratefully into a chair in the crowded tent and looked up at her anxiously. 'You're looking for that Freeman, aren't you, maid? But what will the maister say – he won't want you hobnobbing with anyone other than gentry now.'

Becky said firmly, 'He knows I have to live my life as I want it. I told him that. Don't worry, Ma, he's not going to take me away from you. I promise I'll always be here.'

Thirza smiled and nodded, then turned away to accept the teacup passed to her by one of her acquaintances behind the long trestle table. Becky left, saying she wouldn't be long, and then went out of the tent to mingle with the crowd. It was easier than she had thought to ask the simple question, *Have you heard anything of Joseph Freeman? He's been working somewhere on the moor,* but every reply was *no,* and after a while she found a quiet spot on a secluded bench in the field where the pony races were getting under way, and sat down, wondering what to do next. But not just what to do next, for what to believe had become the all important, nagging question. Had Nat Briggs been telling the truth, after all? Was it possible that Joseph had, indeed, run? And if it were true, what should she do?

She sat and watched the races, listening vaguely to the beating hoofs on the turf, the shouts and the cheers as someone's favourite won, and was still there, lost in thought, when Dinah appeared at her side. 'I been looking for you. Your Ma said as how you'd gone off – she be worrying. Said I'd find you. Shall we have a look at ole Uncle Tom Cobley on his grey mare – it's Ned Foster all dressed up this year in his ole smock and top hat. Go an' see, shall we?'

Becky came back to the present, looked at Dinah, so pretty in her flower trimmed hat and newly laundered but faded blue dress and, with a surprising connection of thoughts, wondered why Will wasn't with her. She realized quickly – of course, he would be looking at the stock, among his fellow farmers, exchanging views and opinions and even slapping hands over a sale, perhaps.

'All right, Dinah, I'll come, but where's Will?'

Dinah dimpled. 'Buying another cow. And sheep. Maister saw him this morning an' said he must.'

Becky's worries momentarily faded. All was going to be well with the farm. Father was keeping his word. Together then, they left the race course and its heavily breathing ponies, and went back to the Green where Dinah turned off into Gypsy Rosie's tell-your-future stall, grinning at Becky and saying, 'I got sixpence. Find out the name o' my sweet'eart, I will.' The grin grew even wider. 'Hopes as how it begins with W.'

Becky's returning smile was warm. Will and Dinah? Could it be? But why not? A family wedding would be lovely. But not hers.... Her smile died. She must find out about Joseph. Looking around, hoping still for a sight of him, she saw Rupert Fielding walking slowly towards a group of newly arrived gentry leaving their traps and carriages, and thought wildly that perhaps he might have some idea of how to find out the truth of Nat Brigg's story.

Quickly, she headed in his direction and then, there was a tall man striding along with his back to her, fair hair curling over his jacket collar, walking towards her father.

Becky ran, her body suddenly warm and light and full of hope. Joseph hadn't gone away. It was all lies. He was here. Now. *Here....*

CHAPTER 19

Bill Narracott harnessed the pony and told Joseph he'd be leaving for home before the end of the day. Grateful for the lift from Hexworthy, Joseph at once set about looking for Becky. Surely, among the crowds of farmers, families and villagers, she must be here? Everyone came to Widecombe Fair. Of course she was here – but it was like looking for a pin in a stook of hay. He walked slowly across the Green, and then into the Old Field where the sheep and cattle were penned. Or perhaps she was already in the refreshment tent. He turned aside and then someone bumped into him. Davy, his workmate from Hound Tor. A big grin, a rough voice, saying words he couldn't believe. 'Mornin' Joe, heard 'bout the Yeo maid, have you? How her's really Mr Fielding's bastard daughter? Cor, the Yeos kept it quiet, didn't they? But now 'tis all over everywhere.' The grin broadened. 'Sweet on her, weren't you? I recalls her coming to the inn lookin' fer you.'

'*What? Mr Fielding's*—' Joseph couldn't say the words for surely they were wicked nonsense. His Becky was a Yeo, sister of that oaf Will, daughter of gentle Thirza. He glared at Davy. 'Don't believe you. Where'd you hear this pack o' lies?'

The friendly grin died. ''Tis true, I tell you. Heard it from Jim, who said the Reverend Mr Gould was talking to the reverend from Manaton. "Do you know 'bout Rupert Fielding's daughter being a love child?" he said.' A hard stare, followed by a punch on the shoulder, and then gruffly, 'Well, if you doesn't believe me, go an' ask someone yerself.'

'I will.' Joseph swung away. Only one person to ask and that was Fielding.

He strode back into the Green and there he was; the maister, the tall chap, walking slowly with a cane, talking to someone newly arrived and just leaving his trap and groom, another man in breeches and bowler hat, gentry, all of them. Well, Fielding must stop chatting to his smart friends and talk to him instead.

And then – 'Joseph!' He heard her voice, turned and stared. Becky Yeo, all dressed up, running towards him, smiling, her face alight with wonder and joy, hands out, reaching for him. He stood motionless, unable to move, unable to think straight. In that long, heart-stopping moment she came to his side and, 'Joseph!' she said again. Helplessly he watched her smile disappear. He saw fear and anguish in her wide eyes and wondered what to say to her.

No words came but flooding emotion made him grab her outstretched hands and pull her with him as he strode towards Rupert Fielding, standing in the small group of farmers and gentry. He felt her shock, sensed she was full of fear and horror. He just needed one word – *no* – from the maister. Only wanted to know she wasn't the bastard daughter, that she was still Becky Yeo who was waiting for him to return to her.

He flung himself into the chatting group, Becky still at his side, imprisoned in his calloused hands, and said roughly, 'Mr Fielding, I gotta speak to you.'

The talk stopped abruptly, eyebrows raised, shocked faces frowned and one elbow lifted threateningly, ash plant in hand. But Rupert Fielding's expression, as he looked first at Becky and then at Joseph, showed concern. He said rapidly, 'Excuse me, gentlemen. I'll see you again later,' and, nodding at Joseph, limped unevenly away towards a free space at the bottom of the Green.

There he stopped, turned and said heavily, 'Well? What do you want?'

Before Joseph could find words to reply, Becky pulled herself free from his grasp.

Sucking in a long breath, she caught at his jacket with flailing hands and cried, 'I thought you'd gone! Nat Briggs said you were a thief and that you'd run, but I knew you hadn't – I've been looking for you all over and now you're here. But why are you looking at me like this? What have I done?'

Her voice died to an anguished whisper. 'Joseph, what have I done?'

Rupert Fielding put out an arm and drew her towards him. 'I'm sure you've done nothing wrong, Becky. I think that Freeman has just heard the wretched gossip and needs to have it confirmed.' He stared at Joseph. 'That's it, isn't ?'

Joseph let out a slow exhalation of held breath and began searching for words. 'Yes. That's it. Gossip, all over the place. That she's—' For a moment he looked at Becky and she saw his face soften, but his voice was still a deep, unhappy growl. 'That she's your daughter, your love child, a Fielding, not a Yeo. That you turned her into a bit of village gossip and she'll never live it down.'

Painfully, Rupert straightened his back. 'Well, yes, she's my daughter, and I'm proud of the fact. I know I wronged her mother, and I'm sorry about it. But I'm making up to Becky and her family as well as I can.'

Joseph's face was grim, his hands balled into fists and fearfully Becky watched him trying to control his fury. A second's pause and then he said, voice low and full of disgust, 'They're calling her a bastard, but you're the real bastard, Mr Fielding, Not her. Not my Becky.'

'Watch your language, Freeman,' Rupert Fielding snapped. 'Just remember, I can get you put off any farm where you look for work.'

'That doesn't bother me, 'cos I'm going to take her away from you, take her somewhere where I'll look after her and love her for the rest of our lives. So you can just forget that wicked moment, all those years ago, forget you fathered a daughter, because you're not fit to have one.' He reached out both hands, put his arms around Becky and drew her close to his chest.

Rupert Fielding was breathing hard. He said sharply, 'And how do you propose to care for her? I hear you're a wanderer, a gypsy;

why, you turned down my work because I imagine you thought it too hard for you. Well, I'll never let Becky have any thoughts of marrying scum like you.'

Becky was in tears, clinging to Joseph, pulling away from her father, full of the certain and desperate knowledge that she mustn't let Joseph go away again. Never mind Father – he'd done without her for nineteen years, he wouldn't miss her now. She heard Joseph say slowly, 'You're wrong. You don't know anything about me. But she does. She knows I'm only trying to sort out my life, to get ready to find her a home and marry her.'

And then her father, scornful and with a sneer on his face: 'And where will this home be, pray? A derelict barn somewhere, I suppose … burned out thatch and damp stones – just the place for my girl to settle down.'

'No.' Joseph's voice was quiet and deep as the anger faded and sense returned. He held Becky in warm, strong arms and she felt his heart beating through his jacket. 'I tell you, Mr Fielding, I just need more time and then she'll have everything she wants, a house with good thick walls, warmth, safety, a bit of land, a proper home. If you love her, then help her wait for me.'

Becky watched Rupert Fielding's expression gradually change. He frowned, brows beetling over narrowed eyes. She hoped he was listening properly, accepting Joseph's words and plans. Very quietly, her voice unsteady, she put out a hand and touched his arm. 'Father, I know what he means. And I'm willing to wait. I'll wait till he's ready. Please believe him.'

Silence. Joseph and Becky looked at each other and she lifted her hand to his cheek. 'Thank goodness you're here. I never believed Nat, not really.'

The words were hardly audible and Joseph nodded, drawing her closer to him. 'Such goddamned lies,' he whispered, his voice rough. Then he lifted his head and looked at Rupert Fielding again. 'Think what you like 'bout me, Mr Fielding. But Becky knows the truth.' His voice lowered a tone. 'And I know that I'm going to get that evil cheating man o' yours. I'll teach him a lesson he won't forget, not for the rest of his life. He an' me are due to fight and sooner the better. So you better look after your daughter, Mr Fielding, while I go and find that little hayseed....'

Rupert Fielding looked at him for a long moment, then said slowly, 'Wait a minute – so you think you can teach Briggs a lesson? You think he deserves one?'

Joseph's answer was rapid. 'I know it. He an' me have met up before, but this time I can't let it go. Causing my Becky such hurt. And surely you know, sir, that he's deserving of a come uppance in other ways? So many of your tenants complaining 'bout the little rogue, from what I've heard.'

Becky met her father's eyes, and they nodded at each other. 'Yes,' said Rupert grimly.

'He's turned out to be a cheat, as well as a thief. As you say, he needs taking down a peg or two. But, Freeman, if you simply pick a fight with him there's no knowing what he'll do – and if he runs then you'll be left angry for ever.'

Joseph scowled. 'I won't let him run. He'll feel the power of my arm before he can take a step away.'

'Even so.' Rupert half turned, looked up the field as if seeking help from his still chatting group of friends, then back at Joseph. 'A properly organized fight would be better. Briggs can be brought into it without any doubts of him running – I could get a few men to arrange it. What do you say?'

Joseph thought, then slowly nodded his head. 'Might be better that way. I don't want the little sod escaping.' He looked at Rupert with a new light in his eyes. 'When'll it be, then?'

'Soon. I'll make the necessary arrangements. Find a spot where you won't be seen, apart from the organizers and seconds.' Rupert nodded. 'Plenty of private places on my land. Where are you working at the moment?'

'Hexworthy, Mr Narracott.'

'Very well. I'll let you know. Send you a message by the postman.' They looked at each other in silence and Becky thought that a truce had been reached, although she didn't understand all that it meant.

Joseph took a step backwards, then looked at Rupert again. 'I said some hard things. But I had to say what I felt, get it off my chest. You had to know.'

'I know a lot more now than I did ten minutes ago.' There was wry amusement in Rupert's quick reply and Becky, with enormous relief, saw the vestige of a smile spread across his face as he acknowledged Joseph's half apology. 'And now?' he asked. 'Am I looking after Becky for the rest of the day, or would she prefer to be with you?'

Becky knew there was only one place she needed to be and that was a quiet haven where she and Joseph could be alone, to talk about everything that had happened and make amends for the wrong thoughts she had been forced into having. She turned to him, and smiled.

'Shall we walk?' she asked innocently, but the expression that suddenly blazed into his eyes caught at her heart.

They left the noise and crowds of the fair, seeking quietness and a place where they could be truly together. Halfway up Bonehill they found a broken down linhay beside the ruins of a deserted farmhouse. Clearly the linhay was still used for storage, the hay smelling sweet and feeling soft as Becky sat down, pulling Joseph with her. A glimmer of sunlight shafted through a space in the timbers and she saw cobwebs swinging in the corners. Outside, a paean of larksong was just audible. Smelling the fragrance of late summer filling the small building, she breathed in a sigh of happiness. 'I can't believe you're really here.'

She leaned into him, felt his arms enclose her, warm, strong, wonderful. It was easy to nestle down in the hay, to let him kiss her eyes, her throat, her mouth. To hear the whispered little words of love. To allow her bodice to be loosened, to feel his rough, hard hands gently enclosing her breasts. To know that this was what she had wanted, yearned for, for so long. Ever since she first saw him, heard him sing, saw the wicked light in his eyes, liked the mischief in his deep voice.

Slowly sensation filled her; a longing being answered, their voices whispering, rising, floating, high and strong and echoing, then falling, murmuring. It became a memory deep inside her, her whole body and mind resonating with it. And then quietly it died down. But she would never forget. Never.

They stayed until the sun began to fade, until the last strains of voices singing and shouting down at the fair ended. Until Joseph said, 'Time I went, my Becky. Can't let ole Narracott drive back to Hexworthy without me. Must keep the pennies coming in.' Gently, smiling, he pulled her bodice up to her throat, did up buttons, tied the tapes and then raised her up from the hay. 'You're my love. Always will be. I gotta go now, but you know I'll be back. You do know that, Becky, don't you, maid?'

She felt half asleep after the excitement of the day, of the precious hours here among the hay, but was able to smile her reassurance. 'I know.'

They walked back to the village and then she turned to look for her father's carriage. It was gone. Joseph frowned, and said, 'You mustn't be alone. Never mind old Narracott, I'll walk you to the farm before I start back to Hexworthy.'

Occasional traps and gigs clattered down the lane, passing them with a smile and a friendly wave. The fair was over and everyone was going back to their work and their homes. Becky walked hand in hand with Joseph between the high hedges, walking through the tall shadows made by the sun filtering through the hedge as it slipped down behind great Hameldon's immense shoulder.

They didn't speak for everything had been said earlier. But the warmth and love that Becky had felt stayed with her and she smiled into the sunset. All the worries and nightmares were gone from her singing mind and she simply wanted to get back to tell Thirza and Will about Joseph being here. Perhaps Will would change his mind, would welcome Joseph to the farm. Perhaps....

Joseph broke into her dreams. 'Will you go back to the Manor? Your father expects it, I think. Is that what you want?'

She shook her head, frowned a little. 'I don't know. Part of me wants to be at the farm with Ma and Will, but Father needs a little bit of me, too.' She looked into his grey eyes, turning silvery now in the diminishing light. 'I don't really have a home any longer, you see. Not one where I really belong.'

He halted for a moment and took her into his arms. 'You will, my Becky, you will before much longer. I promise you.'

Nodding, she put her arms around his neck and drew his head down to hers. 'And until then I shall just wait. But it's hard....'

They walked on, turning off the lane down the potholed track to the farm, where Prince started barking as they entered the yard. Becky stopped. 'Goodness,' she said, 'the thatcher's come already – see, his ladder and all that reed.' She looked at Joseph with a glowing smile. 'Father's keeping his word. He said he would do things for the farm. Let's go in, let's see what Will has to say about the fair.'

The farm kitchen was warm and smelt of bacon. Dinah stood by the range, stirring the pot, while Will sat in his usual chair, close to her, looking up at her and laughing. Thirza sat on the settle, busy with some sewing, but when Becky and Joseph entered they all turned and stared.

'So you've come home, maid.' Thirza put aside her sewing and got to her feet, arms extended. Becky went into them, loving the welcome but then wondering uneasily if this really was her home any longer. But Thirza's love was too encompassing to worry too long. Becky turned to Will, also standing up, looking at Joseph with an expression of indecision on his face.

Joseph held out his hand. 'I've brought Becky back from the fair,' he said easily. 'Can't stay, must get on to Hexworthy before the old man realizes I'm not there.'

Will nodded and managed a smile as he shook the offered hand. 'Working there, are you? Narracott's a hard master, so I heard tell.'

'Wants hard labour for his pay, but I'm staying on. Working on newtake walls. Learning how to deal with moor stone.'

Will nodded again. 'Hard, but come in handy one day, I dessay.'

Becky heard Joseph's voice change to a deeper, more intense note.

'Sure it will. As you say, one day.' He looked across the room at Becky. 'But I gotta go now.' His eyes caught Thirza's anxious glance. 'I wish you well, Mrs Yeo. I know Becky's in good hands with you beside her. But I'll come back when I can – if you allow it.'

Thirza said warmly, 'You're welcome when ever, Joseph.' She paused, then her smile grew and her voice lifted. 'But while you're here, you can join in the good news.'

Becky looked at her grandma's pink, happy face. 'What's that, then Ma?'

Thirza threw a smile at Will, standing close to Dinah, and said , 'Why, our Will's gonna marry Dinah. So what d'you think o' that, eh, maid?'

Will cleared his throat, put an arm around Dinah's waist and pulled her from the range. He kissed her soundly and then grinned across the room. 'Asked 'er at the fair. Need another pair o' hands now, see, new stock, more work.'

Becky laughed, delighted to see this new Will. 'But surely she'll be more than that, Will? Say something nice about her, go on!'

Dinah was blushing, and blushed even more so as Will pushed her away from him, saying with a grin, 'Get on, maid, us is waitin' for our tea – pretty words won't get us nowhere.'

Becky went to Dinah, took her free hand, and said quietly, 'Welcome to the family, Dinah. And I hope Will says something nice before the evening's out. You've worked wonders with him already. I just hope he'll be a good husband to you.'

'Course he will.' The few words were enough, for Becky saw, in Dinah's blue eyes, a love that she knew reflected what she felt for Joseph. She watched as Will sat down again, as if no longer interested in Dinah, but his hand reached out and touched her without seeming to do so, and his eyes were sky blue, no longer the steely ice that Becky remembered from her childhood.

As Joseph said goodbye, after asking permission to kiss Dinah, and so making her plump face grow even redder, Becky went with him into the yard, closing the door behind her.

They kissed, a long, parting passionate kiss, with both of them remembering the joy of the afternoon in the hay-filled linhay. Then huskily, Joseph said, 'I'll be back, my love. Soon, I promise. Just keep waiting. Think of me, like I'll think of you, and we'll keep together that way.'

She watched him stride away, down the yard, into the lane, and then disappeared through the shadows now bringing in the dimpsey. The old song whispered in her mind:

'*O'er the wall came a lad, he took all that I had*,' and happiness filled her, remembering their lovemaking and the dreams that it created. She had, indeed, given him all that she had and now she dreamed of marriage, and then a home of their own. But how? They had no money and Joseph was only earning a pittance. Returning to the farm kitchen she paused, hand on the door latch thinking that marriages were in the air – Dinah and Will and then – for it must happen, sometime, somehow – hers and Joseph's.

She could ask for nothing more and realized that this was what she had always been longing for. Marriage and a home. Nothing like shabby but once elegant High Cross Manor, with her father – not even the dilapidated farm cottage, with Ma and the new maister and mistress.

She sighed. This was the dream that filled her thoughts, something that had been hiding from her for her whole life until this minute. She could almost see it – a stone cottage filled with everything she needed to live an ordinary life; no riches, but it would have an atmosphere of happiness that would never die. A place where dreams had led her and where she could be her true self. A home where she knew she and Joseph – and later their children – belonged, and would never leave.

The dream still filled her mind as she opened the door and went into the kitchen where Dinah and Thirza were talking as they prepared the meal. And then, suddenly, a small voice in her head whispered that, yes, sometimes dreams came true – but more often than not they didn't.

In the warmth of the kitchen Becky momentarily shivered, but told herself that, come what may, she must keep her dream alive.

CHAPTER 20

The letter lay on the table before him. He had read it three times and now he leaned back in his chair, eyes fixed on the bookshelves at the far end of the study, letting Felicity's writing, her small, well shaped words in their black ink, run around in his mind.

'*You will be glad to know that Laura is recovering, although she still needs my presence here. Therefore, and this is difficult for me to say to you, Rupert, I have decided that our engagement must end. I find Italy a beautiful place to live, and I feel settled, with lively and interesting new friends around me. And I know you would never leave your old home in Devonshire, so I fear this must be goodbye. I trust you are now quite recovered from your accident. Again, I am sorry, but they say that time heals, you know. With best wishes, Felicity.*'

So that was the end of the proposed marriage. No new mistress for High Cross Manor. No amiable companion to accompany him into shared old age. A heavy sigh broke through his darkening thoughts. Alone, as ever. And he had hoped that Felicity, for all her brusque bossiness and comparative youth, would release him from that solitude. But no. It wasn't to be.

After a pause of some moments, he straightened his aching back, reached for writing paper and began composing his reply. It was short and to the point, saying that he understood and agreed with her decision that the engagement must end. He wished her happiness and then, before signing himself, paused and narrowed his eyes, wondering how she truly thought of him. Sighing, he wrote,

'Sincerely, Rupert Fielding.' No affection, indeed, no more pretence, but reality. He had never become her lover, and now found he wasn't really interested in the life ahead of her. So why not make his feelings clear?

Indeed, as the minutes passed, he began to tell himself that her rejection was a kind of blessing. After all, he was no longer alone – he had a daughter. Becky was part of his life now, a real blessing which he was already enjoying. Leaning back in his chair he allowed a smile to lift his heavy face. Becky was a strong and vital young woman who seemed to have some slight affection for him, as well as an admirable sense of duty.

And that brought Joseph Freeman into his thoughts. A man he had at first thought to be a useless and wild peasant, until their exchange of thoughts at the fair had minimized his dislike, even bringing a grudging sense of admiration in their wake. Freeman loved Becky, that was very clear; as, just as obviously, she loved him. And Freeman had said he was intent on working until he considered himself a suitable husband. Well, time would prove those optimistic words. And in the meantime it wouldn't hurt to introduce Becky to a more respectable society.

Rupert's thoughts shifted then to Nat Briggs who would be here tomorrow morning, coming for orders as usual, and would be told about Freeman's need to fight him. Of course, thought Rupert, scornfully, Briggs would argue and do his wretched best to get out of it. But if the winner of the fight should be awarded a good purse – what then? Nat Briggs, he knew, with a wry curl of his mouth, would do all he could to put his hands on that money.

Rupert considered. Where should the fight be held? A deserted stretch of more or less level moorland was needed. He visualized the various miles of his property and his eyes brightened as he found the very place. That flat piece of downland behind Bonehill Rocks. Out of sight of Widecombe below, away from passers-by, half hidden by the huge rocks with enough level turf for two men to work out their fury. Somewhere easy enough for watchers to gather unseen. His landowning friends, always ready for some sport, would probably be delighted to fund a purse, and it should be easy enough to instruct some tenants who had suffered beneath Briggs's bad temper to prepare the ground and act as sticklers and seconds. He chuckled. There would probably be a large audience, all intent on hopefully seeing Briggs get what he deserved. Was Briggs bound to lose? He was a slight man, while heavily built and taller Freeman would have a natural advantage over him. But knowing Briggs, Rupert suspected he might well have some tricks up his sleeve. No, it would not be an easy victory for Freeman. But it would be a fight well worth watching. For a moment his thoughts took him back to youthful similar bouts, money being lost and won, and old feuds avenged. He was looking forward to it.

With a new purpose ahead of him, Rupert felt a return of his old strength. He pushed Felicity's letter into the top drawer of the desk and left the study to call Tom from the yard, give him his own letter to post and tell him to harness Justice; he had some calls to make amongst his friends and a word with both Tom and Eddy about likely estate farmers to help organize the match. Striding into the yard he recalled a few words of that letter. *Time heals*. Yes, he felt it might well do so.

Nat Briggs left the maister's study next morning in a state of confused fury, half of his thoughts veering towards enraged resentment – he, the estate bailiff, being threatened with dismissal in this way? – and half planning how to ensure Freeman's downfall. Because it was vital that the fight that the maister was organizing must end in his own victory.

'There will be a goodish purse, Briggs, you can be assured of that,' Mr Fielding had told him, looking down his long nose and leaving no doubts as to his distaste for the man standing before him. 'But just remember that your situation as my estate manager rests on the outcome. I would have sacked you long before this on account of all your nasty little cheats and frauds – and don't forget that you still have to repay those embezzlements – but I needed your work to continue for as long as possible before replacing you; reliable estate managers are hard to find. So if there is the slightest chance of you cheating or breaking rules in the fight, then you'll be out. Understand?'

Silently seething with rage, Nat's reply had been quietly subservient. 'Yes, sir. O' course. No question of it. You should know that I'm an honest man mostly....' The expression on the maister's face forced an explanation. 'I mean, money's always hard to find, and sometimes, it's a bit of a temptation to—'

'Get out, Briggs. Get on with that work over at Worth's farm. Those pigsties must be repaired without any more delay. And be polite to the farmer and his wife. I've had complaints about your behaviour.' A last freezing stare over the desk and a final order as Briggs headed for the door. 'Just make sure you're up at Bonehill on the day and at the time I plan.'

Nat stomped downstairs, thundered through the kitchen, ignoring the stares of Nellie Mudge and, outside in the yard, wary words from Tom Abbot. He kicked the cob, hardly controlling his pace as he reached the lane and headed for the main road and Hexworthy. Those bloody pigsties. That bloody farmer, Worth. And when that's all done, he must make plans about the fight. Freeman's name brought Becky into his mind and again his rage exploded. This was probably all due to her, the bitch persuading Fielding to look on Freeman more kindly. Well, when the fight was over, the watchers would know who had won, and who would remain estate bailiff without any more to do about it. Just wait and see.

Becky and Thirza climbed into the trap which Tom Abbot had driven into the yard.

Dinah, feeding Flower, the pig, waved as they headed out towards the lane and the road to Moretonhampstead and Becky said, 'What can we buy as a present for Dinah?'

'Some'at for the wedding, p'raps,' Thirza said thoughtfully. 'She's got nothing new – wonder what she'll wear?'

They looked at each other and laughed. 'Her ole blue,' they said together.

Thirza thought for a moment. 'I haven't started sewin' that material you bought the other week in Newton – why don't I make that up for her? Just make a size bigger'n you, maid, for she's got a proper curvy figure.'

'That's a good idea, Ma. And I'll buy something she can wear with it when she walks up the aisle – something pretty she'd never buy even if she had the money. We'll have a good look around.'

They did. Once the trap was left beside the White Hart Inn, with Tom saying he'd wait in the tap room for their return, Becky and Thirza went from shop to shop, enjoying the freedom of not working and of being together. They chatted as they went, as companionable and loving as they had always been and Becky saw that Thirza had left behind her much of the quiet unhappiness that had been building up over the years.

She thought about their recent visit to Grace's grave, under-standing now that the past can easily cast a wretched spell over the present if it is allowed to do so. Just like the grave beneath Bowerman's Nose – folk repeating the old story until it seemed to be still living. How much better, she thought, to let the past rest and just live each day as it comes. And this was what she was trying to do with her own life. Grace's sad death was behind her, although never to be forgotten. She knew that Father would always need a part of her, and this she would never deny him, even when she and Joseph were together. She wondered how life would be if Mrs Felicity Richards came back from Italy and married Father. Would she, the illegitimate daughter, be welcome at High Cross Manor any more? Or would the new mistress push her back into the old farm home?

But wherever she landed up, she told herself resolutely that it would only be a temporary shelter, for Joseph had promised her a home, and he would find one. And then, of course, another shadow suddenly edged into her mind – what about the fight Father had said he would arrange? Joseph and Nat Briggs fighting…. Becky blinked away the anxiety and said quickly to Ma as they entered the dressmaker's little shop, 'We'll look at a pretty hat for you, Ma – Dinah's not going to be the only handsome maid at her wedding.'

It took an enjoyable twenty minutes or so of trying on before Thirza finally settled on an ivory coloured Leghorn straw, trimmed with ochre and pale gold braid, with a large satin bow dipping over the side. 'But I can't wear this,' Thirza kept saying nervously, looking at herself in the mirror, and then back at Becky for reassurance. 'It's too fine for me.'

'Nothing's too fine for you, Ma. You've done without things for so long, you deserve a lovely hat, and I want you to have this one. A few flowers on the brim and you'll be a picture.'

'Well….' At last the hat was packed up, while Becky searched for a gift for Dinah. The local lace school had arranged its products on a small table at the back of the shop, and there she found just what she was looking for – something expensive and rich, something Dinah would never have thought of buying. Picking it up, Becky felt the soft texture of the handmade lace collar and pictured what it would look like, an elegant decoration of flowers and flowing tendrils at Dinah's throat, catching all eyes and enhancing the simple new dress that Thirza was making.

'I'll have this, please.' Becky found money in her pocket and shook her head when the dressmaker offered to put both purchases on Mr Fielding's account. She had received her wages and wanted to share them with her family. What the future held regarding money she had no idea, but this was an important moment. She longed to give something to both Dinah and Thirza to show her gratitude for all their love and help during the bleak days of the recent past.

'You Freeman?' The postman stopped in the yard, bag over his shoulder, one hand on the pony's bridle, the other holding out an envelope to Bill Narracott, and staring at Joseph, just coming out of the farmhouse.

'I am.'

'Gotta message from Mr Fielding. Ses to tell you five o'clock next Saturday at Bonehill Rocks.' The man stared, curiosity etched on his leathery face as he remounted.

'Thank you.' Joseph nodded and continued on his way across the yard, pausing as Narracott shouted after him.

'What's all that then? Sat'day afternoon? You wants time off?'

Joseph went back to the old man. 'Something very important. I'll make up the time.'

Bill Narracott's eyes, set deep in his weathered face, held a gleam of knowledge.

'Important, eh? I heard as 'ow that Briggs most likely'll get what's comin' to him. That's it, then?'

Grimly, Joseph nodded. 'That's about it, Mr Narracott.'

'Oh ah. An' not before time. All right then, you gets your Sat'day afternoon.'

'Thank you.' Joseph paused. 'But I have to take a couple of mates with me. All right for Mr Hunt to come?'

The old man stared. 'So that's the way o' it. Need your friends around you, eh? Sounds like a fighting match – is that what you're up to?'

So the word had got out. No secrets on the moor, thought Joseph wryly. Well, he could use it to his advantage, perhaps. 'Yes,' he answered shortly. 'I'm fighting Briggs an' I need my mates as seconds and sticklers. Dan'l has said he'll be there if you let him off the last few hours of the day.'

Narracott said nothing but slowly nodded. And it was only as Joseph turned away he called after him. 'Where is it again?'

Joseph looked back. 'Bonehill Rocks. Five o'clock.'

Their eyes met, Narracott nodded, and then they went their separate ways.

Dan'l waited until crib time when they sat in the shade of the wall they were repairing. 'Ole man said all right 'bout Saturday.' He grinned as he bit into a chunk of hard bread. 'Looks like he'll be there. These ole chaps, they like a good wrestling match. It was all the rage fifty years ago but died out then. Now you're starting it up again. But can be cruel stuff. How do you feel 'bout it?'

'I'll beat him. Briggs is all mouth, he won't last long.'

Silence while they drank cold tea. Then Dan'l said carefully, 'Course, he could well be up to tricks – we know what he's like.' He glanced aside at Joseph. 'Look out for a few tricks, lad – tripping, kicking, even gouging if he can get away wi' it.'

'I will. Thanks. And how about letting me see your dad's, what did you call them? Skillibegs?' They laughed at the forgotten word. Then Dan'l cut into an onion and said, 'You want to watch out for him kicking, an they'll protect you. Briggs'll know all about that, probably bake his boots to make 'em hard. You don't want no broken legs, lad, not if you're going to follow the rest o' your plan for the future. '

Joseph leaned back against the wall, his mind busy, knife and bacon forgotten on the turf beside him. 'You mean doing what old Satterly did? Yes, I'll keep out of trouble all right. But I'll need more than just you beside me, Dan'l; need a few more mates to keep control and use their sticks. Think I'll drop into the Forest Inn this evening and ask for helpers.'

Dan'l packed up his bag, corking the bottle and storing both behind a handy gorse bush. 'You won't need to ask. All round here, we wants to get even with that bloody Briggs. You'll see. Men like Andy Burridge, who suffered from losing half his profit over timber sales to the little shit. Try him.'

'Thanks. I will.'

They got to their feet, spat on their hands, and went back to work.

In the farmhouse at High Cross all the talk was of the wedding, arranged for three weeks' time, after the banns had been called. In vain had Will said crossly, 'Gotta get the 'taties clamped first and the oats stored. Can't just be runnin' off to church at any old time.' But his half smile at Dinah took the edge off his words and Becky felt a new sort of warmth filling her and casting out lurking shadows. Will had changed so much since Dinah's arrival, but on the other hand she also realized her place in the family circle was being replaced. No room now for another seat by the fire. No extra bed upstairs for the nights when she didn't want to go back to the Manor. Thirza was busily turning out her bedroom ready for the newly married pair, putting her few belongings into what used to be Becky's little attic. The only sleeping place now was a blanket and some pillows on the settle beside the dying fire. And because of the discomfort and the cold feeling of no longer belonging, Becky usually returned to her comfortable bedroom at High Cross Manor.

The Manor was quiet and Rupert Fielding was out for most of the next few days. Becky waited for him to return, and filled up the time by working on the accounts and then, with Ruth, going into the third bedroom and seeing what needed to be done. But the relationship between them was different. Ruth was uncomfortable whereas before they had worked together quite happily. Becky was in charge now, the daughter of the house and after a few hours of silent, awkward work in the room, she left Ruth to finish off the windows and mirrors and went back to her own bedroom.

After washing her hands and face, changing back into the green dress and tidying her hair, she sat on the bed, looking out of the window and wondered about life. She had to wait for Joseph to do what he had promised. A house somewhere. Their home. And slowly it came to her yet again, like warmth filling a cold body, that this was what she longed for, to be caring for her home, cooking for Joseph, sleeping with him in a small, cosy bedroom beneath the thatched roof.

She watched the sun slowly fade as it slipped down towards the far horizon, and with its light her smile also faded. What if Joseph didn't return? If he couldn't find them a house? If he failed to find the job that would sustain him through the rest of his working life? And then even worse, what if he were injured in the coming fight? It took all her strength to stop thinking such black thoughts. Then there were horse hoofs outside in the yard and Tom's voice, so she hurriedly left the room and went downstairs in search of her father.

She must find out what he had arranged about the fight. She hated the thought of it, but of course she must be there, watching, hoping and praying. All her strength would be needed, and, leaving the house, and raising her head defiantly, she knew that somehow she would find it.

CHAPTER 21

Rupert Fielding met her in the hall, taking off his hat, unbuttoning his tweed jacket, and smiling.

'Tea time, I think,' he said. 'Have it in the drawing room, shall we? I have a lot to tell you.'

Becky nodded. 'I'll ask Ruth to bring it. I hope the fire's been lit – there's a cold wind today. Autumn's on the way.' She walked across the large room, sat in one of the two comfortable, chintz covered chairs enclosing the hearth, and looked around.

Today, for some reason, she found herself being critical. It was a lovely, spacious room, paneled and full of heavy old furniture which shone with polish and smelled of beeswax. On small tables and niches china and silver glittered. A portrait over the fireplace showed a long dead Fielding, dressed in cutaway coat with a white stock at his scrawny neck, posing stiffly with a dog at his side. Long legs were encased in fawn pantaloons and on his thin, hawkish face, greying hair luxuriated.

Rupert, following her in and seating himself opposite, saw her looking up at the portrait. 'Your great grandfather,' he told her.

She felt his eyes on her but continued to look at the portrait. Yes, she understood that this old man with his elegant clothes and stiff posture was related to her, but she felt no connection. He may be an ancestor, but his home wasn't hers. Even the comfort of this warm and beautifully furnished room gave her no real feeling of homeliness.

She pushed aside the uneasy feelings and looked across at her father, still watching her. Leave the business of trying to explain that she didn't belong here until later. For now, 'What news, Father?'

As Ruth came in with a tea tray and Becky sat up straight to lift the heavy silver teapot and pour out, Rupert said, 'Two things. Important things.' He waited for Ruth to leave. 'One is that my fiancée, Mrs Richards – Felicity – tells me that our engagement has ended. She intends to live in Italy.'

Becky waited while thoughts pounded in her mind. Then, 'So she's not coming here after all?'

He reached across for his tea cup and held it in his two hands, watching her face. 'No.'

Becky swallowed a lump that had suddenly formed. 'I'm sorry. You were hoping, of course....'

'To be married. To have a wife to share the rest of my life with. Yes, I was.' He smiled briefly, a lift of the straight mouth and then it was gone. 'So I must return to my solitary state. Except that I now have you, my dear daughter.' The smile lifted again, remained long enough for her to understand that it was a plea for comfort.

'Father—' No, this wasn't the time to tell him she didn't wish to share his life. She tried to copy his smile. 'Even so, you must be feeling sad, Father.'

He put his cup down on a small fireside table and said briskly, 'Perhaps. But one must always find other things to remedy sadness.' His voice rose and she saw a gleam appear in the dark, deep set eyes. 'I must tell you about the arrangements I've been making for the fight.'

'The fight?' Her heart pounded and she stiffened, putting her own cup back on the tray. 'It's arranged? You've told Joseph?'

'I have. The match is on, Freeman versus Briggs. I've been calling on my neighbours, sportsmen all of them, and there's been a good response to the idea of a match. A long time since we saw any wrestling. And I've been to look at the ground – up behind Bonehill Rocks, a sort of small amphitheatre of downland, large and level enough. Ideal. Out of sight and big enough for what's required. Oh yes, and funds are pouring in; the purse should be quite large – ten or twelve guineas, I think.' He grinned. 'Large enough to persuade Briggs not to flee.'

Becky felt sick. So Joseph knew and would be thinking about it and so would Nat. Two men preparing to fight, and Father and his cronies already gloating over the enjoyment they would have from watching. And then, thankfully, the quick, wicked images of violence, of broken limbs and even worse fatalities colliding in her mind vanished, and she was able to say sharply, 'I shall come and watch. Of course I shall. I shall be there to see Joseph win.'

Rupert leaned forward and took a slice of seed cake. Between mouthfuls, he said very firmly, 'You certainly won't. No women at wrestling matches, against the rules. No, Becky, you'll stay here and wait until I come back.'

She got to her feet, stared down at him, already feeling in her mind the awful business of waiting for a result – Joseph winning? Or hurt? Rapidly she said, 'No. I shall be there, watching, Father. Don't try to stop me.'

She saw his frown, watched his mouth set angrily, and knew impulsively that she must escape from this new and unwanted authority. 'Please excuse me,' she said with a break in her voice, 'I have to get back to the farm. My family need me.' She left the room without waiting for permission, found a shawl, and walked straight out of the front door and through the yard, heading for High Cross Farm; her family was there even if it were no longer her home. Because home most surely wasn't here, at the Manor.

Frowning, Nat Briggs thought very hard as he left the maister's study next morning. So the fight was on. Saturday, five of the clock. Bonehill Rocks. Out of the way, but a good enough space for a crowd to gather and see him throw Freeman and break his back. Trotting down the road towards farmer Worth and his pigsties, Nat balled his fists as he rode and smiled. His boots were already fire hardened and newly iron tipped. And he knew a thing or two about kicking in forbidden places. All right, Freeman was big and heavy, but he had no idea of what his opponent could do, given half a chance. That was all he needed, just the chance. The smile grew and he kicked the cob into a canter as he turned off, heading across open moorland. *Joseph Freeman, you're gonna get all you deserve, and mebbe just a bit more.*

Chance, that was all he needed.

On Saturday Becky told Thirza she had duties to perform at the Manor. She would be back in the evening, for her usual visit. She avoided Will's frowning face as she walked through the yard. 'Not goin' to the fight, I hope?'

He looked ready to argue, so she smiled calmly. 'I've been told not to go. Father said women don't watch fights.'

Will nodded. 'He's right. I'll go, come and tell you what's what when it's over. You stay with Dinah and Ma.' His sharp eyes were piercing.

Becky made no reply, just walked away. She heard him call after her, a note of quick anger in his voice. 'You hear me, Becks – you stay at home.'

She waved a dismissive hand as she left the yard. Let him get on with his work; she must live her own life. She would do exactly as she had planned. The little linhay half way up Bonehill would be her refuge. Memory struck then, and she held it close. *She and Joseph, loving.*

She would slip in there before everybody arrived, then, when the fight started, make her way up and around to the Rocks, where she could find a shelter of some sort to hide and watch. Of course she must be there. She felt the blood race through her body at the thought. It would be an ordeal, to watch, to see them grapple, twist and push, using all the strength they could find to get a winning hold and force the other's body to the ground, but she must see it. Must be there, in case.... She took in a long breath that only briefly stayed the knot in her stomach – in case Joseph was hurt. He wouldn't be, of course, he was so big and strong, and compared with him, Nat Briggs was a weakling, but – in case....

The day dawned in true autumn style, a damp wind soughing through branches in the valleys and the drifting mist hiding the tors on the high moorland. Rain was expected and, later in the afternoon, Joseph saw the arriving watchers wearing heavy coats and battered hats. He had come in good time, journeying in Dan'l's horse and cart, along with some acquaintances from the Hexworthy farms, all willing to spend an hour or so helping to organize this unexpected and exciting event.

He watched as pony and sheep dung was cleared away before the stakes forming the ring were dug in, enclosing a fighting area of some fifteen yards. Laughter and loud talk accompanied the work, and he waited impatiently, with a stomach full of nervous energy, for the hour to arrive. More people were coming than he had expected – more support, he told himself stoutly – and most of them, probably – he managed a grin, hearing the rough words being thrown about – only too glad to be there in the hope of seeing Nat Briggs defeated.

There was Mr Fielding and his gentlemen friends, all farmers and land owners, arriving on horseback or in traps and gigs, even the Master of the Hunt in his bowler hat, the air thick around them with laughter and talk. Then farmer Narracott rattled up in his old gig, gathering together a crowd of other farmers, clearly eager to discuss the odds and make bets. Another reason to bring Briggs down and not let people lose money, thought Joseph grimly.

Dan'l Hunt found him. 'Here you be, Joe – me dad's skillibegs. Tie 'em round yer legs, t'will keep the kicks from breakin' anything.'

Joseph, in the shadow of the big rocks, nodded. He strapped on the hay-lined thick pads and felt better. He looked around for Briggs, wondering if perhaps, after all, the little bit of cowshit had fled. And then – there he was, mounted on his old cob, making the crowd give way before him, throwing a word here, a false smile there.

Joseph felt his pulse rate settle. It would work out all right. The fight was on. Not long now, and he would win. His frown was grimly resolute. So much depended on winning – the purse would be useful, his reputation would be established, the possibility of future plans would become clearer, and, of course, he would offer his triumph to Becky.

Beloved Becky. All this for Becky – but don't think of her now.

Standing straight and strong, boots laced tightly, shirt loosely falling around him and breeches secured with a thick leather belt, he looked around him, finding the enclosing moorland a comfort, a reassurance. He knew he had learned to understood the moor and its moods, and thought it possibly understood him. Now it made sense to him that this small, seemingly unimportant event was all of a kind with his other experiences of moorland living. He must square up to the situation, make the most of it, somewhere find extra strength and endurance, and then it would reward him, Bonehill Rocks always remaining in his memory as the last bastion of challenges that life had been continually throwing at him ever since he left the Workhouse. This, surely, would see the very last of vulnerable young Jack Adams.

But voices were calling. 'Freeman! Briggs!' He left the shelter of the rockface and walked out into the rope enclosed ring, surrounded now by eager faces. The judging sticklers stood on the edge of the ring, ready to keep spectators back with their staffs and to ensure fair play.

The man in charge was a large, red-faced farmer from Throwleigh way, whose ancestor William Cann had been a champion wrestler. He marched into the ring, looked around the circle of eager watchers, and then addressed the fighters. 'Freeman and Briggs – no gouging, no tripping, no kicking above the knees. Four falls'll win. Touch hands, if you please.'

Joseph felt Briggs's damp hand hardly touching his, and saw his closely set eyes squinting at him as he muttered, 'I'll get you,' before backing away. Joseph leaned down, arms hanging forwards, eyes fixed on Briggs's thin, tense body taking up the same stance, both of them eager to make the first move.

Joseph sucked in a breath, nodded, and waited. It was vital to know just how Briggs was going to fight; what were his weak points, his strengths? Only a few seconds to wait, then Briggs pushed forward, to grab hold of Joseph's loose shirt. Joseph felt the force of the arms trying to ram him off balance. For a small man Briggs had great strength. There were catcalls from the watchers and Joseph knew instinctively that he must be ready for illegal moves; Briggs wasn't the man to play fair. The warning shouts continued. 'Watch 'is heels – no hitches!'

The sticklers moved with the fight, intent on every step the two men took. Once a stick was pushed between them as Briggs held the flapping shirt and aimed a kick at Joseph's thigh hidden beneath it.

'Unfair!' came the shouts and they parted again. But in the next second Joseph heaved himself towards Briggs with all his force and kicked at his legs. He felt the bone-thudding crash hit home and knew cruel joy.

A shout of approval whirled around his head, but no longer was he listening. He was lost in this brutal, enclosed world, getting into the right position to tackle that small, twisting body, finding a way out of the revengeful, hardened iron-tipped boots that aimed at vulnerable parts of his own legs. There were agonizing moments of yielding and having to accept the pain of sly kicks, craftily and quickly hidden by another easier attack, so far unseen by the sticklers.

Rain began to fall, cooling Joseph's sweating body, soaking into the turf beneath his feet, oozing in slippery little channels and adding to the danger of Brigg's thin, seemingly armour-plated feet always just a few inches away from his own, hitting home. He felt blood soaking through the skillibeg on one leg where the string had come untied, leaving him unprotected.

Not a wound, but a spur. He pressed on with extra strength, determined to floor the man who danced so expertly on thin legs, cleverly using iron tips to find painful spots, unseen by the sticklers moving around them.

Friendly voices helped. 'Come on, Freeman, give that l'il hayseed what for....'

And then, suddenly, he found the way to hold Briggs still, and in that second he floored him. Briggs was on his back, breathless, lying on the now rain-soaked turf, staring up with narrow eyes full of disbelief and fury.

'One fall,' shouted the judging stickler and the crowd roared approval. Briggs pulled himself up, rubbed his back, glared at Joseph, and then took his stance and at once Joseph knew he was in graver danger than before. But he knew now how his opponent fought; quick moves, hurried grabs, forceful unseen and illegal kicks where it hurt, a lithe body that spun away within a second of each attack. Joseph clamped his lips together and planned exactly how to deal with this cheating little wretch. He was ready with his hands now, quick to draw Brigg's shirt so close that kicking legs had no chance of reaching their target. And with that nearness, all his strength streamed out, lifting the body and throwing it down.

One fall, and then two. A third to Briggs, after he managed a sly trip of Joseph's feet and more shouts and an intervention by a stickler. 'No tripping. Any more and we'll disqualify.'

It seemed to Joseph, half blinded by the rain and his sweat, that the fight would never end. He hoped he would last out and win, but realized that it was more than a match; Briggs's staring eyes and rictus expression of hate claimed it was a fight to the death.

Becky was watching, persuaded almost without knowing from her half hidden position at the back of the crowd. Although women were not supposed to watch such fights, she found herself being treated in a friendly fashion. 'Here, maid, step in front – you can see better.' And then she was there, among the fidgeting, shouting spectators, letting their enthusiasm edge into her own mind. Yes, it was brutal sport, but she was being forced into understanding the appeal of watching those two men using all their instinctive knowledge and strength to try and floor one another.

She almost forgot it was Joseph fighting Nat Briggs – but then

Nat fell and she saw the expression on his face as he pulled himself up. An evil scowl, determined on revenge. And her feelings changed. But for all her growing hatred of this brutality, she knew she had to watch. What had Joseph said, when he left her not long ago? *If you think of me, and I think of you, we're together.* She knew he wasn't thinking of her now, but she would send all her thoughts and longings to him, and perhaps they would somehow reach him.

She watched as the rain fell increasingly heavier and guessed that danger had become more acute. The heavy, hard boots were slipping, bodies out of control for that split second that could bring pain and another fall. Nat fell again, but then it was Joseph who overbalanced as he grabbed at the twisting body just out of reach. There were immediate shouts of concern. Joseph was the hoped for winner, but the score was only just in his favour. And then he fell again – this time as Nat lured him into a clinch that was slyly aiming a kick at his body. More warnings, and on it went.

Becky felt her stomach knotting with every move they made. The score mounted. Three all now and everything depended on the next moves and which of them could make the other yield. She could see they were both tiring. Rain and sweat poured down their heated faces, and the arms that reached for victory were growing heavy and slow. Joseph's leg was red with blood and he winced as another sly kick reached for his groin. Becky closed her eyes for a second, but forced them to open again. It would be over soon – the next fall deciding victory. The crowd's increasingly rough shouts scoured her mind clean of everything save her desperate need of Joseph's safety.

And then, as she watched, she noticed a stickler momentarily dropping his staff and bending to retrieve it in a fatal second of lost concentration, and in that moment her eyes moved to Nat and she saw him grin, knew he was up to something wicked, and held her breath. She saw his right hand reach out, fingers extended. It swung to within an inch of Joseph's face, and then swept on towards his eye.

Gouging.

'No!' Horror-stricken, her scream was loud enough to silence the shouts for a second, its echo booming among the surrounding rocks. Silence, and then, as the stickler pushed his staff between the two bodies, separating them, again the voices exploded in fury.

The stickler had to shout to make himself heard. 'No gouging! You know that. Briggs, You're disqualified.'

Becky found herself swept up in a vast movement of heated bodies leaping forward into the ring, breaking the rope and surrounding the two gasping men. Briggs was pummeled and pushed around, while Joseph was helped into the shelter of the rocks. Becky watched, praying that he was safe but knowing she must wait. She left the sticklers and Joseph's friends to offer drying towels, warm clothes and a mouthful of cider, and retreated back to her hiding place within the side of the rockpile.

Her breath was short and painful, her body ached as if she, too, had been at the mercy of those wicked arms and kicking feet, her mind overwhelmed with terrible images. She wanted just to be left alone to recover – and then, turning, saw Nat Briggs being chased out of the ring, limping unevenly over the soaking turf, nearing her in his bid to reach his pony and escape.

Their eyes met. He took a step sideways, scowled, and thrust out his fist. 'You bitch! You did it – you stopped me getting him. Well, you'll 'ave it instead.' Face contorted, he put the last ounce of his failing strength into a punch which caught her on the side of her head and then ran off, into the drifting mist and the pouring rain.

Becky felt a cloud of pain sweep through her head, and, gasping, fell to the ground.

She was falling into a black abyss, falling, falling. Her last horrified thought was *is Joseph safe? And where is he...?*

CHAPTER 22

He was there at her bedside. Opening her eyes she looked straight into his, grey, wide, fearful.

'Becky.' His voice was deep and full of anguish. 'You've come back to me, thank the Lord. What happened? But no, you mustn't talk, not yet. Just rest.' He was on his knees beside her, his hands holding hers, warm and strong.

Weakly, she looked around. She was in her bedroom at the Manor, with Joseph on one side of her and Thirza and Mrs Mudge on the other. If she looked down towards the end of the bed she saw her father standing there, staring down at her, his lined face tight with anxiety.

Her family, her friend Mrs Mudge and Joseph, her lover. What more could she want? The pain in Becky's head pulsed and ached, but somehow she smiled. They were all here, caring for her, and Joseph was alive! She turned to him, caught the expression on his face and knew their thoughts had come together, even though they were silent.

Rupert Fielding was speaking, his voice low and rapid. 'I've sent for Dr Gale. He should be here soon. You must stay where you are, Becky, and just rest. We don't know what happened, but it's clear you had a blow to your head.'

She was able to breathe better now. Longer breaths, clearer thoughts. The pain coming and going but not stopping her from needing to tell them. 'It was Nat,' she whispered. 'He was trying to get away, and he saw me – and – and....' But then it was too much to have to live through it all again. The expression on his face, his terrible words, and then the blow that brought darkness and pain. She closed her eyes and tried to forget.

Thirza was bending over her. 'Poor lamb, try an' sleep. Doctor'll give you some'at for the pain when he comes, but rest now.'

'Yes.' Becky was slipping back into the comfort of drowsy forgetfulness, but Joseph's hands remained holding hers, giving her the warm security of being loved. After a moment or two she slept and the two women at her bedside carefully left the room, Mrs Mudge whispering to Thirza, 'Come down and have a cup of tea while I make some broth for the poor maid.'

Rupert caught Joseph's eye. He nodded at him. 'You did well, Freeman. That evil little bastard tried every trick, but you finally floored him. I understand he's gone now. His cottage is empty, his clothes cleared out and his cob with him. Making an escape – and he's lucky to do so. Many of the spectators wanted to get him.'

Standing up, Joseph slipped his hands away from Becky's, now that she slept. He grimaced as his back complained of undue exertion and bad treatment, and his voice was dark as he said, 'Just as well he's gone. If he'd stayed around I would have hunted him down. Hurting Becky....' He shook his head and his jaw tightened with his thoughts.

Rupert looked at the strong weathered face with its deep-set eyes and tight mouth and understood the feelings that remained unsaid. 'You're all right, yourself? That kick to your leg needs attention. Dr. Gale can look at it when he comes.'

'No need. Something to tie round it, that's all it wants. And anyhow, I have to get back to work. I can't stay here.'

'But Becky—?' Rupert's voice rose.

'She'll understand.' Quiet, clipped words and Joseph walked stiffly towards the door.

'I leave her with you, sir, and know she'll be well looked after. Tell her, please, that I have one more thing to do and then I'll be back.'

Rupert said nothing for a moment, but then, as Joseph's hand reached out to open the door, he said spontaneously, 'Wait a moment, Freeman. Something I want to discuss with you. It's important. Why not spend the night here and give yourself time to recover properly before you go back to Hexworthy? And of course Becky will want to see you again when she awakes. What about it?'

Joseph took a deep, long breath. Tempting to accept this invitation; a sluice under the yard pump, a good hot meal, a bandage or two and then somewhere to sleep off the aches and pains and bad memories of the day. And another few moments with Becky tomorrow. a chance to know that she really was recovering. Slowly letting his breath out, he grinned wryly. 'I can't say no, so thank you, sir. I'll stay and make my excuses to Mr Narracott when I get back there tomorrow morning.'

'I'm sure he'll understand. After all, you're the hero of the day. He won't put you off.' Rupert's voice was jovial and he walked slowly around the room to sit at Becky's bedside, nodding as Joseph left the room. Deep in thought he began making plans. Plans for the future, for himself and for both of them, Becky and her sweetheart. Turning to look at her, sleeping peacefully now, he realized that life certainly brought shadows, but also, surprisingly, allowed the sun to shine and dispel them. It was a new and welcome thought.

Becky awoke with the dawn. Her head still ached, but Dr Gale's pills had given her a good night's refreshing sleep. A scratch on the door and she turned her head. 'Who is it?'

No answer but the door opened and Joseph slipped in. He closed the door very quietly and came to the bedside. 'My love. My lovely Becky. How much better you look now – how do you feel?' His hands found hers and helped her sit up. He pulled the pillow behind her head to make her more comfortable and sat on the bed beside her. Gently he kissed her aching temple, her eyes, her cheeks, and then, lingeringly, her mouth. 'I couldn't go without making sure you were better.'

'Go?' Her voice was very quiet but he understood the emotion hidden within the one word and smiled reassuringly.

'Back to Hexworthy. I have to work, you know that. And then there is something that I shall be doing, very soon – and then—'

She gripped his hand. 'But why must you go? You need to get over that awful fight. Your leg – I saw what happened. And those falls – your back must be hurt?'

His smile faded. 'I shall get over it. And you must understand that I have to go back to work.' His eyes, grey and wide, looked into hers almost pleadingly. 'Trust me, Becky. Trust me.'

The pain in her temple grew stronger. She leaned back on the pillow feeling weak and suddenly low spirited. He had won the match, won the purse, but still he had to leave her. And while she was feeling so sorry for herself – suddenly she was full of black thoughts. Was it so much more important that he kept his job at Hexworthy than stay here and wait until she was well again? Was that the love that he had sworn he felt for her?

'I don't understand,' she whispered, turning her face from him – he mustn't see the easy tears. 'Why must you go back to work? You said it was only repairing walls – surely they can wait for a day or two.'

'No.' He let go her hands, sat up straighter and looked at her with a different expression. Looking at him again she saw resolution, determination, strength – and knew she had to accept his decision. Something in Hexworthy that he had to do and by now she knew him so well that she realized nothing would change his mind. Even leaving her here, in bed, unable to get back to her life wouldn't stop him. He must go and once again, she was left, waiting.

'I want you to stay, but of course you won't. So go and let me sleep.' She heard self pity in her voice and was angry with herself. But the pain and the disappointment was too great. 'Goodbye,' she said unevenly and burrowed into the pillow.

'Becky, Becky, I'll be back soon. I promise. Very soon.' His voice was deep and full of a longing that touched her heart. It was only when she felt him rise from the bed that she opened her eyes and looked towards the door. He stood there, and she knew suddenly that there was something he longed to tell her, but couldn't. Not yet. And so she was able to give him a last, watery smile as she murmured, 'Goodbye, my love. Come back soon.'

Joseph rode back to Hexworthy. At Widecombe horse sales Rupert Fielding had bought a quiet little mare for Becky, and she was in the stable, waiting for her new mistress to recover and then ride out. Joseph, having had Rupert Fielding's permission, saddled her quietly, without waiting for Tom to come down from the tallat, and then led her out of the yard.

'Off you go, my beauty. Let's see how you run.' Clearly, she was delighted to be in the fresh morning air and he settled into a comfortable pace as they turned into the road and headed for Hexworthy. During the ride he thought back to the conversation he and Rupert had had after the evening meal last night.

Rupert had surprised him by apologizing for his unfriendly treatment when first he came to the Manor. 'I thought you were just a fly-by-night making free with my daughter,' he said wryly, lighting a cigar and telling Joseph to sit down. 'Now I know I was wrong and you and Becky are truly fond of one another. I can see that you're strong and trustworthy, and I have a job to offer you once this Hexworthy work is finished.'

Joseph, trying not to show the pain his back was inflicting on him, nodded. 'Thank you, sir,' he said shortly. 'And what is the job?' Those damned library shelves, perhaps, after all, he thought, disappointed but amused.

Fielding's words surprised him. 'Now Briggs has gone I need a new estate bailiff and I think you could do the job. You know the moor. From all I hear about you I know you're a good craftsman, you understand the sort of work that's needed, and I reckon you would be popular with my tenants. '

They regarded one another in silence, while Joseph tried to sort out the many thoughts abruptly filling his mind. Rupert drank his whisky, then said, 'No need to decide at once. Think about it and let me know. And remember, there's Briggs's cottage and bit of land to go with the job.' Leaning back looking through the cigar smoke, he smiled. 'And, perhaps, if Becky and you eventually marry, this would be useful. A ready-made home.'

Like a bell, the word chimed with Joseph's heartfelt ambition. *Home.*

Suddenly the pain in his back edged away and he smiled as he said, 'It's good of you, sir, and I'll think about all you've said.' He certainly would. 'But for the moment I have to get back to Hexworthy. Something's waiting there for me, you see, something that's the most important thing I've ever wanted, ever done.'

Rupert watched the grey eyes light up and reluctantly felt his admiration for Becky's sweetheart to grow. Would he, in time, make a good husband for Becky? Not quite the alliance he was hoping for, but even so. He nodded. 'Very well. And if you feel you've got to get back there you can try out the new mare I bought for Becky.' He grinned. 'Better for your back than that long walk.'

Joseph stood up, stretching his aching muscles and returned the smile. 'Thank you, Mr Fielding. I'll do that. I shall be off early tomorrow, so I'll say goodnight now. And thank you again.'

Rupert stood up and offered his hand. 'Come back soon, Freeman. She'll be waiting. And I shall want to know if you've decided to accept the offer I've made.'

A last look between them, and then Joseph left the room. Rupert sat down, returned to his whisky and cigar and thought how pleasant it would be to have Becky living so close to the Manor if Freeman accepted the job – and of course he would. Why not? He'd be a fool not to. Becky, living nearby; she could carry on doing his accounts, and be his hostess when he had social occasions. Now, Felicity's absence drifted into forgetfulness, for Becky would be here.

Closing his eyes, he smiled.

Farmer Narracott saw Joseph arrive, put the mare into the stable with a feed of oats, and then walk across the yard.

'You'm late,' he grunted.

Contritely, Joseph nodded. 'I'm sorry. Things I had to do after the match. I came as soon as I could.'

The old man's face creased into wrinkles. 'You did well there, boy. Don't worry 'bout it. The grin faded. 'And Dan'l tells me that you've got an idea 'bout doing what old Satterley did all those years ago, building a stone house fer himself in a day.'

Joseph took in a long breath. The old man sounded sympathetic, but could he be sure?

'I am. I've got friends who say they'll help.' He stared into the faded brown eyes. 'And of course I need your sayso to take the time off.'

Bill Narracott leaned on his stick and grunted again. 'An' where you gonna build this house, then? Not on my land, boy.'

Joseph's mouth twisted. He was half there, but this could be the vital part of the agreement. 'Mr Fielding's got a piece of rough land between here and his house. It's on level ground, near a stream. Piles of moorstone handy and ideal for a small holding which is what I plan. He's offered me a job so I'm hoping he won't mind me putting my roots down on his estate.'

During the ride from the Manor, it had touched his mind that Mr Fielding's permission should have been requested before he put his plan into action. But yesterday, and Becky's pain and his own soaring ambition had pushed everything else into forgetfulness.

'Oh ah. Well, you'd better get on wi' it, then. Old Satterly had until dusk to build for his freehold an' you'll be the same, I reckon.' Farmer Narracott nodded and gave what Joseph guessed was the nearest to a good smile that he was likely to get. 'An' I won't dock you of money that you're not earning. A house, eh? Got a wife, then?'

Joseph felt his own smile burgeon. 'I soon will have.' Becky flew into his mind, Becky riding the new mare, trotting over the moorland, coming to see their home. Becky with him, never again to part. *It must be built today.*

'Thanks, Mr Narracott,' he said, and strode away to find Dan'l and the other men who had offered their help. *Get on with it. Get it finished, with smoke drifting up from the chimney, that means the freehold is mine, and then back to Becky, to tell her. To bring her here – home.*

They gathered on the piece of land he'd selected, the three mates from work at Hound Tor and a couple of men living in Hexworthy who had enjoyed the match and offered their help, together with Dan'l Hunt, there with the agreement of farmer Narracott.

'You gotta good spot 'ere, Joe', said Dan'l, looking around him with expert eyes, when they arrived by horse and cart laden with tools and crib. 'Stream near enough to get water easy, those trees up there to keep off the wind and all this moorstone nearby. Let's get on with it quick, I reckon.'

Jackets were taken off and bags of crib tossed down in the shade of a red berried rowan tree. The seven men looked at each other. 'So where do us start?' asked Davy, and Joseph felt his mind suddenly clear. He could already see it, the finished cottage.

'Get the stones together first. Then we'll build the walls.' Already he and Ed were handling the granite, hauling up the big rocks and starting the first line of stones.

They worked steadily with only a brief stop at midday for drink and food. The work was hard, dangerous even, with the humping of the massive rocks causing bruises and cuts. But they laughed and talked as they carted more stones and, as the afternoon passed, collected great armfuls of bracken for thatching the roof. The sun sank too fast for Joseph's peace of mind, but, wiping sweat from his brow, he looked at the building which had grown almost magically since the morning, and knew his cottage would be finished in time.

The walls were only five feet high, but they reached the sloping roof and met the thatch, keeping out the rain which had started to fall early in the afternoon. Inside he built a fireplace and joined with Davy and Dan'l to add a chimney to the inside wall.

It was quite dark, and very wet, with the trees on the top of the hill behind them soughing in a rising wind when Joseph said hoarsely, 'That's it, then. It's done. Just got to light the fire.'

Dan'l produced his tinderbox and kneeled by the hearth, coaxing the slight flame to catch the twigs laid on the granite slab that formed the base of the fireplace. They were damp, but at last the flame leaped and, crackling, the fire began to burn. Joseph, watching, felt emotion suddenly thrust through him. He touched Dan'l on the shoulder. 'Well done. Come outside and let's see the smoke.'

They all stood out in the rain, wiping their faces and staring up at the chimney from which smoke began slowly appearing. Dan'l turned to Joseph and grinned. 'There's your home, then, boy. So come back now and have a bite with me an' Mary.'

Joseph felt torn in half. He had planned to immediately ride back to High Cross Manor to tell Mr Fielding about the cottage, ask about the freehold, and then say yes, he accepted the job offered, but suddenly his body was sending other messages. The painful strains of yesterday's fight had been made worse by today's work of lifting, heaving stones and building the cottage walls. His injured leg was swollen and ached with each step he took. But he needed to go back to Becky…. He thought as hard as his churning mind would allow him, and then grudgingly accepted that rest was making such strong demands that he could only accept Dan'l's offer of a meal, and then get himself back to the tallat and sleep.

He thanked Dan'l and then turned to his other friends, gathering up their belongings before returning home. 'Can't thank you enough for your help. Next time I'm in the inn I'll put in pints for you all.' After hearty words of thanks and handshakes, they parted and went their separate ways.

Joseph's thoughts as Dan'l's carthorse plodded homewards through the dusky evening were happy and celebratory ones that came and went through his weary mind. With the cottage half built now he and Becky could be together. And it was only as Dan'l turned into the yard at Hexworthy that Joseph began to feel anxious about how Rupert Fielding would respond to his grabbing a piece of the estate land without permission. But after a wash, a hot meal and then the thankful fall into his bed in the tallat, everything faded. His last thought was that tomorrow was a new day.

In the morning the pain and muddled thinking had lessened. The dawn was bright and cold and he was up early, finding farmer Narracott and telling him that he must leave today but was grateful for having had the chance to learn about working with stones. The old man grunted, but nodded his head. 'On your way, then boy, an' good luck with what you do next. You're a good worker an deserve some'at better'n stone walling.' He watched as Joseph took the mare from the stable, tacked her up and then rode out of the yard, giving a final wave as he did so.

At High Cross Manor he knocked on the kitchen door and was taken into the warmth by a kindly Mrs Mudge, who took his damp coat off him and poured boiling water onto the half empty teapot.

'So how's Becky? Is she here?' He couldn't wait to see her.

Nellie Mudge returned to her seat by the fire. 'Gone to the farm for a couple of hours, she said. Better, yes, no more headache, but she wanted to be with her family.' She looked at Joseph and saw his disappointment. 'Don't you go chasing off after her now. The maister said as when you come back, he wants to see you – at once. So tidy yerself a bit and then you'll find him upstairs. In his study, I guess.' She grinned. 'Up earlier these days – a lot to do, so he ses.'

Joseph drank the tea, focusing his thoughts. Now he had to explain to Mr Fielding just what he had done yesterday. And then he began to wonder if in so doing he had foregone his opportunity of taking the job offered – would the maister still want him as estate bailiff? He was frowning as he went upstairs and knocked at the study door.

CHAPTER 23

Rupert Fielding heard his knock and met him, halfway across the room. 'I hope you've come to tell me you're taking the job I offered? The estate needs to have a new bailiff very soon. Here, sit down.'

Joseph eased himself into the chair indicated, thoughts busily gathering themselves into what he hoped would be a polite and tactful way of revealing what he had done. It struck him forcibly that if Fielding were to make trouble about setting up on his land, very probably the job offer would be withdrawn. But he wanted the job. Estate bailiff? Yes, he could do it well and efficiently. And it would be worth doing, work that would use all his experience of living and working on the moor. It would complete his life's journey. But the cottage freehold….

'Well?' Rupert's voice was impatient and Joseph took a long breath before plunging into the problem.

'You know about old man Satterly, years ago, building a stone cottage in a day with help from his friends?'

'Of course. It's part of Dartmoor folklore.'

'Well, sir, I've done the same.' A pause. 'And on your land, without your sayso.'

They stared at each other in silence. Until Rupert said slowly, 'Satterly did it to claim the freehold – was that your idea, too?'

Joseph nodded. 'Yes. We got the roof on and smoke coming out of the chimney in a day. Even though the building is only half finished, that means the cottage is mine.'

'On my land?' Rupert's voice was grim, his stare cold.

'Yes, sir. And I ask you to let it stay and be a home for me and Becky.'

Rupert stood up and walked to the window. He stood there for a moment before looking back. Joseph saw the stiffness of the tall figure and prepared himself for a hard answer. What could he do if Fielding refused to give him the piece of land?

For a long moment Rupert said nothing, then suddenly he turned and the expression on his face was unexpected. Not quite a smile, but a hint of approval which sent Joseph's grim thoughts flying.

'Of course, you know that I should demand that you take it down, stone by stone, just as you've built it.' There was a note of wry amusement in the words. 'But I know you've done this for Becky, so of course I can't complain. All right then, Freeman, you can have your cottage and we'll come to terms about the piece of land surrounding it. And you still haven't told me whether you want the job I offered.'

Joseph's smile said it all. 'I take it, and thank you. I'll do my best for you, Mr Fielding. And as for the land – well – all I can say is thank you.'

They looked at each other and then Rupert held out his hand, saying quietly, almost as if to himself, 'And of course the other gift I make you, Freeman, is my daughter's hand in marriage – if that's what you're going to ask next.'

Taking the proffered hand and shaking it, Joseph could only say huskily, 'I was. And, now, with your approval, I shall ask her.'

Rupert walked carefully to his chair and eased himself into it. He arranged papers on the table, frowned at them and then looked up, smiling. 'Well, Freeman, your duties as my estate bailiff start tomorrow morning, early. Here in my study. I badly need your help. We'll discuss payment and I'll give you some orders. But for the moment I think there's something far more important you have to do.'

Joseph caught the light-hearted note in the words, and nodded, as he smiled back at the still handsome but lined face regarding him so keenly. 'Very well, sir, thank you and I'll be here sharp.' He took a step towards the door. 'And now, as you say, I must go and find Becky. To tell her about the cottage and to ask her....' But already he was leaving the room, urgency forcing him to leave without a formal goodbye.

Rupert's voice followed him as he went down the stairs. 'She's at the farm – said she had to help make arrangements for her brother's – uncle's wedding. Take the trap, Freeman, she won't want to have to walk to your cottage.'

Sitting there quietly, thoughts wandering before he delved into estate matters, Rupert came to understand that his life had mellowed to the extent even of accepting Joseph Freeman as Becky's husband to be. A brave, straightforward man who would love her, he was sure of it. And as for the old thoughts of keeping his daughter close, well, he knew now that he was better advised to let her go. *I must live my own life*, she had said, and he could accept that now. No strings attached, but he knew she would never desert him. Love, he knew, for Becky, was unconditional and how fortunate he was to have discovered and come to love her, so late in life. He sat in the sunshine, and felt the new day bring with it a new sort of happiness.

In the yard Joseph helped Tom put the mare into the shafts of the trap and then left the Manor, racing along the road to the farm. In his mind, as he drove, all the past unhappy pieces of his life suddenly began fitting together – and he knew that this was the final piece which made it complete. He must find Becky.

Becky, feeling better, had had breakfast with her father and then, despite his worry as to whether she was strong enough, had taken herself off, out of the yard, down the track and on towards High Cross Farm. As she walked it seemed to her that life had begun a new pattern, her thoughts moving on from the horrors of the wrestling match and the painful blow to her head, to being here in the cool, bright day with the surrounding moorland seemingly smiling down at her. She felt she was approaching something new and distant and wonderful. Joseph was safe – that was all that mattered. He would come back when he was ready, and in the meantime she would spend time with her family on the farm.

There was a lot to discuss; how Dinah's new dress was going, should she really wear that lovely lace collar with it? 'Too good for someone like me,' she said, grinning, but feeling the lace with gentle, admiring fingers. And what about Will having a new coat? 'Go into market and see what you can find, boy,' said Thirza, as she took some long hoarded coins from her skirt pocket and put them on the table.

Becky watched all this, listened, and made small contributions to the conversation as she helped prepare the midday meal, feeling herself content and newly happy. And then her mind told her it was time to leave. So once the pot was on the fire, with Will saying he couldn't stay any longer – work to be done, and then disappearing outside, she remembered that Father would be waiting at the Manor, and perhaps there would be news of Joseph.

Her heart began to race. *There must be – there must be.*

'Goodbye,' she said, kissing Thirza and smiling warmly at Dinah. 'I'll come again soon. And of course I'll be in church on Sunday to hear your banns being read.' She left them with a clear mind, knowing that all was well at the farm, and then reminded herself that all was well at the Manor, too, with Father not being quite as possessive as he had been.

Her thoughts as she walked out of the yard, down the track and towards the road, were busy and serene. A cool wind, brilliant autumn light, fading greenery in the hedges, leaves falling from the roadside elms; stock in the fields and the moor stretching up into the blue sky.

And then, suddenly, the faint sounds of hoof beats approaching. A trap rounded the corner and came towards her, the large, fair-haired man driving pulling at the reins as he drew nearer, his smile a wide and glorious greeting. Joyously, she heard her name on his lips and answered him. *Joseph!*

He halted the mare, leaped out and ran towards her. Arms tight and safe around her willing body; flesh to flesh as his kisses warmed her face. His voice singing in her ears, his joy reaching out to her. 'Becky! I'm building a cottage for us – Fielding has given us the land, I'm to be his new bailiff, and we shall be together. Becky, say you'll marry me?'

'Yes! Yes! Of course I will! Oh, Joseph, at last....'

For a moment Joseph was silent, no words able to show his happiness. And then, slowly all he could say, very huskily, was, 'So come with me, love. I'm going to take you home.'

So much to say, so many kisses, plans to be made, thoughts shared. She sat in the trap beside him and thought ecstatically of what had to be done. The words of *The Sprig of Thyme* ran through her mind, and she understood that, with the gift of true love that she had given to Joseph, she had herself been given in return the greatest of gifts. The cottage he was telling her about to be finished, furnished, made liveable. The new job which she could help him with, working still at Father's accounts. Their marriage – their life together – it was all coming true.

After hurrying the mare on from the Manor, Joseph now let her take her time and recover. They went slowly up the lane, took the rough track towards Bowerman's Nose and stopped for a moment at the grave. Becky found a few petals of fading hawkweed and dropped them on the mound. She looked up at Joseph. 'Poor maid, she had an unhappy life – like my mother.'

He put out his hand, helping her climb back beside him. 'But you don't need to think of them no more, sweetheart. Your life is quite different. You and me will always be happy. Our children will be loved and looked after.'

Dreaming, Becky let the world pass her by as they continued along the lane. She hoped he would carry her over the threshold of their new home, that they would soon have a family. She knew that she was blessed, and offered up a small word of thanks as they continued, in the sunlight, passing Bowerman's Nose and heading for the cottage.

Going home....

With Joseph's free hand holding hers, she looked about her and smiled. The moor – her moor – was ablaze with sunlight.

No shadows today.